PRIVATE
PLEASURES

PRIVATE PLEASURES

Hamdy el-Gazzar

Translated by Humphrey Davies

The American University in Cairo Press
Cairo   New York

First published in 2013 by
The American University in Cairo Press
113 Sharia Kasr el Aini, Cairo, Egypt
420 Fifth Avenue, New York, NY 10018
www.aucpress.com

Exclusive distribution outside Egypt and North America by I.B.Tauris & Co. Ltd., 6 Salem Road,
London, W2 4BU

Dar el Kutub No. 17287/12
ISBN 978 977 416 601 3

Dar el Kutub Cataloging-in-Publication Data

El-Gazzar, Hamdy
        Private Pleasures / Hamdy el-Gazzar; translated by Humphrey Davies. — Cairo: The
    American University in Cairo Press, 2013.
        p.   cm.
        ISBN 978 977 416 601 3
        1. Arabic fiction
        I. Davies, Humphrey (tr.)
        892.73

1 2 3 4 5   17 16 15 14 13

Designed by Andrea El-Akshar
Printed in Egypt

CONTENTS

A DAY AND A NIGHT

1 Underpass — 3

2 Haris — 12

3 Copulation — 21

4 Evening Prayer — 29

5 Nashwa — 32

6 Simone — 35

7 Kagha's Uncontrollable Tears — 39

8 Anwar Gabr — 52

9 A Slap — 58

10 A Killer — 67

11 A Mother — 70

12 A Chain — 75

YESTERDAY

13 Two Killings — 81

14 A Progenitor — 93

15 A Woman — 111

16 A Grandfather — 119

17 An Ascetic — 126

18 Samira — 133

19 A Lover Surprised — 138

20 Flight — 145

EXIT

21 Blast — 149

22 An Older Man — 158

23 Butchers — 167

24 Fantasio — 175

25 CD — 181

26 Umm el-Masriyeen — 190

27 Travel — 194

28 Drowning — 198

TOMORROW

29 Washing the Body — 203

30 Crossing — 206

31 Highly Confidential — 210

Glossary — 211

A DAY AND A NIGHT

1 UNDERPASS

WE WERE ON OUR WAY TO THE UNDERPASS.

Behind us, Giza Square is a raucous, pullulating, raging inferno, filled to its farthest limits with lights, sounds, and shapes and crowded to over-flowing with bodies, objects, and goods of every conceivable kind. The square is a giant, twisted oblong bathed in the evening lights shining from the buildings and tall towers scattered about the corners of its celebrated streets: Murad, University, el-Sanadeeli, Saad Zaghloul, Salah Salim.

Salah Salim was originally el-Rabeea el-Gizi. Its buildings are old and low-rise, some unsound to the point of collapse, their ground-floor premises occupied by the Bank of Egypt, Ghalyun's, Cinema Fantasio, the Samar Café—featureless yellowing brick apartment blocks, their façades bearing a plethora of ancient signboards advertising the offices of famous doctors, leading engineers, accountants, import-export com-panies, medical labs, lawyers.

The office of my father, Idris el-Hagg, Legal Counselor, is there, in the Khawaga Kheir building on the corner of Saad Zaghoul, opposite the fuul restaurant named La Manche.

On the roofs of most of the apartment blocks and towers overlook-ing the square stand tall iron frames supporting neon signs. They dis-play giant images of singers male and female, football players, a well-known preacher from the Gulf, posters for new movies, and flashing advertisements for insecticides, cars, canned cooking butter, bathroom fittings and tiles, hardware and paint, and a lone, looming urinal.

A dim yellow light emanates from lamps on metal posts that run the length of the flyover that crosses the square from Feisal and the courthouse on-ramp to Salah Salim.

Along the medians of the classier streets (Nile, Murad, University), new-fangled signs lit on both sides and showing famous faces and bodies have been erected on smaller poles. One after another, every few seconds, always in the same sequence, they form out of light and color the faces of female Egyptian and Arab singing stars, cell-phone advertising girls, girls modeling nightdresses, makeup, casual and evening wear.

Ancient peeling signs, and uncountable new ones, hang from innumerable elevated points and balconies overlooking the Omar Effendi department store, the Sherifein Markets, the Egypt Insurance Tower, the Nasr Building.

To the north, the lights of the Straight Path minaret and the beacons on the mast of the tall metal tower next to the Giza telephone exchange, over toward the avenue that leads to the university, spread themselves across the sky.

The wide bay embraced by the mosque and its medical center, on the stretch between the bus station and the telephone exchange, is occupied by stalls selling Qur'ans and books on religion, tapes of Qur'anic recitation, sermons, homilies of warning and guidance, scented sticks for cleaning the teeth, perfumes, Sudanese and Indian incense. The incense comes in the form of thin sticks smelling of jasmine and imitation sandalwood sold in long colored packages, or as crumbly pellets in triangles of thick paper.

Level with the noses of the perfume and prayer-bead sellers are tiny square glass bottles, each containing a few drops of musk, jasmine, and amber—fake, imitation, cheap. The bottles are set side by side on gray spreads next to cheap prayer beads of wood, plastic, and stone hung on tall, thin metal hangers.

In front of elderly salesmen wearing short gallabiyas and venerable white beards, arranged on dirty cloths on the ground, are small plastic

4

bags bearing labels in ill-formed handwriting listing the names of herbs and their medical uses—treatments for indigestion and diarrhea, enhancement of the libido and prolongation of intercourse, cures for impotence and infertility, kidney stones and headache, excessive lust and sciatica, night blindness and incontinence, cirrhosis of the liver and Mongolism.

Anyone strolling like us will notice, stretching as far as the eye can see, small collapsible wooden stands under old, tattered umbrellas. The stands hold piles of software CDs for programs both extremely old and very new, CDs and DVDs of Arabic movies of love, horror, and comedy, American action and adventure movies, Turkish movies showing titillatingly dressed women, cartoons for children and adults, belly dancing, and professional wrestling—all stacked one above the other.

Finally, well-hidden but selling briskly under the table, are the porn flicks (down-to-earth Arabic or artistic foreign) in their standard categories of *suftisiks*, *hardikoor*, *stirayt*, and *gaay*.

Most of the salesmen behind the wooden stands are young and wear gallabiyas, skullcaps, and long, bushy beards; a few are teenagers in cheap jeans and logo caps, their chests bared to reveal the freshly sprouted hair.

The throng of salesmen, customers, passersby, and those waiting for buses and minivans forms a chaotic nebula.

The air vibrates to a continuous hum, a nonstop roar drawn from all the square's diverse sources of sound. The horns of Public Transport Authority buses, minivans, taxis, and private cars of every make, color, and size blend with the squeal of tires on asphalt and the noise from the tape recorders of the salesmen all around the square and from the stores, kiosks, and stalls, the throats of peddlers and mouths of minivan barkers and their boy assistants calling "Pyramids!" and "Feisal!," "Beni Sueif!" and "Fayoum!" all rising in successive, stereophonic waves—dense, raucous, clashing.

Arabic and foreign songs mix with Qur'anic recitation, sermons, and religious chants to fuse with a call to the sunset prayer ascending to the sky from the mosque of the Straight Path and another coming from the mosque of Nasr el-Din at the other end of the underpass.

The only sound of the square that's missing is the tolling of the bells of St. George's Coptic Catholic Church on Durri Street, an old building with a dome topped by a metal roundel depicting the Virgin Mary, carrying Christ in her arms and protected by the shadow of the huge cross mounted on the church's tower.

This incredible mass of sounds, lights, and shapes melds with the never-ending undulations of human movement, a movement like that of ants who have emerged too early from their long winter hibernation—men in peasant and Western garb, workers and well-dressed men of the middle classes, government employees and professionals, young people, children, and the old, men in gallabiyas and abayas, in skullcaps and scarves, in shirts and pants, in three-piece suits, in official uniforms, in army and police jackets. Among the crowd are women of all ages in dresses and twin sets, pants and mantles. Some cover their hair, others go bareheaded, yet others are veiled from head to toe.

Wherever you look, a mass of humanity marches through the streets.

Today is Thursday. Thursday and Thursday night are the square's weekly Day of Resurrection and Night of the Last Hour.

Government employees and workers from Upper Egypt pour into the square from all parts of Greater Cairo and the new cities. They come to it from every direction, only to set off from it once more for their villages in the south. Some fill to bursting the nearby railway station and its entrances as they wait for their third-class trains; others distribute themselves among the cafés, restaurants, and stores, wandering here and there in groups or waiting at the bus and minivan starting points scattered around a small green area at the center of the square that is surrounded on four sides by an iron fence and in the middle of which stand three short palm trees.

The sun had almost set, its yellow disc vanished from the square. Perhaps it had buried itself in the desert, way over there, far to the west, behind the Great Pyramid and the Sphinx.

—

The sky over the square is gray, loaded with smoke and dust, and threads of darkness spread out and work their way into it, extinguishing what blueness and light remain. The fall chill, at the end of November, is mild and invigorating.

On our right, a few steps before the underpass, stands the Avowal of God's Unity and Light Shopping Center, its giant glass frontage occupying all three floors of the imposing medium-rise building. Placed across and at the sides of its huge display windows are large spotlights trained on mannequins the size of an average human that end in headless necks. Dummies wear men's sportswear, deluxe and regular, cheaper, white gallabiyas, women's capacious black, brown, or drab mantles, and various other forms of religiously approved "modest dress" and full-body coverings, all of them plain white, black, or dark blue. Miniature mannequins—dummies equally headless—wear up-to-date children's styles. There are no mannequins displaying underwear, nightdresses, or swimwear.

The giant display windows are crowded with shoes, slippers, and leather bags, and kitchen utensils and tableware jostle one another next to radios, tape recorders, television sets, and computers. To take in everything on display, the observer must take two steps back, making a little distance between himself and the glass. Attracted by the vast number of items on show, the window-shopper wandering on the opposite sidewalk, in front of the Zaabalawi tent-mall, will be pulled toward the giant glass windows and cross the street toward the Avowal of God's Unity and Light, as though the windows were giant lamps attracting all the bugs of the world. The zealous consumer will have no choice but to come over here, where we had paused to loiter a little. Leaving Zaabalawi's behind him, he will cross below the flyover to gaze at the paradise of the Avowal of God's Unity and Light, stopping to stare and wonder a while before entering.

At the top of the building, ropes of yellow, red, and blue light bulbs wrap themselves around a large signboard on which is written in neon lights: ☦ *O People, fear your Lord. Terrible indeed shall be the quaking of the Last Hour.* ☦

The colored bulbs throw a meager light on the stretch of the flyover that rises in front of my old school, the school of "Him Who Never Speaks," the Sphinx National School, and on the gas station and aged cafés next to the shopping center.

🔯 *Terrible indeed shall be the quaking of the Last Hour.* 🔯

I am lost . . . scared.

We entered the underpass with slow steps, arm in arm, humming "They done him wrong, da-da-dah, da-da-dah."

We stopped about halfway along the dimly lit passage on the Pyramids Road, on the narrow right-hand sidewalk, where there was barely room for two.

I bent my right leg and used it to prop myself against the underpass wall so I could relax standing up.

A broad smile lit Haris's handsome black face. His mouth is large, his teeth very white. Two are missing, lost in some adolescent fight. Raising his dark-brown pullover—a still-fashionable fall pullover with a V-collar, beneath which he was wearing an overlarge white shirt that hid his thin chest—he reached into his shirt pocket and extracted a joint rolled and ready for smoking. He cracked the knuckles of the thumb and middle finger of his right hand with a familiar movement, and offered me the swollen cigarette with his left. "Have a good one. Light up."

The patches and dribbles of urine on the underpass wall were black, the reek mild; it melted into the odiferous cloud of tobacco smoke that resides permanently under the ceiling of the underpass, fed by the chimneys of the Eastern Tobacco Company, whose buildings stand parallel to the railroad.

The railroad goes over the underpass. Above it is an elevated line for subway trains.

A subway train passed overhead with a faint roar.

Glad looks darted from Haris's eyes as he lit the cigarette for me with his gold lighter. I took two long, appreciative drags and gave it back to him. We passed the cigarette back and forth, taking slow tokes and feeling good, following with joyful faces the progress of the cloud of blue smoke above our heads. In gasps, along with the smoke, Haris's favorite sentence when thus occupied emerged: "What's the sweetest thing in the world? What? Hashish, and smoking in the open air, heh-heh!"

The cars speed through the underpass toward the square in an ascending, seemingly endless, line. There are no pedestrians in the underpass. It is empty except for me and Haris.

Suddenly, a decrepit Brazilian-made Volkswagen minibus crammed with people slowed down, its driver sounding a long blast on the horn as he came to a halt in front of us.

Along with the thick, wrinkled neck that emerged from the driver's window came a huge, ancient face that had long ago taken whatever it had coming to it—a face as long and twisted as Giza Square, with narrow, shifty eyes, a large, aged nose, and a low, abundantly creased forehead under thick, very white hair.

The old man let out a long whistle from his wide toothless mouth and chamfered lips.

"Pssssssssssssht!"

Haris looked up at the old man with a wan smile.

"Halis! Halis! Nayth day!"

Haris replied, through his nose, "Cut to the evening! Come and take a toke."

The cars came to a forced stop in a long line behind the old man's minibus, which was gray and had an open door via which the passengers were fed a constant diet of exhaust fumes, dust, colds, and influenza, not to mention opportunities to fall out into the river of traffic. The door was tied back with strong rope to prevent its being closed, thus saving on wear and tear.

Extended blasts rose from the horns of the cars held up behind the minibus and gesticulating hands emerged from their windows, while innumerable mouths released, at varying rates and volumes, gross insults directed at a certain sensitive part of the old man's mother's body.

The old man made a gesture with both hands, shaking his head dismissively, then let out a long, stupid laugh as though sharing a joke with himself.

He winked with his right eye and said, with the coquettishness of a zebra, "Fankth, Halis! I'm good. Good and all lit up." He craned his neck with its bulging, bluish veins, indicating the large, elaborately wrapped and befrilled spliff of strongly scented marijuana dangling from his left hand in the air beside the window, and waved it at us.

Suddenly, he trod on the gas and the minibus juddered and moved off, its rusty body shaking and rattling, the driver's hysterical laughter and the terrified gasps and cries of its panicked passengers rising as they swayed and bounced, cannoning off the backs of the seats and the sides and roof, shoulders and heads banging together, bodies falling on top of one another.

Releasing the steering wheel to make a dumb show of brushing the sounds of the passengers off his ears, the old man waved to us with both hands and emitted a "Ho ho!"

"Thee you, boys! Thee you!" he shouted at us.

Haris made an abrupt two-handed gesture in the air, as though ridding himself of an obnoxious nuisance.

"See you."

My mood spoiled by the old man, I handed the cigarette back to Haris.

"Ugh!" he half laughed, gesturing after the aged driver of the decrepit minibus. "Sayyid Uqr. The biggest asshole in Giza and suburbs."

"Yeah, yeah," I said, shaking my head.

Uqr's minibus disappeared out the underpass in the direction of the flyover, the cars behind him still hooting continuously, the heads of men and women sticking out of the windows, spitting in the air, and keeping up a nonstop barrage of abuse.

The minibus climbed the slope of the flyover in front of the Sphinx School and set off at high speed, like a projectile shot from an ancient cannon and destined to burst in the sky over the square at the very moment, a few seconds later, that it would leave our sight.

Haris gave me what remained of the cigarette, the "last kiss," exhaling from the depths of his lungs and producing a faint snoring sound through his nose.

A train passed overhead on its way to Ramses Station, letting off a high, prolonged whistle. The rhythmic sound of its wheels on the rails was deafening and we put our hands over our ears. We squatted on the paving stones of the sidewalk.

Ponderously, the train with its many cars crossed the bridge as though stamping on our heads, smashing them and flattening our bodies against the asphalt. As it drew away, we sighed in relief and stood up again.

I took the filter that Haris had made from a Marlboro Red pack and inserted into it the last millimeter of the cigarette.

Haris turned his back and went off. He left me coughing and spluttering like an old man—my usual dry cough. He exited the underpass and crossed over to Nasr Street, at the beginning of Pyramids Road.

I took my time over the last kiss, sucking the final toke down slowly, with relish.

2 HARIS

WITH HIS LONG, HURRIED STRIDES, he was always ahead of me, hands swinging right and left, long legs moving forward as though wading through mud.

I'd be behind him, moving like an aged elephant, my steps slow and heavy.

From the back, Haris looked tall, with a large oval head stuck directly onto narrow shoulders, and a thin body. His black hair was short and kinky and sprouted from his huge head like esparto grass. His neck wasn't simply very short, he seemed to have been born without one. As a specimen of the human race, Haris deserved the heartfelt lamentations that Aziza poured over him on every conceivable occasion, as she gazed at him with her wide honey-colored eyes and exclaimed, "Your poor mother!"

To look at him from behind was to be made aware of the idiotic contradiction between Haris's body and the beauty of his face with its piercing, extremely black eyes, straight nose, and full lips, to deduce from his hurried movements that he was aware of his body's misshapenness, and to discover that he hid a lack of self-confidence and a latent self-contempt behind his comically exaggerated motions.

Twenty long years ago, Haris had shared my desk in elementary school. He was the son of Uncle Hasan, janitor at the Sphinx School, a large, goodhearted old man with a black face, an ample white Nubian gallabiya, and a white turban. His mother, Auntie Amna, sold us halvah, exercise books, geometry sets, and pencils from her little stand to the right of the school's iron gate, close to her husband's bench. Her dark-brown face was sunny and bright, with a serene smile. She'd give us what we wanted, followed by a peck on the cheek as she whispered gently and lovingly, "You're all my children, you little devils."

She had only the one child—the quarrelsome, naughty boy, always in a fury, who shared my desk and my sandwiches and was sometimes my partner in playing hooky, to stroll through the Giza market or go to Cinema Fantasio, wander along Pyramids Road or roam the zoo.

Haris, Auntie Amna's son, had by now drawn far ahead of me, crossed the double median, and was close to disappearing from sight into the throng of people moving along the other side of Pyramids Road.

I kept going at my slow pace, gazing into the faces of the people around me. Unconsciously, my eyes scanned the crowds on the sidewalk as people came and went.

Since leaving the house that day, I'd been searching the innumerable faces on the street for that one particular face, the one that would pursue me for the rest of my life (assuming I had any left to me)—the face that would find me wherever I might go, awake or asleep, the face that had taken up residence inside my head, from which I could not escape, and that I'd been unable to erase from my brain from the moment Nashwa had informed me, the night before yesterday, how things stood with me and of my pitiable situation.

Panic was growing in my limbs, a panic that swelled and came to rest in the pit of my stomach, preventing me from joining the ranks of these people who lived without awareness of death and poured through the streets and squares in pursuit of what is called life.

From the beginning, from the time I first saw Nashwa, I'd been running toward my end. I'd run as a thirsty blind man runs to a river, and because I couldn't see, I'd drunk the sweetest, most delicious water in existence and my whole body had become saturated, up to the neck. Then my foot had slipped and I'd fallen into the fathomless waters.

With every second, every instant, I can feel the corruption and rottenness spreading to new parts of my body and soul. Fear now accompanies me wherever I turn, like my shadow, sticking to me, forming a mask over my face, blinding me, blocking my nostrils and ears, paralyzing each of my senses. Fear of sudden death has become a disability like blindness or muteness or deafness, a chronic and incurable disability not to be gotten around or forgotten. Fear is destroying my brain cells and hindering the beating of my heart.

At the farthest point I can see, on the opposite corner, Haris props his back against a lamppost in front of the Hotel Pharaoh, his thin hand playing with a long keychain.

I hesitate for a long time before attempting to cross the street's two lanes, one of which goes to Mishaal, the other to Giza Square.

I take one step forward and another back, fearful of being hit by a car and dying in the middle of the road like a stray dog.

After some time, and with much care, I cross the first lane, eyes swiveling, focused on the cars coming toward me. I stand on the narrow median and catch my breath.

Two minutes later, I cross the other lane and let out an "ouff" of relief.

There are only about five meters between me and Haris. I see him gesturing with his right hand as he talks to a prettily plump, fair-skinned girl, the front part of whose blonde hair is visible and goes well with her white face, while the rest is hidden under her shiny, colored headscarf. Once a minute she tugs her headscarf forward with the fingers of both hands to make sure it covers most of her forehead.

The girl seems to be afraid of looking like a dumb whore, of the sort one can recognize just by looking at her clothes, which is why she's added to her accessories a colored headscarf of a common kind. This allows her to maintain the desired balance between whorishness and decency, between enticement of those who get the message and a contemporary religious respectability.

Her headscarf functioned as efficiently as a good sewing machine: if she pulled it down to cover her whole forehead, she looked like any ordinary girl student at venerable Cairo University, a university girl who dressed modestly and studied, for example, Arabic Language. If she pushed it back a little, she moved from the study of Arabic to that of English, and if she further increased the area of exposed hair, she moved to acting at the Higher Institute of Dramatic Arts.

The Academy of Arts was a few minutes' walk from there.

It was only her repeated pulling and tugging at her headscarf that made me aware of this stratagem of hers. Her headscarf had no connection to the rest of her clothes—her tight blue jeans, her pink blouse with the top button opened to reveal her cleavage, her breasts, round as large pomegranates, squeezed together under it. She had a large piece of bubble gum in her small mouth and was rolling it around with her red tongue, popping it like a child. Her face, which was completely without makeup, was innocent and attractive.

She looked me over disdainfully, starting at my shoes. The expression on her lips, curled in disgust at the imposition of my person on the two of them, hurt me a little.

More to show off than with any intention of introducing me, Haris spat out, "Rabeea. My friend."

He didn't add another word. I was waiting for him to mention at the least my distinguished position, my high-ranking job, my fame, social and cultural status, and important family (ha-ha), to mention any of my qualities, good or bad—anything that would do as an excuse for a quick landing, a forced landing I was in desperate need of that night, onto the body of this arousing female.

Her lower body was unexpectedly well endowed, in stark contrast to the innocence of her face. The look in her wide eyes was that of a plump blonde calf, like that of the Children of Israel.

She addressed Haris with the authority and confidence of a school teacher reprimanding a dull student: "Cut to the chase, for God's sake, sweetiepie!"

She spoke with the nasal twang and rasped "r" dear to well-off ladies.

Despite the vulgarity of the expression, there was something odd about her intonation and tone, something that didn't fit the rest of the sociolinguistic environment. For a moment I saw her as a stage ingénue in an old black-and-white movie, born and bred in Maadi and playing the role of the vivacious whore from Sheikh's Lane in the back alleys of Giza.

Before she could finish speaking, Haris, who claimed to be a veteran when it came to dealing with "women of the night," had put his large hand on my shoulder and turned me around to face the other way. He gave me a slight push, leaving the girl behind us.

After we'd taken three steps forward, he turned back toward her with a quick snort to show his contempt and fired off one of his familiar ringing laughs in her direction, his thick lips expelling the hackneyed phrase, "You'll be sorry later, bimbo."

"What's it to you, dumbo?"

I admired her deft response, the deployment of rhyme as a part of her vulgar, piss-foreign repertoire.

Looking around, I saw she'd "turned her face inside out like a sock," as they say, as though she'd caught the smell of some dead dog that had spilt its entrails on the sidewalk right there, in front of the Hotel Pharaoh.

Despite her histrionic tone of voice and hammy movements, I decided the anger in her reaction was real, or wanted to believe it was. At the same time, I wanted her face to soften a bit, to relax and resume its former nonchalant expression.

Her broad thighs, stuffed by main force into her jeans, aroused the animal between my legs, which proceeded to push out a little the retaining wall of my pants.

Like an idiot, I drew a broad smile on my face for her. Pleading pathetically, I said, "Don't get mad. It's just Haris."

She'd been expecting more reproach. With sweet exasperation, she said, "Some people are so out of it. Imagine! Me, the princess, Princess Simone, for two hundred pounds. Two hundred pounds! Now that'd be a bargain!"

I didn't ask her slightingly, as I normally would have: "So that's your name today? What was it yesterday, then, and what will you call yourself tomorrow?"

I envy her her line of work, which gives her the freedom to choose her name and personality every day, every night.

With a face like an angry bull, Haris shouted in protest, "Two hundred pounds for an hour! For an hour, makes how much? You want to tell me you make sixteen hundred a day if you work just eight hours like regular people?"

She put on a "fuck you!" expression and asked Haris, "Are you trying to say, baby-face, that you're the same as me? That you think you should make the same as I do?"

Her ringing voice is disparaging and her large backside flicks left and right in rhythmic coordination with the singsong delivery of her so gracious words.

With secret connivance, Haris pushed down on my collarbone with the palm of the hand that was resting on my shoulder.

"Fine. Forget the potty talk and make a deal with this customer here. Go ahead, madam."

She gave an affected and coquettish laugh and looked sternly into my face as she said, "Go ahead and stare, bozo. Take your time with the once-over, customer."

She turned slowly, naively dramatic, placing her hand on her right hip and sticking her backside out in my direction.

"Take a good look. Take a good look, baby" (said with the sexy delivery of a pampered mistress lying at full length beneath her lover's prick).

She looked me straight in the eyes to gauge the effect of her well-turned, very arousing backside, high and upward-pointing in its progress from the tops of her thighs to the nip of her waist, large and cleft like a big white watermelon with a slice taken out of it. I pictured it like that—tasty and suffused with red.

Turning to face me, she exclaimed, with deep-rooted fear of the effects of admiration, "I seek refuge with God from your eye that splits stone!"

Her breasts were suspended in front of my face as she placed her hand on my hair.

"So how much am I worth, customer? Huh?"

A delicious light numbness, a weak electric current, flowed through my body at the caresses of her long, thin fingers.

I gazed into her eyes. I saw in them an ancient, deep-seated sorrow struggling to hide a settled, bitter grief. Shit!

Fearful of our princess's emotional motility, I used her body to distract myself from looking into her eyes, into the things she chose, with overwhelming naiveté, to show and to hide, and began running my eyes over her body, weighing the merits of each of her many curves in my head.

The pocket between her breasts was deep and shiny, pink and white.

Unbidden, the thought occurred to me of burying my head between her breasts and falling asleep where I stood, on Pyramids Road, under the eyes of all, hugging a prostitute who would one day hate me from the depths of her heart.

A long time must have passed while I stood in silence, engrossed in contemplation of Simone, because Haris let out a gloating guffaw.

She laughed along with him and took his arm in hers.

"Okay . . . two hundred, dinner, two bottles of beer, and two joints, baby."

"In God's name, then!" said Haris, with deep and genuine piety. "Don't worry about the fixings. They're all there, God willing, and more."

I felt as though I'd stepped back many years into the past.

It seems I was still awestruck, still bashful as a thirteen-year-old before any bold, brazen female. When I'd run into Magda, my preparatory school teacher, a month ago on the subway and, in a rare moment of nostalgia for my boyhood, reminded her who I was, she'd been amazed. Taking a long look at me, she'd said, "Same shy boy. Always shamefaced."

Ashamed of myself, I took refuge in my own thoughts despite the evening racket, the suffocating crowds, the blaring car horns, the overpowering smell of her perfume (it seemed she'd put on not drops but a bucketful of knock-off scent whipped up by some crap perfume-maker). Resisting the allure of the crude scent, I kept my distance from them, trying to overcome the lust coursing through the lower half of my body and feeling the pain in my belly that hit me every time I tried to rein in my ramping desire.

It seems they misunderstood my silence and why I kept a few steps behind them. They assumed I was feeling defeated and useless. To them I was now an excrescence, with no part to play in the harmonious scene they were creating together.

I was supposed to stay curled up in my private nook, saying nothing, delving into my soul in search of the reasons for my sudden obsession with Simone's body.

I stared dully at the two of them as they shared a laugh on the heels of some scabrous joke Haris had poured into her right ear. Her laughter was loud and genuine and rose without restraint.

Haris took her arm in his with the eagerness of someone who'd won a prize he'd been afraid would elude him and they forged ahead of me, falling into step like old friends, like they'd been lovers for ages.

Aware that "three's a crowd," I walked behind them.

I contemplated Simone's body from behind, trying to control the amazement I felt as I gazed at it.

The movements of her body, her steps, her long strides—all were familiar to me. In the way her body thrust forward and swayed, the way it cut through the space before it and around it, there was something already known. Something intimately familiar. I had heard before the tiny sounds that emanated from her buttocks and the shaking of her gold bracelets, just once, and here, in the very same place. Not long ago I'd seen that back. I'd touched it with my hand and caressed it over and over, and that . . . .

I felt as though this whole scene had taken place before, at the same time and place, a few steps from the Hotel Pharaoh.

They moved ahead of me through the underpass, heading for Giza Square, and I gazed at Simone, the same amazement now inscribed on my face.

My eyes moved over her body from behind like a plow moving through soil it has furrowed a hundred times before. Nothing was missing. There were no new bumps — the same anticipated smoothness of skin, occupying the same surface area that I'd already subjected to minute inspection, the same body outline, same shadow size, same motion, same haughty strut. Everything. Everything.

Maybe what was about to happen in the minutes and hours to come had already happened.

I don't know.

I drew closer, till I was a couple of steps behind them.

For a few moments I listened to the sounds issuing from her body, sounds like those that had entranced me before, the sounds of the women of my life that I'd preserved inside of me. From every woman I'd loved, I had taken into my possession something that I'd fixed inside of me by force, so that I'd possess it for good, so that each would remind me of another.

I desire them all and I don't want any particular one of them.

That way, the torment lasts forever.

Every Simone is something from the past, resembles some part of what I've already experienced. She had something or other—a great deal, perhaps—of Nashwa specifically. Something indefinable, indescribable, impossible to pin down.

I was afraid of Simone, and of Haris, but I kept walking behind them in this pitiful state.

I walk behind them like a parasite, someone alone and forgotten, wanted by no one, no one at all.

3 COPULATION

HARIS'S ROOM ON SAAD ZAGHOUL is ideal for lying low on one's own, just as it is for the clandestine introduction of a woman, suspect or honest, since the permanent crowd standing in front of the stores, large and small, and surrounding the peddlers provides cover. Men and women jostle one another the length and breadth of the street in front of and around the sellers of underwear, women's accessories, fruit, cheese, mish, and bread, children's toys, and anything else you can think of. Some salesmen spread their wares on the ground; others set them out on palm-frond chicken crates or wooden handcarts that they push ahead of them.

We enter Saad Zaghloul in the midst of the crowd, the two of them in front, I a couple of meters behind. I steal a look at my father's office window, lit up on the third floor of the Khawaga Building. Great. He's there, working devotedly on the cases of his paying clients.

The three of us move serenely on, concealed by the crowds of humanity.

Haris's room is the only habitable one in an old three-story house, half of which is in ruins, a pile of stones packed tightly one on top of the other to a height of five meters. The back half stands as tall as it has for the last ninety years. The Gabr family house, which until five years ago was stately and beautiful, has now become just a derelict lot between the two largest and best-known stores on Saad Zaghloul—

Hasan Rizq's (shoes and leather goods) and Shennawi's (readymade clothes designed specifically for one category of women—the "modestly dressed").

The house looks like the wreck of an old man sitting between two blooming, straight-backed youths, a deserted semi-vacuum that breaks the continuous line of old buildings whose ground floors are occupied by shops selling clothes, household goods, frozen meat, herbs, and spices—large stores with façades of glass or marble and brick-red or yellow stone facing. The street is busy from first thing in the morning to the following dawn, the buying and selling, the bargaining and arguing, the making of deals public and private never ceasing.

In fact, Haris's room, on the third floor at the back of the house, would make good accommodation for a local intellectual interested in studying the ancient Gizans' relationship to trade goods.

When Uncle Hasan retired and left his post in front of the gate of the Sphinx School, where he'd been a fixture for forty years, he'd brought his wife and his son Haris to guard this abandoned house. He was paid by the Gabr family, who had moved into new quarters in their imposing tower block on Greater Ocean.

Even after his parents had left for the village of Abu Simbel, south of Aswan, Haris was delighted to guard the old house and stayed on in it by himself. The elderly couple had said they wanted to die in the village where they'd grown up, and Haris had replied, "And I want to live here."

Long unemployed, he had recently started a job as a waiter at the Thutmose Bar in the Hotel Pharaoh, at the beginning of Pyramids Road.

The goodhearted parents had left two years before and the naughty boy, who had taken a degree in history from Cairo University, had stayed on. Alone, day after day, he guarded the house, the deserted home at the center of the commercial bustle and crowds, and three nights a week he served drinks to the patrons of the bar.

He'd chosen the largest room in the house that could be lived in and the farthest from the noise of the street, furnishing it like the cell of a dedicated voluptuary.

He'd tricked it out and made it as beautiful as a bride, to the point that "simply to live in it was pleasure enow," ho-ho.

Tiling made of chips of old decorative marble is covered with a Nubian rug with brown and white squares. Low, shining white couches furnished with luxurious throws, armrests, and silk cushions press against the walls, and decorated leather pillows in a variety of sizes are distributed over the couches and the floor. In two corners of the room, on either side of a wide couch with a red cover that Haris uses as a bed, two large old mirrors of Belgian glass stand facing one another. The stately mirrors are large enough to reflect an entire human body from in front and behind and, by providing images from a number of angles, to follow whatever movements and positions are being acted out on the couch. The mirror frames are a dull brown and made of rosewood, white-and-shiny-black mother-of-pearl, and mashrabiya work.

The computer is on a beech table, in front of which is a seat with a cane bottom and no back. Beneath the glass on top of the table there's a photo of a blonde American woman of fifty with "From Lauren to my darling Haris" scrawled on it.

On the room's four walls, about halfway between the back cushions of the couches and the ceiling, Haris has hung posters and reproductions of paintings and photographs in frames of varying sizes showing naked women—whites, blondes, yellows, blacks. His women are of every imaginable size and weight—sleek and thin, full and fat, huge as tanks. They have one strange thing in common: their gaze. A delicate gaze, closer to tender than lustful, a gaze simultaneously seductive and compassionate, from innocent eyes.

Haris spends most of his income on looking after the room and adding to its beauty. At regular intervals, he renews and adds to his collection of women. Every time I come I'm surprised by a new poster or reproduction of a nude in a deluxe frame. He pays as much attention to the beauty of the frame as he does to the woman inside it and has them all made at el-Qazzaz's on Mahmud Azmi.

The shop is famous, its prices exorbitant, and Mahrus el-Qazzaz, the son, adds to Haris's bill, with an affectionate smirk, the following items:

1. Emolument for averting his own eyes, specifically, from the said disgusting pictures.
2. Emolument for his workers for pretending not to see what they are framing and protecting with glass.
3. Allowance for keeping the pictures out of sight and hiding them from the eyes of his father, the founder of the business, Hagg Mustafa el-Qazzaz.

The Hagg's eyes are large and keen beneath the thick eyebrows and the huge prayer mark that takes up most of his forehead.

In the middle of the room is a low, white oak table covered with a sheet of translucent frosted glass. At either end of the table is a silver candelabra holding six pink candles and a brass incense-burner that emits a constant smell of sandalwood.

Classical music emanates at low volume from four speakers fastened to the walls and operated by Haris via the computer or his stereo tape recorder.

The room has nothing whatsoever to do with the rest of the house, the street, and the Giza market. It has to do with Haris's hidden self and that's all.

Sometimes I picture Haris stretched out on his couch, alone in his room. He presses a button and the white bulb in the light in the middle of the ceiling goes out. He presses another and turns on a small blue spot lamp that is trained on the center of the red spread that covers the couch. He presses a third to turn on other white spot lamps, focused to illuminate in their entirety the bodies of his girls hanging on the walls. Haris distributes the threads of colored light, in a calculated sequence, over his couch, into the air of his room, onto the naked bodies imprisoned in their frames.

Haris prepares the most arousing atmosphere possible before spilling his sperm onto the breasts, vaginas, and buttocks of his naked women.

Every night, morning, or midday, he chooses one, according to his mood and feelings on waking from sleep, or an hour after eating his lunch, or before lying down to sleep at night.

For a while, his rapid glances roam the bodies of his nudes and he starts prioritizing them, dawdling and hesitating at length before choosing. He excludes yesterday's woman first, then decides among all the possible and conceivable colors of the human body, ranging from a chilling whiteness to the borders of hot blackness.

With the scales of his eyes, he measures the volumes of the bodies, which range from 40 to 250 kilos in weight, hefting his women, whose sizes and weights extend from featherweight to elephant-weight, with his hands. He tries to choose between the women of each of the five continents, between a woman from the Old World or the New, or some unknown island. The reckoning takes time, but plays the role of pickles or salad as the starter to a meal. After much time and hesitation, and a little regret, he narrows the choice to three, then two, and finally chooses the bride with whom he will copulate.

First he takes off the white T-shirt that he wears around the house and looks into the face of the chosen woman, staring into her eyes to gauge the impact on her of his naked torso. When (naturally) no reaction appears, he leaves her face to its own devices and moves down to her breasts, then to her belly and waist, coming to a stop at her pelvis, at which point he catches his breath and slowly lowers his pajama bottoms to his thighs, his palms opening and closing at his groin. His lips are parted and he stares at the woman's naked lower half, taking a general snapshot with the camera of his eyes. His left hand reaches the top of his pubes, his left thumb moves toward the sparse hair, his fourth finger toward the root of the thing. Haris's wide eyes zoom in on the woman's crack, where they remain transfixed for a long time. He swallows and wets his lips with his tongue. He straightens his back and parts his thighs and his hands start moving, first gripping, then sliding from top to bottom, slowly at first, then a little faster, then a lot faster, till his whole being is shaken and he explodes with pleasure, moaning, his eyes fastened on the vagina of his woman, who is standing or stretched out on a bed or sprawled on the ground or sticking out her buttocks at him. He gives his thing, which is darker than the rest of him, a pat, closes his eyes, and dozes off. He sleeps and dreams, happy that what he gets up to with his naked women will never ever cross Lauren's mind.

The first time she saw his room, she said, "My, Haris! You're not very picky about your women!" Lauren had left for New York a year ago, on the understanding that she'd come back to him the following winter or he'd settle his affairs and go to her.

We drank two bottles of Omar Khayyam red, Haris's love potion of choice, and took turns smoking a not insignificant number of joints. A number, in fact, beyond my ability to count.

Asking for more, making like a slow-motion movie, I extended the palm of my closed right hand toward Haris, the index and middle fingers parted to form a V.

"That's it, buddy. That was the last," said Haris apologetically, as the final whiff of smoke exited Simone's nostrils.

The room, whose windows and door were shut, had filled with the blue smoke, which collected in the corners and beneath the ceiling. The flames of the six candles that Haris had lit when we entered danced before my eyes. Sometimes Haris could be a real old-time romantic, all sentiment.

Slowly and with difficulty, Simone rose to her feet and looked from one of us to the other, smiling and stoned.

She seemed unsure of something she'd been thinking about for a while, perhaps since we had arrived. She stood there, lips moving, one wetting the other, the tip of her tongue visible between them, no meaningful sound or comprehensible word emerging from her open mouth. She moved fretfully as she stood there looking at us and put her right index finger in her mouth as though puzzled, swaying her body slightly from side to side. Quietly, just as she had stood up, she sat down again in the same spot on the couch next to Haris, even though we hadn't understood what she wanted at all.

I had been staring at her naked toes and her legs, and when she sat down her rounded calves gave an almost imperceptible quiver. After a few moments, which seemed to me like an eternity, she stood up again and faced us with the air of someone making a final effort to gather all her courage and project it through her eyes.

In her vibrant voice, she proceeded to make a proposal that was the very essence of weird, and she uttered it in a commanding tone that brooked no argument.

Addressing Haris only, as though I had nothing to do with it, she said, "You two together. One party."

Haris's face darkened and the side of his mouth tightened with that familiar movement of his jaw.

He protested emphatically, yelling, "No way, whore!"

She placed her hands on her hips and pushed her backside out with a crude movement. "What's the big deal? You're afraid he'll see your a—"

"Ughghghghghghghghghghghgh!" The long, ugly sound escaped my lips.

Haris's features took on the look of the gang leader in an old movie, mocked by his men and his womenfolk.

Haughtily, she moved her delectable body slowly closer to him, till the air he breathed was saturated with her cheap perfume. She leaned over him and reached out with her left hand for the back of his neck while with nimble fingers her right hand opened one by one the buttons of his shirt.

Softly and gently she started playing with the hair of his head, while tender fingers caressed the sparse hair of his chest.

She went on playing with the skin on the back of his neck and with his hair till Haris dropped his eyes and let himself relax completely.

She descended to his black gabardine pants, slowly undoing his fly while giving me a wink.

The white globes of her buttocks were rounded and spilled over the edges of her red bikini panties. She'd sprawled out on a soft pillow set down on a black square on the rug and her full breasts were starting to spill out of her see-through red bra, quivering with the regular motion of her hand.

She bent her head toward him and her face disappeared.

As I stared at them, I felt the pain in my guts grow.

Suddenly, I stood up and took off my shirt beneath Haris's gaze, while he tried to overcome his moans by adopting a severe face, suppressing any sudden spasm of pleasure.

He was chewing his lower lip, pressing down with his tongue, and gritting his teeth to silence his sighs.

Impetuous and crafty, I galloped toward them like a donkey in heat, grabbed her breasts hard with both hands, plastered myself against her from behind, and plunged it between her white buttocks.

I lifted her thighs from the floor and put her into a kneeling position so that she looked like a coddled white bitch quietly standing there, and then I spread her legs apart till her buttocks clenched and quivered.

With schooled professionalism, she raised her backside into the air and displayed her two red passages.

In an instant, without preparation or forethought, I cast everything that was inside me, my whole body, into her, till I could feel her blood vessels dilating, the bones of her pelvis grinding, and her, moaning, beneath my successive thrusts.

4 EVENING PRAYER

THE EVENING PRAYER IS AN "AUDIBLE" PRAYER. The imam speaks in an audible voice while reciting the opening chapter of the Qur'an and the two chapters that follow during the first and the second prostrations.

The opening chapter is being recited by the most beautiful of the voices of my childhood, that of my boyhood idol, Sheikh Hubb el-Deen.

The sheikh's delicate voice is as sweet as honeycomb. It casts a protective shade over the house and emanates from it, because the zawya's loudspeaker hangs above us, at the top of a tall pole stuck into the roof of Haris's room.

The Mercy zawya is two buildings away from us, in the building containing three large, well-known stores. Between it and us are forty meters of electric wire that stretch from the zawya's microphone in the basement to the ancient loudspeaker above the house.

After sixty years of reciting the Wise Narration, the venerable sheikh's voice is still melodious and full of beauty for all that it is weak and fails to carry.

Out of his love for humanity, with all the strength in his heart, and from the depths of his soul, Sheikh Hubb recites.

Sheikh Hubb recites the Opening with the detachment of one who bids this world farewell, ready to meet his Maker.

"Aaaaaamen," respond the few worshipers behind Sheikh Hubb el-Deen in the small prayer hall, which holds twenty at most.

The Mercy zawya was built by Hagg Shawkat in the basement of his building. As soon as he'd put up the small wooden pulpit with its two wooden steps, covered the floor tiles with plastic mats, and put in a single squat-latrine and a small basin with three faucets, he went in person to Sheikh Hubb el-Deen's home, where he gave the sheikh's hand and graying head a long kiss, in the hope that he would agree to act as muezzin and lead the prayer.

On Sheikh Hubb el-Deen's agreeing to be the imam of the zawya, a few traders, artisans, and workers from the market who were the sheikh's followers moved there and gave it life.

The sheikh loved it because it was small, tucked away, and out of sight of the clamorous and crowded market. There he found a refuge in which to apply himself to the service of God, indifferent to this life and its affairs, leaving the world on the outside, behind him.

The zawya is accessed via a narrow wooden stairway next to the door to Hagg Shawkat's emporium with its floors bursting with sanitary ware, ceramic tiles, and marble.

During the first prostration, after a brief, reverent silence, the sheikh recited, from the depths of his effulgent heart, the chapter entitled

"Forgiving," and the worshipers asked for intercession on his, and their own, behalf.

His recitation was full of the fear of God and the people wept in their prayers till I could hear their sobs pouring down upon me from the loudspeaker above the room.

Their souls shake with apprehension, moan with pain, and pierce the ceiling with a low keening that spreads, then gathers directly above my head.

5 NASHWA

I COULD FEEL that Haris had fixed his gaze on my face in amazement, was staring at me in astonishment. I could see his phantom standing there unmoving, like a tall black reed.

I'm behind her, my eyes half closed. I gather all the powers of my body. I quiver and shudder like a wild stallion. I whinny from the depths of my being and all that is inside of me and outside of me shudders as one, shaking and roaring.

I hone every one of my senses. I polish them and smooth them and sharpen them like a razor blade. I boil them in my heat, vaporize them, distill them, and concentrate them into a solid essence that I form into a single mold, body, substance. I smelt this substance outside and in, in part and in whole, and convert it into one power, one sense—that of touch.

I gather an uncountable number of keenly sensitized nerve cells and place them within the half centimeter at the tip of my furthest extremity and then place my love-crazed, greedy self on top of them. I etch the eyes of my heart into the center of my beast's head and wipe my soul, with its slow gaze—its slow, focused, wholly rapt gaze—all over its face.

Moments, seconds, and I'm gone from the Other, the room, the world.

Nothing remains in my world but the head of my outermost extremity and her passageway. I disappear in pursuit of my cells of touch, which leap out of me like swimmers in a long-distance race. I guide my skillful swimmers toward the entrance to her passage. Gently I knock on the door and push through it. I thrust in the direction of the threshold, then of the entranceway. I push on toward the center, then the depths. I flirt with the ceiling and the walls, I knock at the angles and corners, and pound on the floor. I push and push till I reach the end of her open passage. The creatures of my touch scatter, move, and graze on the ground of her velvety smooth barrier, taste her soft, delicious flesh, drink her sweet water, inhale her fragrance, which exhales an intoxicatingly attractive smell. My creatures glide, gambol, and gallop over her soil, playing, jumping, and running, are watered and irrigated by her honey so that they become drunken and drugged, swaying and dancing from excess of pleasure. Little by little, my speed increases. Deliberately and with studied care, I tenderly split her in two. Mercifully, then resolutely and with all my strength, powerfully, and finally crudely, with a violence that sweeps all before it, I dig down into her, I break on through to the end of her end, to her deepest point. I plow her till I reach her innermost place.

Deeply, deeply, I enter her, with the whole of me, with all the strength of my despair, with black vengeance.

It was Nashwa I was having sex with: Nashwa who had taken on Simone's body, Nashwa who was hiding inside Simone's body, Nashwa who had melded with Simone's skin, blood, and flesh.

I was with Nashwa concealed inside Simone's body.

I was having sex with Nashwa, Nashwa alone, no other woman.

In Haris's face, its eyes trained upon me, I beheld extraordinary surprise and prolonged shock. His eyes were open to their widest, appalled. His lips trembled slightly and he stood up, straight as an ebony statue.

I hear the sound of slapping dough, an African jungle rhythm. I listen intently to the drumbeat that mounts with each entry and exit. My body picks up the beat as her labia play again and again on the drumhead of our melting, our pulling apart, our coming together. The rhythm of our encounter speeds up. My hands' cruel grip upon her hardens. My legs and my knees and my feet, which are planted on the ground, shake from the uncontrollable acceleration of my movements and my careening impetuosity. My whole body explodes and shudders with insane desire and overflows like a river that breaks its banks, sweeping all before it.

She moans and lets out violent, deep, protracted sighs as she turns her head toward me, her eyes opening to their widest.

Rosy and glowing, she fixes her eyes on my face in ecstasy, absorbed in pleasure's pain. Shocked and afraid, astonished, she gazes into my eyes.

Suddenly, Haris screamed and let out a roar of fury mixed with fear that shook his body.

He picked up his pants and quickly put them on. Then he left, slamming the door behind him, while I made love to her as though it was the last copulation of my life, as though I was going to die in one minute, as though fighting off my inescapable end.

My soul leaves my body slowly, exits through the pores of my skin subtly and quickly as I scream with pleasure and pain.

My soul rises, rises to the sky with agonizing slowness.

6 SIMONE

I FINISHED AND SLUMPED OFF, hiding my privates with my pants.

After a silence as long as death's, she laughed. Her voice rang out in plentiful, false merriment, the roof of her mouth vibrating with a resounding horselaugh. Her body shook long and hard with the force of her meaningless mirth as she picked up her brassiere and put it into her small silver bag.

She slapped palm against palm in a mime of helpless mirth, now gesturing toward the door through which Haris had exited, now toward my naked chest and the pants on my lap.

As I stretched out on the couch and lit a cigarette, I smiled at her, from the heart.

She put her blouse on over her sexy, warm flesh. She hadn't yet closed the buttons. Her large round breasts swung slightly in front of my eyes, revealing two small brown nipples, still erect.

My body struts in a gauzy quiet numbness. All of me is drugged and sleepy.

I take a few slow, luxurious drags on my cigarette, indifferent to the fact that the smoke is mounting toward her face and her long yellow hair.

I turn away from her and lose myself in my thoughts.

I know that Simone will soon begin, after the manner of other goodhearted *filles de joie*, to tell the story of the tragedy that drove her off the straight and narrow. There's bound to have been some great calamity in her past, some heavy-duty disaster. No woman in this part of the world, or in any other part perhaps, chooses the sex trade of her own free will. We don't have any examples of "free" sex workers who practice the profession out of a sense of conviction, or out of love for the craft—respectable, mature, well-balanced women who choose to offer sexual services as a career and who make it their profession to bring happiness to wretched, wounded men, with a physician's dedication and the skill of a great and learned surgeon. Here, the physician always, and unfortunately, feels that her patient doesn't value her as she deserves, doesn't treat her with appropriate respect, doesn't acknowledge her dedication, feels no gratitude for her sublime services. The caregiver wants to feel the patient is grateful to her, wants him to praise her fervently as he mounts her in return for his money. . . .

As though reading these cheerful thoughts, Simone cut through them with the words, "The money alone isn't enough, baby."

You get on and hand over some money, like you would a bus fare or a taxi fare or a plane fare, according to the means of transportation and its tariff. Do you despise the taxi driver for being a taxi driver?

Don't despise me either.

This being so, I'll make up an explanation for why I've made myself into something for others to ride. It doesn't matter whether what I tell you is true or not, and it's not important that you believe me. Generally, I lie, and you know that I'm lying. I don't want you to believe me. There are no true stories, customer. The story is invented to produce an effect, so just respect me, don't believe me. So long as I pleasure you with my body and my story, what more can you ask for?

In return for your banknote, you obtain one sexual orgasm plus one of another kind for free—the orgasm of listening to a fascinating melodrama that cleanses you and releases you from your repressed emotions and bad feelings, that flushes your eyes with the tears of pity. What more can you ask for, baby . . . greedy boy?

She told me to pay now. Pay the respect before and after the cash, baby. She said she didn't want anything more.

Simone, now turned philosopher, emptied the bucket of her mighty thoughts over my head, resting on the pillow, and over my face, which was staring into the light inside the lamp suspended from the middle of the white ceiling.

She seemed like another woman, someone completely different. A woman one could take to an intellectual, political, or literary salon and sit quietly next to, feeling proud as she takes the microphone and confidently, arrogantly, and with impeccable logic comments on each issue raised.

She said, "I bet you've listened to lots of stories about whores. I've listened to a few too, and I'm not going to make one up specially for you. That's not part of the deal, baby. There is a true story in my past but I'm not going to tell it to you now. Maybe one day I'll charm your ears with it, but you're just a baby, baby, and you won't believe me and you won't understand. Anyway, you have to respect me even if I don't give you any reason, justification, or prop. I don't need your sympathy or your pity. Give me my money and, over and above, before and after, the respect I deserve."

The philosopher achieved the effect she desired. Instead of milking my sympathy and pity and tickling the customer's vanity with some tawdry story of a pitiful woman with a still-suckling orphan to care for that had lost its father in the flower of his youth, or of a woman in flight from a scheming stepmother, cruel father, and ten siblings, or of a noble innocent husband in prison and his sick mother who needed an incredibly expensive operation, or . . . or any other story that might emerge from dirty reality or the fertile imagination of a goodhearted *fille de joie*—instead of all that, Simone attacked me and branded me a baby. Me, a baby?

She philosophized, put forward an ontological analysis of her existence as one example of a unique phenomenological condition about which, it appeared, she'd thought at length, and graciously bestowed on me her final conclusions.

To which group, category, kind, or class of *filles de joie* did this satiating, contemplative "Simone" belong?

With contempt, she said, "That's it, baby. Time's up. *O refwar!*"

I clung to the tail of her blouse like a child clinging to its mother's dress. "Don't . . . don't go yet."

"*Suri*, I really have to rush. Next time we can stay and have a nice chat!"

She spruced up her clothes, put her colored headscarf over her hair and pinned it with hairpins, and ended up looking exactly as she had when I'd first seen her—a modestly dressed young woman with a modern look.

She gave me a sweet smile and a nod, ruffled my hair, patted me affectionately on the back, and, in contrast to the normal ways of prostitutes, kissed me gently on the cheek. Then she left.

I too shall arise now and go, to catch up with him who fled from before my countenance . . . with Haris.

7 KAGHA'S UNCONTROLLABLE TEARS

WHEN I ENTERED THE ROOM, Haris gave me a strangely suspicious look. Unlike Shawqi, he didn't get up, didn't put out his hand to shake mine, and stared unwaveringly at my face with veiled anger. So I behaved as though he wasn't there.

After Shawqi's greetings and Kagha's hugs, I sat down in my place; in my usual corner on the colored plastic mat and on top of the black leather pillow, I sat myself down. I stretched my legs and bare feet out in front of me as far as they would go, deliberately directing them toward the face of Haris, who was sitting on the couch.

I leaned back against the wall, smiling at Kagha, who was next to me. I rested my head, closed my eyes, and let out a deep sigh, savoring the pleasure of lying down in the warmth of my companions, whose faces were just as they had been for the last twenty years or so, the essence unchanged, though the features were now more deeply etched, and transfigured.

Each contemplates the faces of the others, the faces of the children and adolescents we once were, in a day that now seems to us long gone. Our faces are old, familiar, an open book. From the beginning, each has followed the other's face, watched it as it became another person's, as the first fuzz sprouted, watched it lose its childish cast, the eyes becoming a little deeper set in their sockets, the fine hair appearing on the hands, the forearms, and the chest, the first signs of rebellion and of a lack of deference to the old. Each of us has heard the other's voice grow husky and rougher, heard it utter words of anger, refusal, and revolt.

Like all adolescents, we were children obsessed with dreams who thought that this country, these people, in fact the whole world, the entire human race (ha!), were in need of their hands and their minds.

We were naive dreamers, sick idealists, poets.

Add another ten years to our ages, and hundreds of experiments and experiences, and our circumstances and our heads have changed. The look in our eyes is a little meeker now. We avoid gazing directly into one another's eyes, avoid stripping the other naked with a cheeky, unwavering look. Without conscious agreement, we've started to fear, to beware of letting our eyes meet. Like those of partners in a terrible, ancient crime, the eyes of each of us flee the other's questioning stare. We have crossed into manhood (manhood!) and together passed the boundary line of the thirties, like a junior soccer team that's become the club's first team, like at the Saha Youth Center, for example, and we play together, like a team, in harmony, with a little tripping and selfishness, yes, but still together despite all the differences and widening gaps, the quarrels and wrongs, the mutually inflicted pains and the aborted hopes.

Here and now, among them, I think about all of that because I'll never again be able to drink of the cup of their companionship. I am eating up the minutes and hours as fast as I can, using lips and teeth, skin, hearing, and sight. I'm avidly eating up the days that remain to me with the greediness of a hungry man, with the impatience of one long deprived, with the voracity of one eating the last of his supplies. Maybe these really are my last supplies and will be followed by a long darkness, in which I shall lie stretched out forever on a bed of dirt, where sleep is restful and long.

I don't have time. I don't know if I'll be here next Thursday or not.

Intense feelings of pleasure course through my body at the familiarity of the room, the familiarity of the faces and bodies, of the voices, and of the ancient, deep-rooted smell of the place. These are my buddies, grown fewer over the years. Hussein el-Kinik, Amgad Murad, and Khalil Zahir have left us, gone their ways without us. They've abandoned us, leaving behind lots of memories and a little sorrow and pain at their departure, though we never permitted ourselves to shed even a few tears for them. "Men don't cry." That's what they taught us, so we put on a façade of strength and swagger, and grew older.

No one has come to fill the places of those who've left. No one sits where Hussein sat or after him Amgad or after him Khalil. Amgad died of heart disease. Khalil disappeared in mysterious circumstances and no one knew anything about him, and Hussein el-Kinik, a founding member of our gang, took a decision long ago to avoid us and ignore our existence.

A few months ago, I was standing in the crowded subway train on my way downtown when I heard that powerful voice of his that I knew so well. I turned and saw him sitting, his thin body wedged between two men of around forty, both huge and wearing dark gallabiyas. Their beards were long and their faces glowering. I saw him and I knew him but he didn't see me. Between his open hands was a small copy of the Qur'an. He was reading out loud, reciting in an angry voice that rose above even the noise of the crowd and the subway: ✿ *I shall surely roast him in Saqar, and what will teach thee what is Saqar?* ✿

He was totally absorbed, his expression brooding, his black beard long and bushy. He was wearing an old sports jacket over a white gallabiya and on his feet were aged leather sandals. He was reciting both for himself and for the people around him, as though to say, "You have your unreformed and godless lives and I have my immovable faith." I called his name and he raised his eyes without pausing in his recitation and saw me staring at him. For a few moments our eyes met and we exchanged a long silent look before he dropped his gaze and ignored me, gazing once more into his open Qur'an.

I smiled at him and at myself and said nothing, while his face bore an ambiguous expression that I found impossible to fathom.

We'd added no new members to our group and had continued to meet over the years for our weekly get-togethers, which we were rarely strong enough to forgo.

Kagha patted my thigh gently, pointing with a smile to a bottle of whisky, three-quarters of which they'd drunk, and I smiled at him.

On the large round low table set in the middle of the room were a vast number of empty beer bottles and four large plates of appetizers: sardines, miluha, and fiseekh, plus a serving plate spread with green onions, limes, arugula, radishes, and a tall pile of pita bread. Finally, there was the bottle, of a whisky rare in Egypt: Maker's Mark. A costly bottle, no doubt brought by Kagha, our shaabi singing star.

Kagha's real name was Imad Ali Ali Ali—that was the name we used to declaim in all its glory in our classroom at middle school. His voice was always nice to listen to and he studied at the Higher Institute of Arabic Music. However, because of the state of the music market and the singers who were already out there, he'd ended up working at a small nightclub (more a popular café, really) called Kamananna, located off Pyramids Road at the Taawon intersection.

When Boss Abd el-Badeea, the owner of the nightclub, auditioned our friend (he heard him do "The Gondola"), he was very taken by the husky catch to his voice but advised him to forget the songs of "General" Abd el-Wahhab and "Hagg" Ahmad Munib that our friend loved and follow the path of "Professor" Shaabolla.

Boss Abd el-Badeea's other condition was that he alone, and without reference to our friend's wishes, should choose the new singer's professional name. Abd el-Badeea spent a whole week turning over in his mind nouns, adjectives, and verbs, days of the week, months, seasons, places, times, and diseases before settling on a truly fabulous stage name for his new nightingale.

"The place is his, the singer is his, and he who nameth his own singer doeth no wrong, ha ha!" said Haris, speaking with all the wisdom of a waiter at the Thutmose Bar.

On the new singer's first working night, the boss unveiled to the small crowd of club regulars, and to the singer as well, his brilliant coinage. Boss Abd el-Badeea, in his check suit and with his broad belly, stood on the small round dance floor at the center of the establishment, cleared his throat, pulled himself up to his full height, and, like a television host announcing a singer in the main auditorium of the Egyptian Opera House, declared in ringing tones, "And now, respected clientele . . . now we present the Curlew of Shaabi Song, straight from the *conserfatoor* and all that jazz, the migrant songbird returned from our beloved Gulf, the scintillating, the dazzling . . . Kaaaaghaaaa!"

Every time he told how Boss Abd el-Badeea had given him the stage name that had become the only one he used, Kagha's eyes would fill with tears of laughter.

Every Thursday our feet hurried over here of their own accord, to Shawqi's room on Sheikh Zahran Lane, off Rabeea Street in Giza, his hermitage since childhood, all on its own on the roof above their small three-story house. The roof was spacious because nothing else had been built on it and the room was small and intimate.

I want to fix the images of these places in my head, to etch them forever into the folds of my brain. I know them as I know the lines on the palm of my hand and the features of my mother's face, and I have no hope of continuing to dwell in them.

Cans of fiseekh, sardines, and miluha, and wooden flats of herring, are stacked next to the party walls of the two neighboring houses and run the length of the balcony railing that looks out over the lane, from which you can see, and smell, truncated bits of the Nile and the Abbas Bridge that peep from behind the tower blocks on Greater Ocean.

Why do Egyptians refer to the Nile, a freshwater river, as an ocean?

The smell of fiseekh was cloying, as old as the fiseekh trade, which dates back to the pharaohs, and strong and penetrating, but we'd gotten used to it, just as we had to Shawqi's own fishy smell. Shawqi is an accountant at a pharmaceuticals factory in Sixth of October City, but the odor of fiseekh has yet to be supplanted on his body by that of pharmaceuticals.

At the few times of year (Shamm el-Naseem and the Feast of the Breaking of the Fast) when there was a call for fiseekh and sardines,

Shawqi puts on a wide Upper Egyptian gallabiya older than the one he's wearing tonight, winds a length of white cloth around his head, covers his fingers and palms with a pair of long rubber medical gloves, and stands in his father's shop, Friendship Fiseekh, right at the entrance to the vegetable market.

Shawqi stands in the store, behind the old wooden counter, not to keep the books and tally the taxes but to sell fiseekh, like a regular fiseekh-seller's assistant, while his father, Hagg Farag, with his huge frame, sits to the left of the shop door on an old bamboo chair that creaks beneath him. His Upper Egyptian gallabiya is of the highest quality, as are his black silk scarf and the turban wound around his large head. The hand in which he holds the plastic hose of his waterpipe is stained orange from a long lifetime of salting fish and turning them into fiseekh and miluha.

Boss Farag smokes his waterpipe and drinks black, heavily sugared tea, his dark-brown face, chiseled as that of a pharaonic statue, assuming the expression of one worried by an intractable problem. Like a venerable and grave politician, he explains to those seated around him drinking tea at his expense the perilous nature of the current political situation and the indifference of the government to the human-made disasters that forever afflict the impoverished and (to put it in the simplest terms) humble but decent Upper Egyptians.

The elderly Upper Egyptian grows excited, his hands moving all over the place. He waves and gesticulates, and sometimes jumps up, threatening the safety of the rickety chair. His face flushes and then pales as he yells a torrent of words that may be filtered, strained, and finally boiled down to the following: "We Upper Egyptians always get the short end of the stick. The government soaks us in dirty kerosene, sets fire to us on broken-down trains, and throws us to the sharks in the Red Sea."

In the purest Upper Egyptian dialect, which forty years of living in Giza has failed to dent, he talks, theorizes, and chats to himself without allowing any of the traders and sellers sitting with him to interrupt. Should anyone try to do so, he rounds on him angrily, saying, "Hold your horses, cousin! Hold your horses!"

His appetite for words knows no bounds. He speaks in a deep, harsh voice, which Shawqi has inherited, and straightens his turban on his bald head as the words stream out over the heads of his silent and well-mannered listeners. It has been a long time since Boss Farag last allowed anyone to quibble, challenge, or offer an opposing opinion. On rare occasions only, and then with barely concealed impatience and ill grace, will he accept a well-framed question or polite query.

He's been that way since the day he stopped cracking jokes.

Shawqi turns a deaf ear to his father's ever-evolving theses and theories. The man's political analyses, panting after each new event—the whole mendacious political ball of wax—hold no interest for him.

Patiently and in silence, Shawqi serves the customers in the store, selecting, weighing, and wrapping the fiseekh, sardines, herring, and miluha in old newspapers that his father has read from beginning to end.

Shawqi works devotedly and energetically, hiding his embarrassment, concealing his shame, his fear of being unmasked.

"Sorry. Not me," he says in a low but harsh voice that issues from his large mouth accompanied by a terrifying frown that he makes by drawing his eyebrows together and pursing his fleshy lips beneath the thick black mustache.

"You're quite wrong. I'm a fiseekh-seller, not an accountant and not a sweet-seller," he says with a short, rude grunt.

With unshakeable singleness of purpose, Shawqi snubs any acquaintance from work or member of his circle who may happen to go to Friendship Fiseekh to buy the cured fish or be driven by curiosity to go there and hail him—to tell him with a sly look, "Now I know all about you!"

Shawqi has no friends from either work or church. Without us, Shawqi has no friends at all.

Child and boy, Shawqi Farag has been known by a nickname: he was famous in both school and neighborhood by the name Fiseekha, or, as a pet name, Fassookha.

Now Shawqi has grown up, is over thirty, and has treated his hands, once stained orange from salting fiseekh, till they've turned brown and look almost natural, and everyone refers to him as "Mr. Shawqi."

If anyone tries to joke around with him and call him by his old name, his expression makes a U-turn. He says nothing, makes no reply to his interlocutor, so that in the end the latter shoves off of his own accord.

Thank God they hadn't started smoking without me.

The large brown piece of hashish appeared after some rapid negotiations with Shawqi, who accurately made the necessary calculation, divided it by four, and stretched out his hand to us with the palm opened all the way, each paying his contribution as usual.

Shawqi put the money into his pocket with one hand. With the other he took from inside his gallabiya something the size of a box of matches, wrapped in cellophane, which he gave to Haris. Haris opened it and extracted the glorious Brown Beauty, "shrub of the Sufis," as he fondly called it. He sniffed it at length, with patent pleasure, and gave Shawqi a broad smile to congratulate him on the quality.

Haris took an elegant tobacco case from his pocket—a bronze-colored metal case with, engraved upon it, the face of Argentinean revolutionary Che Guevara with his bushy black beard, a giant Cuban cigar between his lips, and the famous black beret on his head.

He took out the packet of papers and devoted himself to the task of rolling the first cigarette, like a zither player, whose capital is all in his fingertips.

He rolled with delight and skill.

The stuffed cigarettes passed among us quickly, one after another, while our mouths devoured most of the fiseekh and sardines and the mound of loaves, our conversation consisting of a continuous overlapping chatter that went east and west, took off for the north and then dropped south.

After about the eighth cigarette (I say "about" because in my condition I couldn't possibly make an accurate count), the chatter gradually started to die down, till a total, long-lasting silence reigned—"as though," as they say, "there was a bird sitting on top of our heads," ho-ho. Birds galore were circling through the heavens of the room, white and green and yellow, twittering and singing.

We seemed to have forgotten our National Language and replaced it with little moues of disgust, with giggles, and with gestures: the mother tongue of the modern man of the jungle.

After lengthy hesitation, Kagha tried to tell the story of the fallout from a recent fuck he'd copped on Nasr el-Deen, on the tenth story of the huge tower block next to the university, just after the underpass. He tried to open his mouth and extend his tongue, loaded down as it was with sounds, but the words turned to rocks in his mouth.

"Aaaaaaa . . . ."

Imad, a.k.a. Kagha, couldn't find the words to rescue himself, so he stood up, simply and unselfconsciously straightened his red bow tie with the fingers of both hands, and, without removing his expensive black coat, lowered his pants halfway down his brown thighs and undid the zipper.

To ensure the display was clear and well-lit, he stood under the long fluorescent lamp in the middle of the room and with two fingers of his left hand took it out (brown and bloody, shrunken and small), pointed with his right to a round, crimson ulcer rising from the skin of the late lamented, and produced from his mouth the squawk of a sick rooster.

Shawqi sat up from where he lay sprawled on the room's only couch, adopted an expression of mock horror, went down on his knees on the mat, and brought his face close to Kagha.

With all the seriousness of a specialist in dermatology and venereal diseases, he commenced an examination of the little patient, fastening his wide eyes on it without extending his hand. He craned his neck up and down, left and right, to get a look at it from all angles.

A stifled "hmmm" from Shawqi's pressed lips startled and terrified Kagha.

Tense minutes of silence passed as Shawqi extracted all the pleasure he could from torturing Kagha.

Finally, terminating the local examination, Shawqi issued a long "aaaah" while simultaneously banging on his forehead and opening his jaws to their fullest extent. With the authority and wisdom of an aged consultant, he issued a decisive sentence: ". . . your mother, there's nothing wrong with it!"

Haris gave an imitation of Sayyid Uqr's asinine laugh.

A full three minutes after Shawqi's pronouncement, I gave a guffaw and we went on laughing for I don't know how long while Kagha stood there as still as a statue, saying nothing, his face anxious.

Kagha, current master of contemporary shaabi song, is also a highly distinguished picker-upper of girls of the night, though only from clubs other than his own since he regards it as sinful and unpleasant to "sully the place where I earn my daily bread," as he puts it.

From the round-the-clock cafés of Faysal Street and Pyramids Road, Kagha hunts girls whenever the mood takes him and he feels the urge. He never goes to the rival bars and nightclubs unless compelled to do so by the invitation of a singer who's a friend or as a compliment to a dancer who's a colleague. On his many days off, given that he only sings at Kamannana two nights a week, he takes a seat at around four in the morning in any coffee shop on Pyramids Road or Faysal, orders tea and a water pipe, and waits for the girls to return from their jobs in the public clubs and *maisons privées*.

And, since the chic singer is as handsome as Omar Sharif in *Struggle in the Valley* and has known this ever since his face sprouted its first downy mustache, it's merely a matter of time before one of them falls into his clutches.

"An hour maybe, tops."

With a pride in his identity equal to that of any authentic Arab of ancient lineage, Kagha proudly intones, "Listen. These broads really don't want much. From apartment to apartment, from a guy with a rag on his head to a guy with a rope around it, you don't want to know. Old men with cracks in their legs as deep as Snake Canyon . . ." and he laughs so hard he falls on his back.

We urge him on, so as to find out the whole philosophy, hoping it'll be something we can use someday.

Let's be clear on one point: Shawqi's in no way a thief, even if he does keep two cigarettes for himself, the way he's doing now.

—

Kagha went on, "Swear to God, once, at the Night, the open-air restaurant, a girl bought me dinner and opened a bottle of good Chivas whisky in my honor, just so she could keep looking at my face!"

"Heavens above!" we responded in unison.

"Thing is, she was locked up three nights a week with this very old guy. She told me just his face made her throw up everything in her stomach five times."

With malice implicit and explicit, Haris remarked, "She's a whore. That's her job. She should choose her customers too?"

Kagha's face flushed with anger and he jumped up without a word and went out to the toilet that Shawqi had devised on the roof, next to his room.

We knew Kagha's theories on the need for life at any cost, but his sympathy, call it affection even, for prostitutes seemed absolutely incomprehensible.

We'd been raised on the philosophy common to Giza's native inhabitants—shop owners, government employees, small-time professionals, and salesmen both established and mendicant—and that philosophy goes as follows: "You can get pleasure out of sleeping with a prostitute and trying out outrageous things and positions you could never do with your wife and hold her in deep and visceral contempt at the same time. The important thing is not to let her take you for a ride on the price."

We gloated over Kagha because a malignant disease had, no doubt about it, taken control of his central self-esteem system.

After you are gone, Kagha, songbird of the Pyramids, who will care for the wretched, who wipe the tears from the eyes of the goodhearted prostitutes and the Sphinx, the Nile, the Ophthalmic Hospital, the Abbas Bridge? Who . . . ?

We improvised a funeral dirge of drawn-out tune and few words appropriate for bidding farewell to Kagha's manhood and seeing it to its last resting place. As he returned from the toilet, he overheard our funereal elegy. He hadn't yet zipped up and he yelled and screamed, with all the resolve his fury could muster, "Never! Never, you dogs!"

We laughed harder and danced in place.

Turning his towering body toward Shawqi, tears in his eyes (for the first time we discovered that he had mournful eyes from which tears could flow), Kagha put his hands on Shawqi's shoulders and asked him imploringly, in the husky voice of a beggar, "On the soul of your father, who isn't yet dead, there really isn't anything? I'm clean, right?"

After deep thought, Shawqi replied, "The best thing would be to ask Gabr, the police officer. He knows everything!"

"LOL! Right! Anwar Gabr is the only one who knows everything," declared Haris, guardian of the Gabr family's former home, staring pointedly and with hidden menace into my face.

A chill ran through my body. All of them laughed except me.

With the mention of the officer's name, my mood turned sour. I grew dejected and my chest tightened as if a knife had been plunged into it. I felt a choking sensation, as though two hands were slowly but surely taking a grip on my neck.

I'd pretended to forget about him. I *had* forgotten about him, had become oblivious to all thoughts of him, and his image had all but flown my head.

Now he suddenly leapt out at me with his smooth white face, his shining green eyes that he got from his Greek grandmother, Rose, his suave smile, his ruddy, fair complexion, his soft, low voice.

Anwar had been a boy of medium height, fleshy, who strutted through the schoolyard always accompanied by two huge students, relatives of his, to protect him from the molestations of the wicked older boys — students who'd just reached puberty, in whose bodies the fires of rampant lust had broken out and who could find no target other than Anwar's body on which to fixate.

That was Anwar Gabr at our school ten years ago.

I'd never been in the same class with him. Haris, Shawqi, Hussein, and I had always been among the high achievers, while he was an average student. He was well known at school because we all knew his father's shop, the famous Gabr's Butchers in the vegetable market from which on rare occasions we'd buy (it had the best and most expensive meat in Giza).

Now Anwar was an officer celebrated for his noble qualities, gallantry, and mild manners, who never turned a blind eye to the needy and who helped all, and the butcher's store had five branches in Giza alone.

The officer had long ago moved out of their home on Saad Zaghloul in favor of their tower block on Greater Ocean and one no longer saw him in the cafés of our adolescence and haunts of our youth. He rarely visited our old playing grounds in the heart of Giza and yet, despite this, his name was on everyone's tongue. Even Shawqi mentioned him when stoned.

I hadn't known she was his wife. It was only yesterday that she'd let his name slip. I didn't know if he was aware that I was having sex with his beautiful wife, copulating with her with no pangs of conscience, no feelings of guilt. She wasn't anyone's property, she was a free woman!

Kagha sobbed at length, laughing through his tears, while Shawqi and Haris laughed like lunatics. The walls of the high-ceilinged room gave back the sobbing, the laughter, and the guffaws. Kagha wept for fear of the curse, afraid his penis would be rotten forevermore. He wept because he wanted— by fathering righteous offspring (offspring more righteous, that is, than he personally was)—to make sure that his memory wasn't wiped from the records of this world. Kagha attended Friday prayer regularly at the Sheikh Ramadan mosque at the beginning of Station Road, where he would pray and beseech God to grant him numerous children (boys only) when one day, God willing, he got married. He dreamed of having babies some day. Babies who wouldn't drown in the sea the way my child Ahmad had, at Maamura in Alexandria the summer before last.

The three grew tired of smoking and being stoned and laughing, of eating and talking and weeping, and submitted and became silent and still. The place fell quiet. Time came to a stop, like a grave too narrow to hold more than a single body.

The darkness descended upon me where I sat cross-legged in the dust inside my narrow grave, alone, above my head a short stone marker that did not bear my name. Calmly and silently I stared at the wall with empty sockets, eyeless.

I was on my own, entirely alone—alone with myself.

8 ANWAR GABR

IN MY MIND'S EYE, I SEE ANWAR GABR, face to face.

I summon my willpower and call him up before me so as to know him. I gaze on him and strip him of his uniform. I make him walk the way we do, a cipher on the street, like any other human being.

He comes to me wearing a shirt and pants. There's nothing to distinguish him from the rest of the passersby. He walks with the stride of the native son, confident of his ground. He approaches with disdain from the direction of Greater Ocean, makes his way through the alleys and lanes till he reaches Bayumiya Square, crosses it to the start of Khufu Street, walks the length of it, turns off into Sheikh Zahran Lane, and climbs up to the roof and to Shawqi's room.

I want him to come and confront me, man to man.

"Come here, man!"

He comes, confident and conceited, smiling with the arrogance of a revered military leader. His face at first looks cloudy, fuzzy, then seems on the point of breaking into a hysterical laugh. He looks the way I saw him all of yesterday night and at dawn on that great all-encompassing spider's web, the Internet.

I pursue him for more than twenty hours straight, switching from one well-known search engine to another: Yahoo, Google, MSN, AltaVista, Maktub, Moheet, Masrawi, Al Arabiya, Azzamn, and on and on.

I smoke voraciously, consume cigarettes without number. I smoke and I pant, the sweat pouring off me in my cold room. The chills of dawn sting me through my window, which is opened onto the street. If I close it, I will suffocate from the smoke of my own cigarettes, continuously ignited as I crisscross the Internet north to south and east to west (if that world may be said to have directions and lines of longitude and latitude). Unconscious of everything around me, I strive with hand and eye, with all my senses and my brain, the letters of his name the only thing in my world. Like some violent psychopath, I pursue him with Arabic and Latin letters across open, naked, transparent virtual space. I search for him, for anything that has any connection to him. The thousands of results I get fill me with a bitter despair. The adrenalin level of my blood rises and I fight the despair and keep searching as savagely as though I were going to eat the computer itself and swallow it.

After fifteen hours of continuous, exhausting search, I arrived at that particular small corner of the infinite world of images, of audio and video, of words. At least twenty persons bore the same name and practiced approximately similar professions. Perhaps I had finally arrived. Unsure, skeptical, I read the letters of his name and stared at the shadowy face, visible only from the left side, a low-quality profile.

Is this the person I want, the one I'm looking for?

Maybe. I don't know.

What I'm looking at is the person who stands before me now in Shawqi's room. The same face that he wore in the video clip published on some blog.

The blog is small, low disk-space, free on Yahoo! GeoCities. Its home page is all primary colors shining from ropes festooned as though to decorate the walls of a house or a store or a new Laundromat—five ropes of little colored lights such as might be used to celebrate the nuptials of an old-time village headman form a border that is sanctified by the colors (red, white, black) of the national flag: the insulation-brick façade of a small restaurant, in a vegetable or meat or fish market.

The blog places above the façade a neon sign with the name of the restaurant: "Eat and Praise the Lord!" It serves only fuul, falafel, potatoes, and pickles. The walls of the restaurant are black and white ceramic tiling from floor to ceiling. The counter is a wide piece of brown marble and behind it a large cooking stove with four wide burners has been placed. A tall blue gas cylinder leans against the wall. On the stove is an astonishingly large aluminum pot full of fuul and a frying pan in which oil is boiling, waiting for someone to throw in the falafel patties. The oil boils, waiting for the sudden hiss.

The person cooking the fuul is a young man in his twenties, a thin smiling youth with a wide mouth. He looks energetic and jolly in his green plastic kitchen apron. He has falafel paste in his hand. The boy is caught on the verge of throwing the patties into the boiling oil, looking at the patrons with a wide smile.

At three wooden tables without cloths sit day laborers, porters, and vendors, wearing gallabiyas and mustaches, countrymen with skullcaps and dark-brown faces scorched by the sun, artisans' assistants of various ages, Upper Egyptians, and an old woman sitting alone in a black gallabiya with her hand against her cheek.

Government office workers, preparatory and secondary students male and female, and two women form a crowd before the owner's desk. They are handing him money and hold in their hands small plastic bags containing the fuul, falafel, and other sandwiches they've bought.

On the bare floor tiles of the restaurant are two-handled woven baskets containing chisels, mattocks, a spirit level, a plasterer's trowel, paint brushes, pliers, and various other tools.

The customers' feet are clad in old shoes, rubber sandals, plastic and leather slippers.

On the wall facing the browser are two large frames holding photographs, one of President Gamal Abdel Nasser as a young man in a short-sleeved safari suit, smiling, his hand on the shoulder of his oldest son. The other is a half-length portrait of the owner, laughing with his mouth open as wide as it can go, his left thumb hooked through the buttonhole of a silvery satin waistcoat worn under a cashmere gallabiya, his thick mustache bristling. It's the same straight-backed boss who is to be seen sitting behind the small semicircular desk in an Upper Egyptian turban, with an enormous belly, his hand grasping the mouthpiece of a water pipe whose smoke partially hides the crowd of customers in front of him. The boss is completely at home sitting that way, content and happy at the crowds of people around him. His desk drawer is open and his hand is taking money out of the hand of the person before him.

On the boss's forehead is a notice that says, "Click here!"

Two words written in red on the boss's broad, brown brow.

I clicked there.

"This is Boss Shatta, owner and manager of the Eat and Praise the Lord Restaurant, and . . . ."

The "Captain" tells us his name and starts giving us a taste of his noble voice. The sound is of poor quality and he uses the signature phrases and performance style of Captain Mimi el-Shirbini, the soccer commentator. He promises his honored visitors the hottest private scandals, with new items and revelations about goings-on in the Protected City.

With the phrase "new and highly confidential," the boss leads the visitor to ten video links.

After a quick survey of the ten links, I found him, found Anwar Gabr.

On the video, which was of poor audio and visual quality, a man of around thirty, in an ordinary shirt and pants, was holding a long black whip, which he was using to flog a beautiful girl of about twenty.

With repeated gestures of his right hand, he orders her to take off her blouse. The young man's face is blurred out. The girl is crying and moving her neck to right and left in refusal. The lash administers a single light blow to her chest. With a gesture of his hand, the young man repeats his order. With tears in her eyes, sobbing quietly, the girl pleads with him and her hands stroke her chest in entreaty. This time the blow from the lash is harder and reaches all the way down to her belly and waist. The girl undoes the buttons of the blouse, her face hidden in darkness. The young man gives an ugly smile as he stares at what can now be seen sticking out of her brassiere. Her breasts have come out of the bra and between them is a deep pocket, bronze-colored and exciting. The young man swallows his saliva and the girl, in an extremity of embarrassment, tries to hide her nakedness with her hands, placing both of them over her breasts. The young man strikes her, bringing the end of the lash down on the white brassiere. The girl convulses and beats her cheeks with her hands. The lash rises into the air and descends on her knees, then on her thighs under her baggy white pants, and she screams. The young man takes hold of the end of the lash with his free hand, threatening her with a movement of the index finger of his right, a frightening look in his eyes. Unspeaking, he stares angrily at her. There is an awful terror in the girl's eyes. Slowly, the girl's hands, shaking, reach for her bra. She tries to take it off from the front but cannot and gazes at the young man, defeated. The young man's lips move, forming some insult. Slowly, hesitantly, the girl reaches behind her back and undoes the clasp of the bra, tears flowing, head bowed. The young man's lips are parted. He sucks on his tongue with pleasure. Her breasts are full, the nipples small, her chest gleams, her eyes are completely fixed and drowning in tears. The young man's face is that of a masturbator halfway to climax. Suddenly he laughs, cracking the whip against the tiles, then aims it at her breasts and nipples. The girl screams again and again in pain and terror. The young man twists his body and moans like someone ejaculating. His arm is stretched to its fullest extent and he waves the whip, bringing it down on the naked chest, the sound as it bites into her flesh ringing out in time with her screams. The young man is drunk on the girl's screams of terror. He throws his body around. He is maddened with pleasure. He screams and the blows of his whip increase in intensity. The young man moans and strikes with all his force. The girl is curled up over herself, her hands on her head, her brown skin marked by the blows of the whip. The whip leaves permanent lines and curves and long bright-red welts. The lash has gouged its marks into her skin like a chisel into stone. The girl is weeping and screaming. Her weeping seems likely to squeeze her guts out through her sides. The blows of the lash increase in violence, following one another in quick succession and with extreme force. Her small body has become a bloody red lump from which issue appeals for help and screams emanating from a hell of torment. The girl screams and screams in terror and pain too awful for any to bear.

Suddenly, at that instant, the image pauses and there is nothing more.

Some sixty seconds of bestial, hellish sadism fit to wrench the heart from one's body and turn one's hair white.

I got up, shaken, placing my hand over my mouth, and ran to the bathroom, where I emptied my guts, my whole body shaking with each spasm of my belly, each gaping of my mouth, each eruption of food and drink from the pit of my stomach. As I shook, my head would almost smash into the basin, and I came close to pissing on myself.

Once I'd gotten rid of everything in my stomach, I took off all my clothes and stood under the showerhead, letting the water pour over my body for almost an hour. My body shivered and I raved on and on, like someone delirious with fever. I raved until I calmed down, and no one heard me, not my mother and not my wife.

I was by no means certain that that young man was Anwar Gabr and I would never be in a fit state to return to that scene of horror.

I hadn't seen Anwar Gabr for close to fifteen years. If we were to subtract fifteen years from the face in the accursed video, would it turn out to be the handsome, innocent face of the Sphinx School student?

I don't know, and it seems I never will.

9   A SLAP

NASHWA'S INSOUCIANT, LAUGHING FACE will be with me forever. It falls into the chaos of my mind to cover Anwar's, concealing it and pushing it from my sight, from the darkness of my thoughts, from the ceaseless churning of my mind inside my black brain.

Yesterday's events still grind me under their weight, bend my body to snapping point, torture my soul, and there is no way to escape from their feverish domination of my very cells, my sight and hearing, my evil, stupid heart.

The self-annihilation microbe is normally associated with what is called (since no other word can sustain, tolerate, or denote the required meaning) the human heart. The self-annihilation microbe, the erasure of the self, is coextensive with, and forms a unity with, the implacable desire for the love of another, a specific Other who carries in his heart, in his very being, a similar microbe. By the time these two have been drawn to and come into contact with each other after overcoming the resistance or interference of all the numerous other human microbes such as egotism, jealousy, and malice, time will have run out and no possible outcome will remain than the unification of the microbe of the ego with the microbe of the Other. It will no longer be possible to escape the inevitable end—the thing called "love," or what I call "the evanescence of the self," or, in yet other words, the death of the ego.

The precious microbe that was the product of my meeting Nashwa, of Nashwa's meeting me, moves through the veins and arteries, the blood and the flesh, and spreads its white light throughout the body, making it radiate light, shine, incandesce. The fertilized microbe is coextensive with the skin of the body in its entirety. It marks it in its waking and sleeping, in its presence and absence, in its moving and staying still. It surrounds the body with a pseudo-sacred halo visible to the eye (visible, that is, to those who possess both sight and insight, to those who have both eye and heart), but the heart is weak, the body feeble, the spirit small. The individual, being human, isn't strong enough to bear too much pleasure or beauty, isn't strong enough for love, isn't strong enough to follow the road to its end, and, on reaching the lesser pinnacle, finds no alternative but a bitter attempt to free itself, to destroy the self of its own free will, to destroy the self through the self for the sake of the self.

If one is unlucky, if one is accursed like me, pathetic like me, and the destruction doesn't come from inside, from the heart, from the lover's very self, he becomes the other's abject slave, beseeching him to put an end to all this unbearable torment with a bullet of mercy, a bullet of revenge, of vengeance or blind hatred, it doesn't matter what. In the end, the other will be doing me a favor beyond price if he makes haste to kill me. The job of my liberation, the favor of setting me free from my asphyxiating dilemma, is on his shoulders. If the other grasps this, he will never grant me comfort, will never kill me. He will leave me as I am, suspended, paralyzed, waiting for his help, or waiting for my own courage, which it seems will never break through, never triumph over my cowardice, never rise and become strong enough to release my soul, never be strong enough to kill me and put an end to my suffering.

How far I still had to go to reach that stage! I didn't have the desire to end my life now with another's hand and I would never be strong enough to end it with my own. At least for a few more days and nights to come, if I could, I would continue to desire her with every limb of my body, would still want her, want Nashwa.

Yesterday I went to her at her family's apartment on Nile Street, at about seven in the evening. I went with longing and impatience, even though I'd left her only a few hours before.

We'd had breakfast together, standing, in front of a handcart.

On the sidewalk of the Abbas Bridge stood a wooden cart painted in a multitude of gay colors. On the front it said in green letters, "Eat fuul and praise the Prophet!"

The cart offered a breakfast consisting of fuul in all its forms—fuul with regular or linseed oil, with eggs, with tomatoes, or with sesame paste—served in small stainless-steel dishes, along with two loaves, a lime, and pickles.

The fuul seller was an old man in a clean white apron, with a bent back, who stood on two upturned crates of Coca-Cola behind a large copper fuul kettle.

His emaciated body shook and he was so glad to see Nashwa that he snatched off his small white skullcap and gazed at her with deep-set smiling eyes surrounded by wrinkles and topped by eyebrows like two white lines.

"Goodness gracious me! How pretty you look!" he told Nashwa, giving her a wink. She smiled at him and said, "So give us extras then."

Under his cotton-like hair, the creases and wrinkles in his face increased in number as he smiled and nodded at me in a kind and friendly way, saying, "No offense, sir. It's just that I always really wanted to be in the candy business!"

She polished off a dish of fuul with linseed oil, limes, and two loaves and said, "Mmm! I haven't had fuul for ages." The fuul seller, his hand never leaving the ladle that was thrust into the kettle, his body never ceasing to rock back and forth between the kettle and the dish in his hand, raised his face to look at her. "Come every day, sweetness," he flirted. "I'll be waiting."

I took her arm in mine, even as she was still smiling at the fuul man, and we left in high spirits.

At the Pigeons open-air restaurant, empty of customers that early in the morning, we sat alongside one another on bamboo chairs, her hand in mine, our faces to the Nile. We didn't speak.

We drank tea and got up and started walking.

We crossed the Abbas Bridge to the other side, her right arm around my waist, my left arm under her long hair, fingers and palm resting on her soft shoulder, face gazing into face, eye into eye. We spoke of the jolly old man and how good his fuul was, of the cold that was sure to come now that December had started, of the expected return of her husband, and of the movie *I Love the Movies*, which she'd seen a long time ago and I hadn't.

We tired ourselves out with walking, with the bursting of the heart with love and of the mind with conflicting ideas. The number of passersby and people crossing the bridge on foot was beginning to increase. We went back to her street and I walked with her all the way to the entrance of her building.

"Come up with me," she said.

"I'm exhausted," I said. "Worn out. I need to sleep."

She gave me a quick kiss on the lips, right there in the street, and said, "Come tonight. I'll be waiting for you."

I walked the short distance to the house, oppressed by the thought of her husband's return and wondering how I'd live without Nashwa. Would I be able to go back to my old life, the way it had been before her? Would I this, would I that? Eventually, I found myself in my bed and slept as soundly as a murdered man, with no dreams and no nightmares, my churning brain sleeping the sleep of the dead.

For no reason other than my biological clock, I woke with a start, breathing as hard as someone just about to fail to save his child from drowning. Quickly, I got myself ready to go to her.

In the living room, I smiled, kissed my mother's head where she sat in her wheelchair watching the six o'clock news on Channel One and knitting me a new black pullover, and left the house.

I went to her as proud as a peacock in my new red wool shirt, freshly shaved, expensive Gucci perfume wafting a meter ahead of me.

I wanted her madly. I yearned to make love to her for five hours straight.

—

The balcony of Nashwa's bedroom looks out over the Nile. Pots of roses, jasmine bushes, many kinds of cactus, and other plants whose names I don't know are distributed over the tiles and on top of the wide wall.

I stand there, resting my body and arms on the balcony railings. I light a cigarette and look at the Nile.

I see a fisherman in a small boat throwing his large net into the water by the bank beneath the Abbas Bridge. A child is rowing skillfully, keeping the boat balanced. Gracefully, the thin fisherman spins on the tips of his bare toes, the air filling out his gallabiya and making his white turban flutter.

In the middle of the water is a yacht like a small two-story palace with a swimming pool on its deck. It glides slowly over the surface of the water, broadcasting classical music to its four passengers—three blonde young women, who look as though they might be European, strutting gracefully and coquettishly around an older man seated majestically at a well-stocked dining table, a huge cigar in his right hand, a glass in his left, laughing. Racing skiffs speed by, the young male and female athletes who row them doing their evening workouts. Slowly moving sailboats and a few motorboats launch skyward a complex mix of shaabi songs, loud music, and engine noise. The boats are packed to the gunwales with families and young people on outings, eating and dancing, singing and waving to the others in the skiffs, the rowing boats, and the yacht.

No one is dancing or waving from the deck of the luxurious *Effendina*, a boat moored within eyeshot on the other shore.

I wait for her to come out of the kitchen.

I know her husband is about to return from his long trip but I don't know where he's been or where he'll be coming from. I don't even know where she lives with him, where the marital home that supposedly exists is located.

Nashwa doesn't wear a wedding band with her husband's name written on it like other women. On the index finger of her left hand there is a thin gold seal ring bearing a white lotus flower; otherwise, her long thin fingers are bare.

—

In all the six months of our relationship, she has never mentioned her husband's name or his work.

She said it was the one secret she would keep from me, and I had to accept that if I wanted her.

I wanted her to the marrow of my bones. I accepted, forgot that she'd ever had a husband, and we drowned together.

We had only a few hours of freedom ahead of us, she said. We had almost daily rendezvous at her parents' apartment. Even now, the first storm of love hadn't abated within me, the fires had yet to die down.

Six months we spent together in her family's home, eating, drinking, and having sex endlessly, every day, every night.

Six months of passion and lust stretching on forever.

Nashwa is the essence of all the women of my life. In her is every woman I have ever loved and desired. She is the ne plus ultra of women in beauty, in bed, in tenderness.

I want her madly.

Her tongue never let slip her husband's name. She never mentioned him in conversation and I didn't insist on knowing. I was drugged, permanently intoxicated, and wanted to stay ignorant till I died.

Nashwa's face is unequivocally attractive and seductive. Her thin eyelids are two rising crescent moons. When she talks they descend over her tapering honey-colored eyes. Her voice is thrilling, emerging from between full lips that mimic the shape of a rosy bird. Nashwa, the most beautiful woman I had ever had sex with, the most lustful and daring in affairs of the bed, had tricked me and driven me to this pitiful madness.

Not once did I notice anything in her parents' house that would point to her husband's identity. The apartment had belonged to her father and mother, who had died, leaving her with no one but her elder sister Abeer, who lived abroad with her diplomat husband. Abeer had been with us at the Sphinx School. We knew her—beautiful and well brought up, of good family, and very bright.

The apartment is small, extremely ordinary. It doesn't speak of wealth, or even a comfortable level of income, but neither does it speak of poverty—it's the family apartment of a deceased engineer. An old family photo has pride of place in the main room. It shows two beautiful young girls sitting at their parents' feet. The mother is a young woman with shiny black hair who bends forward gracefully, her honey-colored eyes looking lovingly at the heads of the two girls. The older father stands erect in a black jacket and knotted tie, the sternness of his features somewhat softened by the smile of a conservative and dignified paterfamilias.

There is no photo on the wall showing her alone, or with her husband.

She came from the kitchen wearing a short white nightdress, her bronze-colored, succulent body shining beneath it, a copper tray with a bottle of champagne and two glasses in her hands.

We sat on the bed as usual and I pulled from my pocket a knuckle-sized piece of best-quality Lebanese hashish.

We submerged ourselves in drinking and smoking and making love until, without realizing, she let slip his name, not knowing what she was saying or what it meant to me. I don't know what, at that instant, appeared upon my face that scared her so much and made her leap from the bed and run to the corner of the room in terror.

Naked, I went over to her, stood in front of her, gazed down at her as though I were seeing her for the first time in my life. Silently, the long reel turned in my head. Many faces jumped up at me from the darkness, some of which I longed to see as much as I longed to see my own face of twenty years before. His was there, among the faces of my boyhood and adolescence.

I asked her what her husband did.

She had come down, her high and her intoxication gone. In a low, husky voice she said, with contempt, that she didn't know and didn't want to know.

She moved toward me. I approached her, staggering, losing control, and without thinking slapped her right cheek.

Shocked, for a few seconds she said nothing.

With a small, delicate hand, whose fingers and palm I had covered with kisses a few minutes before, she returned my slap with weak blows twice, three times, four times while I stood frozen in place, amazed at what I'd done. She screamed at me, "You're a coward! A coward!"

There was no hope.

I left the apartment at a run, my heart leaping inside my chest and making my whole body shake. I bounded down the stairs and ran flat out over the Abbas Bridge, as though fleeing a terrible fire that had broken out all over Giza.

I had to get to the other bank of the river as fast as I could. Far to the east, the Muqattam Hills looked like a single, huge, gray rock looming over Cairo, filling the height and breadth of the sky and covering it like a low, endless ceiling.

I crossed the Abbas Bridge, my breath coming in gasps, my body trembling, terror in my heart.

I had to get to the hills, like Noah's fugitive son who denied the Lord and his father's prophethood, the young son who wanted to climb the hill to save himself from the flood and found no safety, no refuge. As I kept running toward the hills, I thought that my ignorance, my blindness alone, would not justify my fall, would never rescue me. I cursed my scandalous cowardice, my implacable amorousness, and my imbecilic frivolity for blinding both my sight and my judgment and preventing me from giving thought to anything, even my life.

Just like a stupid rat that has devoted its efforts to get at the piece of meat inside the trap and entered it, its lips twitching with greed, but hears, as it settles down under the tasty morsel, a sound like a thunderbolt, the sound of the door of the trap crashing shut, so Anwar, that skilled stalker, had shut the door on me, leaving me with my coveted piece of flesh, my greed, and my passion, trapped and waiting to be hung using a thick rope suspended from an iron beam over a deep hole, or to be crushed like some miserable rodent under a huge heavy boot, or drowned in black, fetid water, or . . . or to have my throat cut by a thick hand from behind, slowly and languorously, to have my neck sawn through by a rusty serrated blade until my head fell off into the dirt.

10 A KILLER

HOW WAS I TO GET DOWN from Shawqi's room on my own?

I woke alone, after each of them had gradually fallen asleep, with Shawqi stretched out on his wooden settle with its hard mattress, Haris on the plastic mat, and, on the other side of the mat, Kagha, his suit in a mess, his red bowtie still in place. He had been the last to fall into the bottomless well, after some staccato sobbing. He had fallen asleep fearful of impotence and sterility, without confiding to me, as he usually did, any new personal secrets selected from his endlessly titillating night life.

The room was warm with their breathing and snores, the air nothing but blue smoke, a great umbrella that sheltered the sleepers as they swam through worlds of images and dreams. I don't know how much time passed while only I was awake. I looked at their outstretched bodies, listened to the loud sounds of their breathing and Haris's continuous snoring, like the croaking of a frog, my thoughts playing tag in my head as they sped after one another like racecars on a final lap. The image of the racecars passed before my eyes slowly and deliberately. Time was slow. Very slow. It barely moved. I could feel the hardness and smoothness of my nails. My ears picked up the sounds of rats racing one another on the roof and crashing into cans of fiseekh. Sounds of a weasel. Chirruping of crickets under the mat. I heard a low moan and the bleating of a sheep, alone and terrified in the middle of the night.

The roof shone bright as a clear sky in which fly doves and sparrows, in the dawn.

After a long while, I suddenly got up, I don't know why. I moved as quickly as though I were fleeing from an airplane that would in a minute explode. I went down the old stone steps at the highest speed possible, or so it seemed to me. I had just one thing in my head—the necessity of getting to our house on Bank of Athens Street in two minutes. I don't know why I had to get to my room in just two minutes. I was staggering a little as I grasped the rotten banister, was falling into a deep chasm with a head that was heavy, so heavy, and clouding eyes.

No light on the stairs, and the small bulb in the entrance casts a meager glow. I grab the front door, open it, and feel for the edge of the threshold with the toe of my shoe.

The lane is dark, the street unlit. The cold is biting and I, furious at the riffraff lying stretched out on the plastic mat and sleeping the sleep of the dead, can feel nothing but my hot forehead and burning ears.

I encounter him for the first time. He's there, emerging from the Khufu Street extension behind Bayumiya Square. His butcher knives, which are secured to the top of the broad belt around his waist, jangle as he walks. The butcher knives and the little boning knives inserted with professional skill into his tall plastic boots gleam. His empty white hands cleave the air before him. His sculpted face is hard, his eyes unblinking. He walks slowly and with confidence, a filthy, blood-stained skullcap on his head.

No sooner had I emerged from the lane and taken a few steps, which brought me to the beginning of Khufu, than I saw him coming toward me from the opposite direction as though he'd been waiting for me. Against my will, my feet remained rooted to the spot. I looked right and left. I gazed at his approaching figure. I wanted to know who he was, to see him, and the bleating of the sheep coursed through my veins, responding to the clinking of his knives, which was slowly growing louder.

He had reached Bayumiya Square. The mosque was behind him. I caught sight of his face, revealed in the light of the bulbs around the minaret at a distance of fifty meters, but my eyes were half-closed. I tried to get them all the way open but all I could see was the looming bulk of his body as he drew closer to me. There was nobody in the street but us. He was in the middle, halfway along it, and I was at the corner, waiting for him to get closer. My knees weren't trembling but my armpits had started to sweat. There were about forty meters between me and him. His step was confident and slow. The bleating of the sheep tore at my immobilized body. My hands were empty and naked, my eyes bulging from their sockets. I could endure it no longer. Still looking behind me, I turned my body and ran. I raced the short distance to Shawqi's house and ran back up the stairs as fast as a child chased through the streets by an angry bull. Without taking off my shoes, I threw myself down in the unoccupied space on the mat between Kagha and Haris, feeling the delicious warmth that rose from their two bodies as they drowned in sleep.

I drowned too, but in my own self, wishing I could drown in sleep like them.

All I saw during those long hours that I spent gazing at the ceiling was the face of the butcher wading through the mire, knives jangling, slowly and intently approaching: the face of the professional killer coming toward me.

11 A MOTHER

As SOON AS DAY BREAKS on the roof and the sun's rays enter Shawqi's room, falling on the bodies of the three sleepers, I put on my shoes and go down, leaving behind me the ceaseless symphony of their snores. I walk the short distance from the lane to our house in Bank of Athens Street like a sleepwalker. I struggle to open my eyes, and the bright sunlight hurts them. I put my hand to my forehead to ward it off. Yielding to force of habit and familiarity, I make my way over the dirt, asphalt, potholes, and bumps that my feet know so well, their daily shifting shapes and distances preserved in their memory.

The streets of Giza are quiet on a Friday morning and few observe how I stagger and weave. I stumble and trip my way from the lane to Khufu, Salah el-Din, and finally Bank of Athens.

In my head, time is a macerating ocean that never moves, neither flowing forward nor running back, unruffled by wind, a tranquil thing that never progresses but, with extreme slowness, revolves, showing me its back, moving around on its axis like a drill, spinning in a vacuum in no direction. In my head's time, past, present, and future are a single solid mass.

My legs are numb, my head like a mill that groans and grinds to no purpose.

I enter the house like a broken robot that moves without knowing where it's putting its feet. My wife, as usual, is in the kitchen, my mother in the living room. Her wheelchair, with its rusty wheels, is rickety but it embraces, tenderly, her entire emaciated body. Her body is a small rectangle, like a trunk with no lower limbs. My mother sits in the ancient wheelchair, her damaged half hidden from view under a blanket whose nap has long ago worn off, a sweet smile on her face—the smile of one who has submitted utterly, who can do herself neither bad nor good. The thin brown face has set slightly into the old smile. Her features never relax, her jaws never move, her tongue never stirs inside her mouth.

Her entire presence seems to have been transformed into a pair of eyes.

Her eyes are black and wide and shine with a permanent low brilliance. Her eyes are linked directly to the center of understanding in her heart. In them is an ancient, chronic sadness. She has been struck dumb by repeated hidden shocks of which I know nothing—or did she choose her silence herself? Maybe she has chosen to remain silent because of all she has seen and suffered. I don't know.

Her hands, and only her hands, work fast and skillfully. In her lap is a large ball of white wool and in her hands two large needles. She has been knitting one white pullover for a long time. She isn't knitting it for anyone in particular, not for me or my father, and all that's taken shape so far is these two short sleeves. When she's finished, she will throw it mechanically, as she might a worn-out rag, into the wastebasket; then after a few minutes she will start another, always the same size—my father's, or mine when I was twenty.

I'm the only one who picks up the new pullovers. They make me happy, as they would a child. I take them and kiss her head and hands, but she doesn't understand.

In the spacious living room, in her wheelchair, she has constructed an entire life, a life consisting of a single scene.

Sitting in the living room on her chair, she knits her old wool, her eyes the liveliest thing about her—unmoving, trained on the screen of an ancient TV, a black and white Telemisr that has stood in the same spot in the living room since I was born, a set that is on, without interruption, from around ten in the morning to twelve at night. My mother sits like that, hands working at the threads of wool, her wide eyes on the TV, which is turned on but without the sound. There is no need for sound because her ears are damaged. Nothing disturbs the peace of this corner of the world but the sound of my wife's footsteps as she comes and goes between the kitchen and the living room, her eyes not lingering long on the sinful TV. My wife, like my father, has always been keener to prevent others than she is to prevent herself from watching such filth—those nonstop TV images that incite people to depravity, moral collapse, and unbelief.

When Afaf first came to the house and wanted to put a stop to the filth, my mother—for the first and the only time in her long history of submission and silence—moved her head right and left in refusal. My mother, who can't hear, moved her chair all the way up to where the set stood on top of her ancient decorated chiffonier and turned the sound off altogether. As she gazed at Afaf with that familiar look whose meaning none of us understands, the TV fell silent.

Afaf was happy to have been able to combat sin "with hand, tongue, and heart," as the Tradition has it.

My mother doesn't go anywhere. For more than a quarter of a century she has huddled right here, four meters from the chattering box, following the flow of pictures on the screen with intense interest, her hands working on their own. In the large kitchen, Afaf moves with the skill of a circus acrobat from dishes to pots and pans, from refrigerator to gas stove. The kitchen is her chosen world. In it, Afaf makes a new woman of herself, creating, inventing, trying out new things. If you could see her face as she tastes a stuffed vine leaf, you'd think she was having an orgasm of unprecedented intensity. Afaf spends twelve hours in the kitchen, day in, day out, going and coming, cooking hot dishes and cold, savory and sweet, light and rich; cooking and cooking, and everything she sets on the table is tasty, delicious, but no one praises her food, not even the mute mother.

Impelled by her faith in the Compassionate One, Afaf used to bring a small table up to my mother, on which she'd place her dishes, her latest inventions, but my mother ate to remain alive, to not die, no more.

72

Afaf wanted her to taste her devoted daughter-in-law's cooking, she wanted her blessings, she wanted my mother's voice to reach the heavens. My mother would eat and Afaf would follow the movement of her jaws, the movement of her teeth soundlessly grinding up the food. Afaf wanted to hear my mother's blessings but my mother's blessings never left her closed mouth. Afaf gazed at my mother's face to know whether she was praying for her in her heart or not. Afaf wanted my mother to move her hands, to raise them to the heavens, to raise them straight up, palms opened wide. She wanted her to move her lips, to make even a little opening in them. She wanted her to mumble as though giving Afaf her blessing. But my mother would not.

Once Afaf had despaired of any message being dispatched skyward sealed with the signature of a disabled old woman, she stopped looking at my mother's face altogether. Afaf would put the food in front of her and go to the kitchen to make the dessert (ashura, prepared out of season) and return after a few minutes and remove the food, of which my mother would have eaten only a few mouthfuls; remove it with a taciturnity matching my mother's long silence.

Afaf is content with herself, delighted that God has looked down on her from the Seventh Heaven and seen how devotedly she serves her disabled, aged mother-in-law, has seen her show understanding for the poor helpless woman, has approved of her deeds and granted her dozens of signs of His grace.

From its place on the wooden shelf between the stove and the refrigerator, Afaf's Malaysian tape recorder works nonstop, turned to maximum volume. The recorder (the most expensive thing Afaf owns, given her by my father), screaming in the kitchen, fills the apartment and whole house with verses from the Noble Quran, with recitation and the tongues of sheikhs whose names I don't know. Their voices are coarse and hard, angry and full of distaste. They loudly and warningly declaim the verses dealing with the coming judgment, the torment of the grave, and the red flames of Hell—voices desolate and empty, barren as the desert; desert voices entirely suited to the desert I inhabit with my wife.

Afaf is as pleased with herself as an ant that lives in a nest it has deluded itself into thinking is the center of the world. Her certainty, that immovable rock, falls on my head night and day. She seems always happy, pleased with her lot in life, like a white swan fluting in the midst of a flock of black ducks.

When my father—her mother's husband—told her he wanted her as a bride for his only son, she looked as bashful as a virgin in purdah and said nothing. With amazing speed, my father had taught her the virtue of obedience, starting from the moment he entered their household as a husband to her widowed mother.

She thought of me as an identical, but negative, copy of my father—an ugly copy, the secret of whose processing, whose operating principle, eluded her, which is why she had been content with my having given her a son to make her virtuous and noble life complete, with no need for anything like emotion, sex, questions, or doubt. But she'd drowned him. He'd drowned in the sea and she hadn't been able to save him.

Afaf struts around in the paradise of felicity that she has created for herself, having first placed me on top of the tent pole, a noble scarecrow with a wooden sword in hand to swipe at any gay blade who may venture too close, to protect and shield her, to put into her hand the money she needs to make her strange dishes, but nothing more, nothing more.

Ahmad drowned in the sea, and with him drowned every feeble straw that connected us.

I went up to my mother's chair, knelt on the floor, and looked into her eyes. I had never understood the expression in her eyes.

Even though I knew she didn't know me and would never hear me, never touch me or pat my cheek, I told her, "I'm . . . scared."

Nothing in her moved. She understood nothing. She felt nothing.

I kissed her head and went to try to get some sleep.

I couldn't. I rocked my body, stretched out on the bed, limbs splayed, with a monotonous motion. I shook myself and swung like a broken pendulum, my brain a forest, dark in the midst of the daylight, from which I could hear the sounds of wolves, bulbuls, grasshoppers, bats, foxes . . . .

12 A CHAIN

I LIE ON MY STOMACH, my arms open as far as they will go, forming a pitiful cross on the white bed sheet, the back of the cross to the ceiling, its front buried in the softness of the cotton mattress — but still my body finds no rest. I turn onto my right side for two minutes and feel small insects invading via my pajama legs, climbing from my feet to the tops of my thighs, biting and sucking. I don't feel annoyance or pain but they bother me. I change position, ignoring the things crawling over my body, and, placing my left hand under my head, settle myself onto my left side and wait.

Neither sleep nor death comes to me. I glue my eyes to the ceiling and lurch around in the darkness of my soul, stoned without sleeping, drunk like a cripple or a blind man, as though searching for a door out of a maze — like someone looking for an exit from the Cairo Mall building, say.

My eyes ricochet off the high walls of my room like ping-pong balls. I dispatch them in the direction of the wall and a single image comes back at me! A highly entertaining game. We send the eye off in the direction of the wall and it comes back like a little ping-pong ball and we wait to see what will happen. We send the eye off, we send our vision in the direction of the four walls, and the balls return with a single image: a featureless desert wrapped in fog on whose sand lies, at full length, an emaciated corpse. That's all.

My balls don't make it to the ceiling. The ceiling is very high and far away. How far, I wonder?

The balls multiply over and over and strike every exposed surface of my body. They fall on my feet and legs, belly, chest, and face, forming a large pile that covers the bed and my whole body with thousands of copies of a single image, the image of a corpse.

The moment I close my eyes, the white balls disappear, the images disappear.

I can stand the darkness for only a few seconds, then I open my eyes again and they rest, of necessity, on the wall next to me and the game starts over, the balls returning a single image. I close my eyes and I see the darkness. I can't stand the darkness so I open my eyes again and . . . .

Dry cement comes out of the walls, its gray particles filling the air of the room, its smell almost suffocating me, so I stop batting the balls (or my eyes, to be accurate). Now what?

I am incapable of standing up or even moving in the bed, so I look at the closest point on my low visual horizon and find that it's covered with lots of little geckos. I can hear their faint whispering, the sound of their sudden scampering over the plaster, their organized scattering and rallying in corners and nooks — tiny tiny geckos the size of ants and no doubt hideous to look at. They move aimlessly, with a disturbing randomness, and as a result bump into one another, but they don't fall on my face. Because they bump into one another, the geckos quarrel and wrestle and fight, the strong eating the weak. It's to my advantage that the geckos should fight because the strongest is certain to eat its fill and consign the others to its stomach, making it the sole remaining gecko on the whole surface, which is a lot better than the first situation, since it makes it possible to imagine one large gecko, a huge and imposing gecko, standing, in all its dignity and majesty, in the circle of light that surrounds the bulb, a gecko that would remind me of how the ceilings of most houses, government-built apartments, villas, government buildings and departments, clubs, and hospitals look: each occupied by a single gecko, large and imposing.

I give myself a pep talk.

76

I tell myself, "Fleeing from conflict will never turn you into a detached onlooker, quite simply because you have a role in the movie, perhaps the most important one. You're not just an observer for whom the play has been put together: the dramatic action, renewed eternally on a daily basis, has to concern you; you have to know. If you restrict yourself and remain nothing more than a witness to the unceasing duel, your whole life will be spent outside the ring, sitting on a seat of silence, death, and nothingness. If you spin a cocoon and shrivel up inside yourself, it will never be enough for you to live even a basic life."

Ha ha ha.

You're the ones from whom I hide my meager body, afraid of being caught in the bloody spume from your battles, in your Sturm und Drang on the playing field, on the arena that's been opened up for rapine, for daily killing, for polishing off the weak and the disabled, the dreamers and the lovers.

The faces of Anwar Gabr, Haris, my father, Simone, and my son Ahmad pass before me but the only one that lasts is Nashwa's.

Your face.

Shall I tell you the bottom line?

I'm just a buffer, trying to stop the vengeful killers from mutilating my body, which died a long time ago. I'm the dead guard who watches over a rotten, dried-out corpse thrown into the middle of the streets and the squares, the river's water and the desert's sands.

Do you understand any of this?

I doubt it.

You're an utterly stupid bitch and the only cure is for you to have your wide eyes gouged out.

Don't come back at me and say, "What's it to do with you?"

"Take care of your own shit. Take care of your own shit."

That's what I say, arrogantly and with withering distaste, to anyone who doesn't care for my screw-you appearance, who looks twice at the color of my shirt, at my trainers, and especially at my strange hairstyle, inappropriate for a respectable man of my age and status.

—

"And what the fuck's it to you?" I'll say to anyone who stares at the silver chain with its cat pendant that always hangs on my chest.

It's a cute chain with a black cat, seated and poised to pounce. The cat is on my chest, its mouth half-open as though permanently on the verge of pouncing. Nashwa put the black cat on my chest for no particular reason and said, "It's just a present, a memento," and kissed me on the lips.

"What's it to you?" I say to anyone who doesn't care for the way I gulp my beer, the way I smoke tobacco and hashish, to anyone who protests my being stoned, my bad manners, the crude language I use when I talk, which is little enough in any case. I say it to anyone who looks at the fly of my pants if I forget to close it when I come back from the toilet. I'm an aggressive type. Watch you don't get too close to my flesh or I'll kill you with a heart as brave as that of a Greek hero.

Anwar Gabr was a real Greek. He carried their blood, from his grandmother Rose, or his mother.

I shiver, I shake, I jangle like a pile of sheet metal, but be not deceived by the external signs of weakness: in my heart, baseness and depravity are joined, along with the courage of a viper fighting for her young. Kill me and fear not, if you are able, before my bullets reach your sick, pounding, self-fearing heart.

"The trembling hands of the fearful and hesitant will never find the strength to build."

Tee-hee-hee-hee.

YESTERDAY

13   TWO KILLINGS

YOU STILL REMEMBER.

Twice the pistol's muzzle was held hard against my forehead. Four hands held my fate in their grasp—hands capable of killing me easily and without emotion. In the viselike grip of four hands, the pistol pressed so hard against my forehead that the tip of the barrel dug into the skin, making the place between my eyebrows bleed.

Both times the distance in time between my brain and its disintegration—its detonation, its vaporization, its pulverization—was only a few fractions of a second, an instant, that of a single, easy pressing of an index finger on a trigger that would lead to the bullet's penetrating my forehead, the explosion of my skull and its contents, and my falling with a crash onto my back on the ground, with no resonating cry or gasp or death rattle, my face covered with blood, my corpse slack and stretched to its full length, a cadaver.

But that, for better or for worse, hasn't happened so far, hasn't happened yet.

Twice. Each time my nose filled with mucus, my lungs and chest filled with the searing smell of burnt gunpowder, the sound of death whistled in my ears.

The black pistol rested quietly on my forehead and the hands of the angel of death squeezed my neck. The grip of his palms and fingers was like iron. For an interval beyond calculation, he held me firm, held me rigid where I was, had command of me and possessed me, but before taking me, he loosened his grip little by little, removed his fingers from my neck and drew back, leaving me to release the air pent up in my chest and breathe again. He pulled his hands away, leaving on me a mark that has never been erased and that will not disappear till he returns to me once more, one final time, on a day not long from now, when he will come and take me and not draw back.

The first time I was the hippy, happy youth par excellence.

I'd graduated from the philosophy department at Cairo University a few months before, awarding myself the title of Junior Epicurean Philosopher. I was the supposed provider for a family (provided for in fact by my father and mother-in-law) with no job and nothing to do. And much obliged, of course, and very grateful to the government for its openhandedness and amazing generosity in excusing me, as an only child, from military service.

Hussein el-Kinik's military service status was "on call" for three years. It was in the minibus crossing the Maryutiya Bridge on the way back from the Rimaya Military Service District, official certificates (whose purport was that we were to remain civilians alert to the call of the nation and at its disposal at any time) in hand, that a light went on in Hussein's head: why not offer ourselves to the carpet and papyrus bazaars in Maryutiya and Saqqara as salesmen to the tourists?

Hussein bent over and whispered in my ear, "Good money, plus field work in our languages. A sweet deal all around, dude."

Hussein is endowed with numerous positive points: as a recent graduate of the Spanish department, Faculty of Humanities, Cairo, he's good at Spanish; plus, he has English, naturally. A quick thinker, cheerful, a little shy. I'd gone along with him partly to boost his morale and partly to fill in some spare time and keep myself amused.

I was unemployed—damaged goods, like an infertile male. My time was all my own and I had nothing to complain of but boredom and emotional sterility. After four years of marriage, the distance between me and Afaf had become very wide, which was no big deal, no big deal at all.

Just like any head of a family off to earn his daily bread along with the rest of God's creatures, I'd set out with Hussein to make the rounds of the bazaars, looking for work.

Hussein would come by my house at around nine in the morning, shaved, in a clean, gaily patterned short-sleeved shirt and Wrangler jeans, Adidas on his feet, Ray-Ban sunglasses over his eyes, a Levi's cap on his head, and a silver bracelet around his wrist.

Every morning, full of energy and good spirits, we'd get on the Volkswagen minibus in front of the Sphinx School, get down at the Maryutiya Bridge, and set off on foot.

The Maryutiya is a canal as long and wide as a branch of the Nile. It extends southward from the Pyramids all the way to Saqqara and from there to Dahshur. On his right, the walker will find European-style villas, their red pitched roofs waiting for the heavy snows that one day must surely fall, as well as a scattering of sumptuous palaces and large bazaars selling carpets, tapestries, and papyri.

We would check out the bazaar before presenting ourselves to the manager or owner. By virtue of his experience working in a bazaar there the summer before, Hussein had an eye for such things and was my guide. He did not, however, want to go back to the same bazaar he'd worked in, because the Mister, the owner of the place, had robbed him and never paid the two months' salary and a thousand pounds in commissions he owed him.

Hussein judged the bazaars by floor space, size of building, cost of fittings, type and price of goods, size of workshop, number of workers, and names of the tourist companies whose buses were parked in front and which would determine the degree of affluence of the clientele and the grade of guide accompanying the tourist group, from all of which would follow the salary to be expected and the commissions to be hoped for.

For six days our journeys yielded nothing but abject failure, as most of the bazaars were swarming with salesmen our age, all of them university graduates who knew languages. Hussein's Spanish and few months' experience were of no help to him (supply outstrips demand, my friend).

In our despair, we started to think of each day's trip as a form of physical and mental exercise. He would take my arm, or I his, and we'd walk, going over together every part of our lives to date, each opening up to the other, on the way out and on the way back, smoking and making fun of ourselves, joking and laughing at our wearisome uselessness.

Wherever we looked, there was the sun, dipping toward its setting over the desert about Saqqara. Over the course of the day we'd made the rounds of about ten bazaars, tiring ourselves out walking and getting depressed by the bazaar owners' and managers' repeated rejections. Most of the owners were middle-aged men, elegant and arrogant as the lords and priests of ancient Memphis, with faces ruddy, plump, and frowning, and expensive scents—of lavish wealth, power, and high birth—wafting off them. They shook their heads, pouted, and said, as calmly and slowly as ancient gods, "Off with you! Go seek your fortunes elsewhere, the two of you!"

When we got to the triangular intersection at the entrance to the desert where the road to the Saqqara step pyramid begins, we decided this would be our last try, our last stop on the route, after which we'd go back to Giza, never to return.

That last stop was the Tutankhamen Bazaar, a huge yellow stone building with arabesque windows and a carved double-leaved beechwood door in the Arab style, the whole topped off with a striking dome. At a large desk scattered with pharaonic figurines and dominating the spacious premises sat a brown giant of around forty, handsome and appealing, his long fluffy hair descending to his shoulders, a gold chain with the face of a lion on it hanging around his neck.

As usual, Hussein addressed himself directly to the manager, saying, "I'm a Spanish major, with *birfikt* English, okay French, and work experience."

The man inclined his head, smiling and welcoming, and pointed to me. I said, "I'm English and Swahili."

84

"And what?"

"Swahili, sir. I speak Swahili. Don't tell me you don't get customers from Swahilia."

On the intellectual level, I was going through my surrealist phase.

"A brother African country, sir."

Mr. Muhsin, younger brother of the businessman who owned the bazaar, laughed, said he looked forward to seeing the customers from Swahilia, and hoped that in the meantime I'd be his personal jester. He appointed us as trainee salesmen, to be taught by the winsome Subhi.

The most senior and expert of the bazaar's salesmen, Subhi had a body as graceful as a ballet dancer's. With extreme amiability, lissome movements of hands and waist, and a low, musical voice, Subhi taught us the elements of the craft in a couple of days. In the workshop, he made us memorize the patter in English and French—brief, simple words summarizing for the customers how the carpets, woven by children's fingertips from the imagination of peasant artists, were produced. In the gallery, he gave us practical training, entertaining us with graceful and acrobatic displays of the art of showing off the "piece": how to send it flying through the air over the customers' heads and then deftly catch it; how to place it on the ground, turn somersaults, hop around, and leap over it with the movements of a gymnast and so display its aesthetic qualities; how to expose a piece of silk at right angles to the sun's rays, causing the customer to let out a long "Wow!" of delight as he stood there, astonished at the shifting play of the colors on the surface of the cloth. He taught us the proper way to unroll the carpet and then roll it up again like a handkerchief and put it in your pants pocket. Subhi went to great lengths tutoring us in the rules of tourist attraction and the principles of luring, persuading, and finally, with a wholly imaginary discount, seducing the customer, and he also went into a long, comprehensive, and boringly detailed explanation of the most efficient older and newer techniques for getting the client well and truly plucked and trussed.

Daily, throughout those two months, Mr. Muhsin would boast to us that he, in person, was a direct descendant of the pharaohs of Memphis.

He—specifically and beyond any doubt whatsoever—was of the lineage of the great god Min, the god of coitus of the pharaohs of Memphis, whose children still copulated and procreated in Mit Rahina, only a few steps from where we stood.

One evening when making merry, stoned on opium, he took out of the desk drawer a moderately sized limestone statuette of a man with a short, very thin body, legs like those of a polio victim, and a tall, broad torso; an older man, stretched out on his back, his member, thick as a cudgel, emerging from its root between testicles the size of large oranges and stretching up over his belly and chest until its mighty head hung over the man's face like a sunshade. Hussein and I were dumbstruck and stared at the awe-inspiring ancient stone. "Observe well the statue's features," said Mr. Muhsin. "The face is pure pharaonic, calm and dignified as a glorious god." Mr. Muhsin said it looked exactly like him. "This statuette is an antiquity," he said, "and authentic, just as I am authentic."

Smoothing his long black hair with two thick hands he went on proudly, "I, the god Min, and anything with even a whiff of him about it, are in huge demand, both in Europe and America."

Then the Mister went into peals of mirth that shook his huge body, and he bent over and fondled the place between his thighs with the fingers of his right hand, as was his wont when laughing or happy.

Tutankhamen consisted of a long sales room with an area of about five hundred square meters. It specialized in handmade carpets, Gobelin tapestries, and silks. Its high walls were covered with top-quality items, most of them made by Rayyis Hamama, two other self-taught artists, and the children of Saqqara and Mit Rahina. The majority of designs were traditional and stereotyped, showing the pyramids, the Nile, palms, Karnak, and pharaonic kings and queens.

In the basement was a workshop containing ten handlooms at which sat some thirty children, none of them over nine years of age, who worked with nimble fingers that were capable of fashioning the most delicate of knots. The sons and daughters of peasants, quiet and clean, silent and well behaved at their work, they did not go to school and were good at chatting up the foreigners.

At Tutankhamen, the least expensive piece cost ten pounds while the most expensive, a square of pure silk six meters by six showing the pyramids and the Sphinx, was priced at a quarter of a million dollars.

We worked hard and well and after two months hadn't been paid a penny. At the end of the day when the muzzle of the revolver was put to my forehead, I'd had strong hopes that we would be.

The day had passed quietly without many customers. Hussein and I were sitting on the night guard's wooden bench, the palm groves and broad fields of wheat and corn at our backs, as well as a towering, ancient dovecote of mud, partially demolished and untenanted. Facing us was the wide-open door of the bazaar. We were passing the time in the usual chat, which turned on the money we were expecting from the Mister that evening. Tranquility and peace had settled around us and light gusts of khamasin wind blew in our faces.

A black Mercedes Phantom pulled up in front of the door of the bazaar. Behind it was a truck of the sort used for moving furniture, with a large back, high and locked. The Mercedes was quiet for a moment but the rear door of the truck was flung open and half a dozen armed men with battered faces jumped out. Their predictably coarse bodies bore scars, boils, razor cuts, deep gashes. In a flash, they spread out and occupied the entrance to the bazaar, the gallery, and the workshop, brandishing long machine guns and revolvers. Others, wearing faded beige jackets, with stooped backs and worn faces, looking like typical porters, moved into place. In seconds, the armed men had surrounded the workers at the bazaar, confining them where they were—Abu Shameela the elderly guard, Rayyis Hamama, and the children in the basement; Subhi and the other employees inside the gallery.

Lithe as a panther, one of them leapt in front of me and yelled, brandishing his revolver, "Who are you? What are you doing here?"

I must have tried, quite unconsciously, to stand. He gripped the pistol with both hands and rested the end of its barrel on my forehead, between my eyes.

In a deep, calm voice he commanded, "Put your hands up. Up."

I raised my arms, opening my hands as wide as I could, and swallowed with difficulty, reduced to speechlessness by shock.

Eventually, I managed to produce, in a trembling voice, "I'm . . . employed here . . . as a salesman."

With lightning speed, the silk, the luxury handmade carpets, and the Gobelin tapestries—the whole contents of the bazaar—disappeared. Even the moquette on the floor was ripped from the tiles and loaded into the back of the large truck.

The pistol continued to rest quietly on my forehead, the muzzle hurting the skin. My body was rigid, my hands raised in the air in entreaty, the searing smell of gunpowder mixing with the air as it entered my chest, my face caught in an expression of surprise, profuse drops of sweat dripping into my eyes and onto my cheeks.

With professional lack of emotion and total indifference, the man watched me, eyes steely, face hard as a rock.

All the while the pistol was held to my forehead, I could think of only one thing. I was trying to picture what would happen after this professional killer pulled the trigger and the bullet pierced my skull.

Sometime after my demise, my father, uncle, and other relatives would come and gather my bloody corpse from the asphalt, put it in an ambulance or hearse, and take it home. They'd lay it out on my bed. In God's name and with prayers, water, soap, and the perfumes of the dead, they'd wash the dear departed, wrap him in a white shroud, and place him on a wooden bier borrowed from the Righteousness Mosque. Rough wood beneath me, above me a green velvet cover.

I'd be placed in a wooden box and lifted onto the shoulders of four of my friends and neighbors. The wailing of Afaf, my uncle's wife, and the women of the quarter would see me off as I came out of the door of the house. The people would take me into the Righteousness Mosque. They'd set the wooden bier down next to the prayer niche. They'd say the funeral prayer over me and ask for mercy and forgiveness for me and for themselves. They'd place the bier on their shoulders once more and set off in the direction of the cemetery. The mourners would walk behind me along the road to my final resting place. They'd open the tomb, take me down into the depths of the earth, and lower me to the floor, wrapped in my white shroud. In my ears and anus, in my mouth, my nostrils, and my eyes, there'd be pieces of white cotton; wafting from my corpse and my shroud, the penetrating scents of the perfumes of the dead. I would be laid down in the dust. "Son of Adam," they would whisper sadly, "from the dust you came and to the dust you now return."

My arms are crossed over my chest, my head and body face the direction of prayer. They exit, closing the tomb's metal door on me, and depart, returning to their lives.

I am alone in the dark now, stretched out in the dust, tranquil, all my senses dead, and I have ceased to be aware of myself and my presence. Then darkness. A darkness as long as the life of the terrestrial sphere.

Or might there be some kind of light, a weak illumination whose presence I would become aware of as it stole into the tomb? With what would I feel it? Which sense would be the first to be reborn, or created?

Just as I started stumbling around in the darkness, the muzzle was removed from my forehead and the killer, brandishing his weapon in my face, drew back a little to stand shoulder to shoulder with his master— a man slight of stature when seen from behind.

I take a gulp of air like a drowning man who has popped up to the surface, dry the sweat on my face with my shirttail, and my eyes start seeing again, which means that I behold Mr. Muhsin two meters from me flung on his back over the hood of the black car with his hands raised in the air. His huge body is shaking violently, his terrified face is bathed in sweat, and his teeth are chattering. The muzzle of a long machine gun is in front of his nose, held with both hands by a short, thin man wearing a white linen suit and exuding a heavy perfume.

With the deliberateness of one who decides men's fates, he says, "Tell your brother our partnership's dissolved. Don't worry. I'm not going to plug you like a sieve, any of you, this time."

—

89

When they'd finished loading everything from the bazaar, they jumped into the back of the truck and the older man threw his machine gun into the Mercedes. His small face became visible. He seemed familiar to me—a public figure, a politician, a businessman, someone who appeared on television a lot, something like that. He got into the Mercedes, unhurriedly turned on the engine, and they left in the direction of the Maryutiya Canal and Pyramids Road, Mercedes in front, truck behind.

I sat back down where I was, on the bench, stunned and silent.

On the dust, in front of and beneath the bench, a small pool of urine had appeared. Hussein was sitting next to me, hiding his head in his hands, his body curled over and rigid, his eyes on the ground, the crotch of his expensive pants wet. Subhi came out of the gallery dancing violently with spasmodic movements that jerked his neck hard to right and left. He looked at us with the eyes of a madman, laughed hysterically, turned around, and started running down the road toward the desert, his laughter trailing behind him, echoing in my ears.

Hussein and I were owed two months' salary and a big commission on three sales worth more than three thousand pounds but we never went back there again, ever.

Five years later, the muzzle of the revolver was placed against my forehead a second time.

I can see myself sitting in a luxurious leather chair in the office of the headmaster of the Dawning Age private school on Station Road. My head is raised, my body an unmoving lump, my eyes unseeing. Against my forehead rests the muzzle of a small revolver held by a fat hairy hand that emerges from the wide sleeve of a gallabiya. An older man of imposing appearance in an abaya of the highest quality—a hulk of a man, with a large fat face preceded by a solid belly, and a white shawl that encircled his face and hung down over his shoulders.

The director had told us, smiling broadly at the "Hagg," that he was going to do a round of the classrooms and that he'd be leaving me with Mr. Mansur, member of the local council and father of Mohamed Mansur, my student in the third secondary class.

Our conversation hadn't gotten beyond the exchange of pleasantries when the Hagg suddenly rose to his full towering height, walked slowly toward me and, producing his small revolver from beneath his abaya, placed its muzzle on my forehead. He then started speaking in a ringing, metallic tone, his voice cold as ice.

He said that anyone looking death in the face would be well placed to imagine the fires of Hell that awaited unbelievers such as myself who summoned men to atheism, decadence, and depravity; that he was capable, by means of a simple squeeze, of gaining a heavenly reward from God; that he had, praise God, been endowed with the means to put an end to abomination with his own hand; and that I should listen very carefully. He yelled that the conduct of his son, Mohamed Mansur, had changed greatly. He had stopped going to the mosque for prayers. He drank cheap alcohol, smoked marijuana, and talked bizarre nonsense about God, the Last Day, and God's Messengers. Most recently, affirming to his companions his new philosophical stance, he had gone around proudly telling everyone he was an existentialist, of the sect of Sartre.

"Meaning, my dear sir, that he's an atheist and a free thinker, meaning that he's an unbeliever, my dear philosophy teacher."

I felt my body go rigid and my heart stop beating.

"You are a teacher of unbelief, not a teacher of philosophy."

I tried to defend myself, saying beseechingly that it hadn't happened, that I taught the government curriculum, nothing more, and had nothing to do with his son's behavior.

The council member said, "The government are unbelievers and they teach unbelief."

He removed the revolver from my forehead but continued to brandish it in my face as he bent down and gazed at me with his large, malicious black eyes, and proudly announced, with fake erudition and overweening conceit, that he knew, praise God, the laws of God, and was going to carry out God's sentence against me.

My breathing stopped and my throat turned to stone.

He pronounced his judgment, saying that, legally speaking, I was responsible for his son's atheism, for he who teaches unbelief is an unbeliever; that I had abandoned the community of Islam; and that the preacher of unbelief was an atheist. However, unfortunately, he could not carry out God's judgment against me without first asking me to repent, meaning that I had either to repudiate my unbelief and trespasses and repeat the two professions of faith, or else . . . .

I grabbed the lifebelt thrown me and interrupted him by quickly reciting the two professions, mechanically and in a loud voice. I repeated them once, twice, and a third time.

The man looked at me with contempt, spat on the ground, and returned his revolver to the pocket of his white abaya.

As he left the office, he ordered me in a voice of thunder to "find yourself another job, and cleanse yourself, filth."

The moment the Hagg left, the headmaster arrived and sent me to the administration to end my contract.

How had I chosen the wrong path?
Why hadn't I listened to what my father had said?

14   A PROGENITOR

MY FATHER.

A thick black beard, trimmed with exquisite care, the few white strands scattered here and there among the long hairs giving his round white face a special benevolence and kindliness that are confirmed by its lack of any mustache other than a thin clipped line above thin lips.

A man in his mid-fifties with a cheerful face, of medium height, stout, always elegant in his office clothes — three-piece suit, black or navy, no third color summer or winter, and tightly knotted tie, usually plain.

In the pocket of his shirt is a small tooth-cleaning stick that he takes out every hour and passes over his teeth, three, four, even five times, then returns to its place. The delicious smell of musk clings not just to his clothes but to his very skin and rises off him, wafting to a distance of several meters.

His right hand is never without a set of black amber prayer beads that his delicate fingertips count off to an incessant low-pitched murmur of "Glory be to God! Glory be to God!" that he keeps up day and night, everywhere — at home in the living room, in the kitchen, and in his bedroom, whether he's alone or in the presence of others.

He is lying on his bed, watching his wife putting her makeup on in front of the large dressing-table mirror. Warda is still attractive and provocative. On their own, involuntarily, my father's fingertips pass over the beads and he whispers, with profound gratitude, "Thanks be to God! Thanks be to God!"

The counselor goes to sleep at twelve midnight and wakes at six a.m., regular as the sun.

With long fingers, he lovingly coils his prayer beads and places them in the pocket of his garment when he gets up to perform the prayer. He and his wife perform the dawn prayer at home the moment they wake. The four other prayers he performs at the Righteousness Mosque.

The large, shiny black beads always move in the same direction, descending then ascending between the fingers of his right hand as he traverses the alleys, lanes, and streets of Giza with steady tread, raising his hand in greeting to all—tradespeople male and female, craft masters, butchers, salespeople in hole-in-the-wall stores and in shops, women who have spread their wares out on the ground, housewives and young girls sitting on the front steps of their houses: "Peace be upon you! Peace be upon you!" The greetings are incessant and interspersed with murmurs of "Glory be to God!" for it is quite a long way from his second wife's house on el-Fatih to Saad Zaghloul, where his office looks out from the Khawajah Kheir building over the square.

In the office, the movement of his fingertips over the beads slows down, the slower rhythm helping him to listen carefully and focus on the many words of his ever-anxious, garrulous clients.

The moment Sheikh Fathallah el-Zahiri raises his deep, stentorian voice in the call to prayer from the Righteousness Mosque at the distant, western end of the square, he descends, preceded by a scent of musk, from his office on the third floor, using the building's old staircase. His eyes are fixed on the mosque's small green dome, the fingertips of his right hand are on his prayer beads, and he repeats, in awe and submission, "God is most great! God is most great!"

He passes through the crowds and the din of people, cars, and vendors, crosses under the flyover, and walks, prayer beads dangling from his hand, in the direction of the sellers of books, perfumes, and CDs who conceal the entrance to the building. After climbing the six

94

marble steps, he enters the large mosque, where he prays, with Sufi-like reverence, behind the imam, in the first row. As soon as the prayer is finished, he takes his prayer beads out of his jacket pocket and retraces his steps, returning to the office having performed both the prescribed and the supererogatory prayers ("Thanks be to God! Thanks be to God!") and having observed humanity striving after its daily bread in the square.

The movement of his fingertips over the prayer beads helps him to come up with practical solutions to problems faced by the lawyers' syndicate. He discusses these professional matters with his colleagues in the garden of the Lawyers' Club opposite the Giza Court of First Instance.

The prayer beads are in his hand, too, as he sits in his usual corner, far from the television, at the Samar Café, where he goes on a Friday to meet some of his friends after the sunset prayer.

A long time ago, before my father opened his own office, he worked in that of Maître Umar el-Gibali, the famous counsel, in the Star of the East Café building opposite the government offices complex that presides, majestically, over the corner of Station Square and el-Rabeea el-Gizi Street. A thin young lawyer, a stickler for order, always on time.

When I was young, my summer vacations always had the same rhythm, form, color, and taste, rendered relatively sweet by my father's presence. The last vacation I had with him was when I passed the primary-school exam with distinction and had two months free before entering first preparatory.

Each morning at about seven, he'd come to my room in his old, vertically striped blue pajamas, the heels of his flip-flops slapping against the floor tiles of my room, and wake me with little touches on my cheek and a smile as tender as a mother's.

"Rabeea . . . Rabeea!" his soft voice would come to me in the depths of my dreams. With difficulty, I'd interrupt the dream by opening my eyes, stretch, put it off for a while, and then get up and start the lengthy search for my slippers.

He'd put some money into my hand so that I could go and buy breakfast, repeating, as he did every day, his traditional injunction: "Take care of Mama!"

Every morning he consigned my mother to my care. He didn't sleep in the same bed with her. For as long as I could remember, he'd slept on a small camp bed in the guest room, the third room in the house, which lay between my mother's bedroom and his office-library. Before the last tones of the alarm clock, set for six-thirty, had died away, he would have woken easily and without fuss while I would bury my head in a pillow, putting another on top so that I couldn't hear the continuous shrilling of the alarm.

He'd go to her and wake her up, and then the good husband would pick her up in his arms like a child and put her in her wheelchair. Gently, he'd push her to her place in the living room three meters from the television and turn it on.

Early in the morning the television has no picture. The electrons, protons, and neutrons of the twenty-one-inch screen cavort there chaotically, forming no image other than that of a silver twilight. Transmission hasn't started yet. The television buzzes and buzzes. In two and a half hours, as the onset of government transmission approaches, the chaos will be transformed into shades of white, black, and gray crossing the screen laterally and the buzzing into a continuous whistle in preparation for the national anthem, conducted by bespectacled Maestro Muhammad Abd el-Wahhab—baton dancing in his hand— who's dressed in a general's uniform to go with the military band.

My father turns the television on for her like that because my mother will watch the black screen and wait for it to light up—it doesn't matter what with, even if there's nothing there, even if there's no picture. The sound doesn't matter because she won't be listening to it; though sometimes my father forgets to turn it off and I am too afraid to lower it or turn it to silent, or to change anything that my father has done, without his permission.

I was an obedient, uncomplaining boy. Gradually, I got used to the continuous buzz of the television and learned to put up with the emptiness of the screen while we waited for the transmission to begin with Muhammad Abd el-Wahhab and the Noble Qur'an.

Half-asleep, I would grope my feet into my slippers and start moving. I'd find him in the bathroom with the door open in front of the ancient washbasin in his white sleeveless undershirt, the foam thickly layered on his chin and cheeks and around his lips, the black, luxuriant hair of his chest matching the crisp, curly hair of his armpits.

He'd be shaving and humming plaintively under his breath Abdel Haleem Hafiz's "Blundering Fate."

When he noticed me, standing in the doorway half asleep, I'd smile at him and he'd take hold of the cologne spray ("Five 5s") and, directing the nozzle toward me with a laugh, spray my face ("shooshshshsh!"). As he left the bathroom, he'd jokingly cuff the back of my head, saying, "Wake up! Wake up, lazybones!" and go and get dressed.

I'd take a dump, wash my face, put on my clothes, go to Izzat the fuul seller's, buy fuul, falafel, and potatoes, and go back and place breakfast in front of my mother. We'd eat, me and her, and we'd watch the buzzing television with its silver screen and no picture.

Sometimes I'd tell her of my dreams and the frequent nightmares that assailed my sleep. I'd watch her face and be sure, with the innocence of a child, that she knew me, and could hear and understand me.

My father would have left the house on an empty stomach.

After a quick review of his case papers, the counselor would, at half-past-seven, depart our house via its iron gate wearing shirt, tie, and pants, numerous files and folders under his right arm, and on his face—inevitably—his permanent, sad smile.

He'd walk with long energetic strides from Bank of Athens to Nasser and from there to Ahmad Mahir. That street, which was extremely noisy and crowded for most of the day and night, would still be quiet, the stores, small shops, and boutiques that lined each side still shut. He'd reach the beginning of the vegetable market, where the Friendship Fiseekh store was situated.

Boss Farag would have opened his store and would be standing in front with his huge body—like a young elephant's—his wide, clean gallabiya, and his white shawl over his head, in his hand a long plastic hose connected to the faucet inside the store, laying with copious water the dust of the extensive open area in front of the store and the entrance to the market.

To the left of the open door to the store was a square table with a small plastic tablecloth on top of it and next to it three wooden chairs with cane backs and seats, the table and chairs borrowed from the Captain Café, separated from Friendship Fiseekh by two stores—the Peace Grocery and the Crossing notions store.

"Good morning, Farag!" the counselor would say, placing his myriad paper and plastic files down on the table and then seating himself on his customary chair, the middle one, between that of the boss and the one reserved for any potential client.

The boss would give him a big smile and say, "And a great morning to you, my dear friend!" without interrupting his spraying.

The counselor opens his folders and files, pulls the cheap blue-and-white ballpoint pen from his shirt pocket, and busies himself with his papers while waiting for clients to arrive—small-time merchants and market vendors carrying a few summonses relating to tax accounts, commercial fines, cases involving fights, and so on. They hold the counselor's legal skills in high esteem and know exactly when he will arrive and where to find his improvised office. They bring him papers to examine and ask for legal advice, or ask him, for a trivial fee, to take care of matters himself at the Tax Department or Giza Courthouse.

The counselor works with wholehearted dedication. With patience and a sweet tongue, he replies to the questions and inquiries of the advice-seekers and clients. Next to him sits Boss Farag with a copy of *al-Ahram* newspaper, which he reads silently, raising his eyes from time to time to voice his opinion, like a clever lawyer's assistant, and discuss certain points of the law with the counselor and his clients, puffing tobacco the while and wagging the mouthpiece in a rhythm appropriate to the complex nature of his legal discourse.

From time to time, the boss orders for the counselor, who is wrapped up in his writing and talking and smoking, a glass of tea from the kid named Zaqla, waiter at the Captain Café.

An hour maximum, depending on circumstances and the number of cases and questions put to him, and the counselor would be done with his legal and accountancy work, would have gotten through almost an entire packet of Cleopatras, and the last client would have left.

At this point, the boss would rub his orange-stained hands, run his tongue over his lips, and his face would assume a happy expression.

With zeal and delight, acting out the parts with his face and hands, Boss Farag would start explaining the political and economic news in *al-Ahram* to the counselor, pausing at length at the accidents page and the court section, to which the counselor would devote particular attention. For around an hour, they would discuss global and local political affairs, with the latest soccer news for dessert.

Finally, it would be time to take some fruit, in the form of any new jokes.

Boss Farag had a large store of the jokes that begin, "Once, an Upper Egyptian . . ." and to this reserve he would add new ones each day, from numerous sources, such as the men and women of the market, his few customers, and the patrons of the Captain Café.

I suspect Boss Farag often made up his own jokes and never let on that he was the author.

My father's laughter would be loud and long and he'd keep it up for ages, while the boss from Samalut fired off one-liners faster than Hamada Sultan.

My father's body would shake with laughter at each pungent new joke that left the boss's mouth in his Upper Egyptian dialect (unsullied still by the vernacular of Giza). As he reached the peak of delight, he would cry hard enough to threaten his dignity as an effendi and shush Farag, placing his hands on his shoulders and saying, "Enough! Enough! God protect us!"

My father used to be, and still is, afraid of too much laughter and the tearing of eyes.

It would be eleven o'clock by the time the counselor rose from his chair, straightened his back, and adjusted his necktie, which he wore over his shirt without a jacket.

"Have a good day, Farag."

"Godspeed, Idris."

And the counselor would proceed with long strides, traversing the many streets of the market area, disappearing from Farag's sight into the crowds of people, handcarts, and peddlers. He'd reach Khufu and quickly cross it to el-Rabeea el-Gizi, a stone's throw from Giza's Court of First Instance, on the other side of the wide thoroughfare.

He'd finish some of the cases from Counselor el-Gibali's office at the court and meet with fellow lawyers and clients until about four in the afternoon. Then he'd leave the courthouse for the vegetable market to buy what was needed for lunch (vegetables and rice or pasta, plus meat or chicken or fish if he'd had a profitable day).

He'd return to the house, go into the kitchen, and prepare our always-late lunch, with me standing beside him, cleaning the rice, handing him the bottle of oil, or watching as he cooked with the skill of a clever housewife. We'd eat our lunch, the three of us together, at the marble table belonging to the living-room set, which my father would turn into a dining table by covering it with a white plastic tablecloth. My father and I would carry the table from the middle of the living room and place it in front of my mother and we'd eat with the television turned on and transmitting away, its programs and chatter pouring over our heads and supplying us with a never-ending flood of images and news items. I loved the newscasts. I knew their times on each of the three channels. I'd wait for them and follow them passionately, admiring the gravity of the readers and their official elegance in their expensive suits and shiny ties.

I'd imitate Mahmud Sultan, my favorite news reader, as I read the headlines on the first page or in the sports section of *al-Ahram*, *al-Akhbar*, and *al-Gumhuriya* over the Sphinx School's broadcasting system, at the morning line-up.

My father ate his only meal at home, talking of the events of his morning and afternoon, lifting his face sometimes to look at me, sometimes at my mother, addressing remarks to her as though she could hear and understand. Sometimes I'd ask him to explain something, or direct some of my childish questions at him, and he'd answer, "You have to understand, Rubbo, that . . ." and set off on a long explanation of things that seemed to me both astonishing and delightful.

Occasionally, with a sad expression, he'd raise his eyes mournfully to my mother's blank face.

After lunch, he'd take a short nap and then go to Counselor el-Gibali's office, where he'd stay, working with the patience and strength of a mule, until about eleven at night.

Once Counselor el-Gibali had left, my father would close up the office, descend to the Star of the East Café, and find everyone seated around the dominoes table, where the person playing against Boss Farag would be weighed down by his losses and gloomy thoughts of the drinks and water pipes he'd have to buy the boss.

The boss, out of sheer bad temper, would entertain himself while waiting for the counselor to arrive by defeating three or four mid-level players, but the real play only began when the counselor came. The defeated player, happy to escape the boss's face and far-reaching hand, would get up, ceding his chair to the counselor with a smile, and join the audience, which would brighten in anticipation of a pleasant and enjoyable spectacle.

The counselor would sit opposite the boss and light a cigarette in readiness for the nightly confrontation.

The pleasure of playing and the joy of watching lie in the strength of the two players. The counselor and the boss are experienced and fierce opponents. They have no time for the American four-hand form of the game.

In 101 dominoes, it's a single player facing another, brain against brain. They play set after set, for cups of coffee. Serious and severe, they devote themselves totally to the game, oblivious to the world around them, each using every ounce of his mental faculties to calculate and keep count, slamming each piece down with a hand that is first raised as high as it can be, then falls like a fierce eagle onto the surface of the Formica table, which magnifies the sound. They strain their intuition to work out in advance what pieces are in the other's hand, what's exposed and what's hidden.

They play skillfully, with ear-splitting crashes, and the onlookers constantly intervene to support one or the other by making his opponent angry, or clapping and making sarcastic remarks, enjoying the vicious war between the two top players.

One night the counselor would win, on another the boss would come out on top, and the game would go on until no one was left in the café but them and their audience. Once the loser had paid the night's tab, they'd set off together and, with the boss's hand emerging from the wide sleeve of his gallabiya and hooked through the counselor's arm, walk thus linked, talking volubly as they went. At Sheikh Zahran Lane, the boss would embrace the counselor and say, "Good night, Idris."

"Good night, Farag," the counselor would respond, giving him a kiss on each cheek, and the boss would disappear into the darkness of the narrow lane, while the counselor kept going until he reached Khufu and then Salah el-Din. Having crossed el-Durri, he'd turn right onto Bank of Athens.

He'd open the metal gate to our building with his key, then the door to our apartment, humming "Blundering Fate" in the darkness. Without turning any lights on, he'd enter his room and go to sleep alone.

My mother is asleep, the apartment large, and I, as usual, am alone, unsleeping in my bed, afraid.

I hear the sound of his singing and his footsteps. My endemic fear disperses with his arrival. I lift my eyes from the magazine in my hands.

Moments pass, and I stop reading the illustrated story. I throw the magazine away with all my strength, then pull the blanket over my head and sleep reassured (praying only that the nightmares don't assail me), for my father is there, under the same roof.

—

Things went on like this until my father went away to work in the Gulf.

A modest contract, arranged for him by an acquaintance of Counselor el-Gibali's, gave my father the opportunity he'd wanted for so long and had worked so hard to get. My mother and I were left in the safe hands of his older brother, who had just been released from detention and had resumed life in his apartment on the second floor with his wife, Abla Camelia, who taught science at Giza Girls' Preparatory, and their daughter Muna, aged three.

Regularly each month, money from my father would reach my uncle Musa, along with a cassette tape on which my father would direct to me, in a low voice, a few words of greeting and longing, and lots of advice.

I'd be overjoyed at hearing his voice and at the thought of recording my own.

Like a proper singer or broadcaster, I'd hold the microphone of my uncle's recorder in a firm grip, place my lips against its black globe, and do a test: "Hello, hello. Two, four, six, eight, ten. Sound test. Hello, hellooo." Abla Camelia, Muna, and Uncle Musa, gathered around me, would make fun of me as I got ready to record, clearing my throat with an "ahem" like any grave newsreader. I'd start by providing my father with a summary of the main news stories and recent events at home and at school, in our street and the district, and then move on to the commentary, taking each resident of the house in turn:

"And now . . . the news in detail.

"My mother's well, don't worry about her: there are men here (striking my left fist against my chest) to look out for you and yours. My grandfather's ill but he isn't going to die or anything and his wife's got epilepsy, that's what my uncle says. And Muna can go down the stairs on her own now. Abla Camelia has received a promotion, now she's a Teacher First Class. And I, as you already know, am top of my class. I came first in the midyear exams. And Uncle Musa is going to teach me to play chess."

I'd end the news by reminding him of the absolute necessity of his bringing a color TV, a tape recorder, a fan, a Raleigh bike, pants, shirts, a black three-piece suit in my size, and a red tie.

My uncle would laugh and clap and say, "Bravo, Rubbo. You've got a very distinguished voice. You'd make a fine broadcaster."

During the first months he was away, my father used to send a tape every month and he'd say he missed me very much and loved me a lot and promise me he'd be bringing a mountain of presents and expensive things. Then the tape started arriving every two months and he'd talk about how busy he was with all the work and his difficulties and his fights. After a while, the tapes became rare, and consisted of terse enquiries as to how I and my mother were, plus an extremely short discourse on the bitterness and loneliness of exile and the money he had to make.

Two years before he returned, the tapes stopped altogether and he made do with sending the usual sum of money to Uncle Musa.

"Mister" Musa, English teacher at the Saidiya Secondary School, wraith, well-known Gizan political activist, was a number of years older than my father and spent his days worrying over the Nation, the People, and the Poor.

He was routinely sent to prison. Each time they took him into detention, he'd spend a few months or a year or two there, before they released him. He spoke in a difficult, strange manner, and had a short temper—he'd "quarrel with the flies on his face"—but he loved me dearly and indulged me, though he "couldn't spare the time" for me and knew nothing of my secret life on the streets of Giza.

For five whole years, my father never came back, even for a single vacation, and during those five years I lived through oceans and mountains of terrifying nightmares.

My father came home a few months before I got my secondary certificate. Many things about him had changed, as they had about me. I was no longer the child he'd left behind.

His features had changed greatly, as had his general appearance, his clothes, his way of wearing them, and the look in his eyes. He'd let his beard grow and his low, gentle voice, his accent, and the words he used had changed. His presence had become something very different for me, as though he were no longer the man I'd known five years before. Even the smell of his body had been transformed from the heavy smell of tobacco I'd been used to as child and boy to that of musk.

My father rented an apartment, two bedrooms and a living room, on the third floor of the Khawaga Kheir building on Saad Zaghloul, paying what was then an unheard-of amount in Giza in key money at the insistence of the aged khawaga, who, as the result of a simple altercation, "wouldn't budge the breadth of a fingertip," as our ancestors the Arabs had it. During the negotiations between my father and the khawaga and the chaffering over the amount of the key money, and by way of an innocent (or perhaps not at all innocent) slip of the tongue, my father opened his mouth and said, "Khawaga Kh—"

Before the counselor at law could finish his sentence, the old man had bestirred himself, risen from his seat, and was yelling at him in stentorian tones, "No, young man, no! I'm every bit as Egyptian as you. It's not right. I'm not a khawaga."

The rich old man was fair-haired and his eyes were blue like a khawaga's and he was a Copt, known everywhere in the market and the district for the elasticity of his conscience and for being a supporter of the old Wafd Party. He knew nothing about checks, or even how to get to the bank, dealt only in banknotes, and had put up a conspicuous sign in the store where he sold fabrics and upholstery, wholesale and retail, warning his customers, "When the rooster speaks, you can have it on credit."

My father apologized to him, asked his forgiveness, opened the new Samsonite briefcase he'd brought with him from the Gulf, and counted out thousands of pounds for the drooling old man. The khawaga took the money, signed the rental agreement, and, as my father left, congratulated him with the words, "Enjoy, Khawaga Idris!"

My father fixed the paintwork, plumbing, and so on in the aged apartment at his own expense and furnished it in exquisite taste, with an emphasis on sobriety and fashion. His beechwood desk was luxurious and large. On it was a brown, natural-leather desk set, while the pen in the counselor's hand was a genuine Parker. His chair behind the desk was luxuriously upholstered. It was made of metal and revolved, allowing him to spin on his own axis, producing feelings of grandeur and importance. Against the walls of the spacious room were wooden bookcases containing new folders waiting to be filled with legal papers and at the counselor's back was a rich legal library, consisting of huge tomes with spines inscribed in letters of gold.

The clients' chairs in the counselor's office were also new, comfortable, and made of black leather. The kitchen was equipped with a stove and a refrigerator and in it worked an old man who excelled at making my father's sugarless Turkish coffee. Counselor Mabrouk, the counselor's assistant, sat in the living room at a new Idéal desk directly facing any who entered the office. He sat straight-backed, overjoyed at his new job, rubbing his hands together and drawing a broad smile on his face for the customers, whose arrival he awaited with inexhaustible patience.

Finally, after all his struggles, my father had opened his own office, with an assistant wearing an old jacket to take the place of his old assistant, Boss Farag.

Gradually, and for no stated reason, his relationship with Boss Farag began to weaken, until it reached the point at which he did no more than salute him if he should pass in front of his store, with the same, ordinary words with which he greeted everyone:

"Peace be upon you, Boss Farag!"

"And upon you be peace, Counselor Idris! Do stop for a glass of tea."

"It's very kind of you but I'm really in a hurry . . ." and my father would keep going, while Boss Farag blew a thick cloud of smoke from his broad nostrils.

The new office drew in a decent income, as well as a female client aged about thirty-five, comely and a widow, called Warda.

Within three months of the opening of the new office, the attractive widow had become my father's second wife.

My mother was disabled, the Divine Revelation permitted it, and my father was still in his prime.

On rare occasions, when my father was in a good mood and after I'd become a husband and a father myself, he'd talk to me man to man in the spacious living room, leaning forward in his old gilt chair that nobody dared go near, and laying out for me the philosophy he'd arrived at after all his many experiences and trials and that had become his final faith and certainty.

Thrusting his torso forward like Sheikh Hubb el-Din reciting the Qur'an, he'd repeat the words of the Prophet: "Three things of this world of yours have been made beloved to me: perfume, women, and, my greatest delight, the five daily prayers."

My father used a great deal of perfume, prayed at length, and I don't know much about his women. He loved following the Noble Path and would always say "I seek refuge with God" when his foot slipped from the strait and narrow and his godliness relaxed, leading him to practice certain sins (in secret and with full awareness of the consequences of what he did).

My father, the lawyer so well known (now, in Giza) for his piety, integrity, and low workload, had, twelve years previously, come close to rejecting my decision to study philosophy at Cairo University, when he said, in an attempt to scare me with the old saw, "To philosophize is to apostasize."

At the time, I'd gotten the bit between my teeth.

I lied to him and told him that my grades in languages wouldn't qualify me to study anything in the Humanities Faculty other than philosophy. In fact, the faculty accepts everybody, unconditionally.

"Dad," I said, "I'll be studying principles of religion, religious jurisprudence, and Islamic philosophy."

He passed the siwak stick over his teeth, coughed, and said, "Right." Then he fell silent.

After a few minutes, he said, "But you're to have nothing to do with apostates, unbelievers, and Christians. Study the scholars of Islam and no one else."

How was that supposed to work, when most philosophers and intellectuals were exactly what he'd said? I didn't know.

Like a good, well-mannered boy, I whispered, "Whatever you say, Dad."

He said nothing for a moment, thinking, while I sat there in front of him, my hands on my thighs, looking at the floor.

"All right, let me think about it, and if it turns out there's none of that nonsense they call philosophy and so on . . ." He stood up. "Son, there's no call for us to go studying philosophy at all. It's all there in the Qur'an, dear boy."

I didn't argue and offered no resistance.

I was an obedient boy whose father had only recently gotten to know him and it wasn't at all in my interest to be setting him straight. Not then, at any rate.

I stood up too, as it wasn't right for me to be sitting when he was standing.

To this day, I don't know if my father was afraid of my becoming a thinker or free thinker.

He put his hand on my shoulder and finally came out with what seemed to me at the time a very trivial line of reasoning: "As you wish . . . but philosophy won't put any bread on the table."

He smelled my breath, rancid with the tobacco that filled my chest. "And cigarettes will destroy your health. Give them up, son."

My father departed for his new wife's home, leaving me with a head like a rock in the middle of an ocean, battered by every wave.

After a few days, to even the score, my father proposed a friendly settlement that would be agreeable to us both and which he must have been turning over in his mind for a long time. That girl Afaf, his wife's daughter, a pretty girl aged seventeen and so a year younger than me, an empty-headed thing with no possibility of continuing her education, loved nothing more than to stay home. Her permanent presence by her mother's side was putting a crimp in my father's conjugal life. Her presence disturbed the tranquillity of his new marriage and interrupted, in no uncertain way, the exercise of that implacable lust that he had repressed for so long.

Of course, that's not what my father said. He said that I was a man now and that an early marriage was a way to preserve the chastity of the likes of me, especially those who'd set their hearts on studying atheism at a western-aping university.

Getting me married would cost neither him nor me a penny, and the benefits to be gained were many!

Those days, I was proud of my shiny colored shirts, my tight pants imported from the Gulf, the black line of the mustache growing above my upper lip, and the cigarette in my mouth, and I always left the top buttons of my shirt undone, to excite the girls with a glimpse of the thick hair on my chest.

As an authentic young Giza wise guy (and being a wise guy is all about doing things right and knowing how to get what you want, as well you know, good buddy), I thought the matter through and decided I'd come out ahead, for the following reasons.

First, adding a woman to my life could do no harm; on the contrary, it would be of great use in helping me kick my addiction to jerking off.

Second, it would be a help to me to get to know at first hand what women were really like, since they were something of which my life was totally devoid—I'd never been granted the opportunity to have a real, ongoing relationship with a girl of my own age, not at the Sphinx School and not in the neighborhood, with a few exceptions that went no further than quick, stolen touches of the body, and a single one-sided love affair: my passion for and infatuation with Samira Farag. Samira came to me in my waking dreams, after she had flown from me, married, and gone abroad with her husband.

Third, the girl Afaf was tasty, nicely put together, and stupid as a donkey foal, which was something not to be sniffed at given my current circumstances.

Fourth, it would be a good idea to augment my diet with some stews and hot meals as my stomach had shriveled up from all the cheese and canned salmon that were the result of my mother's situation and my own incompetence as a cook, and would lead to a marked improvement in my general health.

Fifth, it would mean a step in the direction of sharp dressing and improved general appearance, via the regular washing and proper ironing of my clothes.

Not to mention that my father would go on paying my monthly out-of-pocket expenses as he had been doing, Afaf would get her normal allowance from her mother, and I wouldn't be required to abandon the study of philosophy and look for work in order to provide for my future bride.

Actually, all the preceding was untrue and of no importance whatsoever.

The sole reason for my agreeing to the marriage was that I would have given anything to find out what sex, excuse me for saying it, was like, even with a goat.

I married Afaf when I was in my first year of college. I was a few days over eighteen and as inexperienced and innocent as a baby thrown by its father into the sea and ordered to swim.

And my father continued down his flowery path strewn with the roses of his comely Warda, redolent with the scents of godliness and musk, while I flailed around in the scary ocean, trying not to drown.

15 A WOMAN

WHEN, AFTER MEALS, you no longer remove the empty plates, pots, and pans from the dinner table with Afaf, carry them into the kitchen smiling at her, wash the glasses and the forks and knives and polish the sink with her, your hand holding hers; when you no longer pick your teeth clean, in preparation, with a wooden toothpick, wash your hands but don't wash your mouth, place your palms on the two pomegranates of her shoulders and seek to encompass her whole body inside your embrace, playing with her long tresses, licking her neck, and kissing her tenderly, whispering into her ear that "the food was delicious, really delicious," placing brief pecks on her lips and tasting the food mingled with the flavor of her lips and savoring the sweet along with the salty, then exchanging long, deep kisses, forgetting where you are as you bend her waist forward in your hands; when you no longer tell her, "Your cooking tastes great and you taste better" as you fall on top of her, pulling off her dress and having sex with her on the kitchen tiles, as you used to in the first months of your marriage—it means quite simply that you've reached the threshold of drought and fallen together into the stagnant pond of estrangement.

It was with the food that the drought started.

She cooks with the skill of a five-star chef. Whatever she makes—be it qulqas or mulukhiya or zucchini (which you hate with a passion)—

is fabulous, appetizing, delicious, and she wants you to tell her that her cooking is good, she yearns to see you beam with pleasure as you gaze at her in gratitude and delight and tell her that you love the food she makes.

She stares at your fork, waiting to see which dish your hand most frequently reaches for, how much you eat of the okra in its ramekin, the stuffed vine leaves, the beef stew, the baba ghanoug, following your movements and your pauses, scrutinizing your face after each cut, chew, and swallow, her eyes never leaving it as she awaits the effect on you of her artistry, waits to see if your face will give expression to what you fail to say, biting her lips as she does so. "Taste this," she'd say, smiling innocently, and the fork in her hand would be extended to your mouth, loaded with flaky pastry cooked in milk with nuts and raisins.

It's always good, the food, delicious and tasty, and you can no longer appreciate it in any way.

After a while, as a very logical and natural result of your indifference and the appearance in you of signs of annoyance at the food, the frequency with which the fork in her hand moved from the dish to your mouth decreased. However, the way she stared at your face and bit her lips while you ate never changed.

She's waiting for a word from you. Love and expectation are killing her. Tell her, "Your cooking's great, you're a clever and skilled cook and a wonderful wife." Tell her you love eating everything she makes and would like to eat her up too, the way you used to.

You no longer whispered sweet nothings to her. You'd gone "as dumb as if you were eating nougat," as she used to say of you—not a letter, a word, a comment. You'd be saying to yourself, "Even though I do like to savor food and appetizing flesh, there are things I like a lot more than filling my belly and cutting, chewing, and swallowing. What she offers isn't enough and she isn't enough."

Most of the dishes she put in front of you turned to ashes in your mouth.

What expression would appear on your face when the taste was unpalatable and insipid, like the taste of your life together?

Did she see you? Did she understand? Could she grasp what was going on with you? Had she come to know you?

In the big bed, which was still brand new, we turned our backs on each other, unable to see if the other's eyes were open or closed. We would go quiet, forbidding our bodies to stretch or bend or change position, or to let out a fart. Good manners in the marital bed are a religious duty, my dear young people.

When you were lying next to her and the desire for her was like a hungry dog barking in the pit of your stomach, you'd hesitantly move closer to her, stretch a hand out to her, fearfully and slowly grope your way toward her, and she'd give a sigh of distaste and move away, sticking her face to the wall, giving you her big rump, and sinking lethargically into herself. You couldn't hear the sound of her breathing. Your hearing was attuned entirely to the rising bark of your lust, which made no sound in her ears, which she'd never feel or sense, never ever intuit or understand. After some minutes, the barking inside you would subside, little by little, till it was completely mute, would go slack and die, and you'd suppress your pain and press your lips together so that no sigh or moan could escape them, and you'd start listening to her, to the sounds of her body, and you'd strain to hear . . . and after minutes of tense silence, your ears would be edified by hearing a low snore, serene as only the snore of one who'd said her evening prayers, plus every possible additional prayer and optional verse, can be.

And after a period of turning your face to the wall and giving her your back, you'd left her the marital bedroom, which had originally been your childhood bedroom and which you'd made no changes to since the day you were born, and had gone, with a lump in your throat and a knot in your guts, to the old camp bed in the guest room, the bed of your father's long solitude. You'd lie down on it and sleep, sleep for a long time, and dream dreams in which this woman who'd obtained an official certificate from the marriage registrar to the effect that she was your life partner made no appearance.

Then. Then what? You arrived quickly at the fidgety stage, at the irritation expressed with a twist of the lips, and from there to rarely talking and thence to prudent silence, followed by the silence of anger, which led to the silence of the dead in their graves.

In the space of a few months, under your own roof, she'd turned before your eyes into something discovered, known, and fixed, never to reveal anything new, never to reveal anything related in any way to humanity's intellectual or spiritual capacities. A fathomless woman, like a smooth sheet of glass that holds nothing and has nothing behind it; a superficial woman who felt no need to ponder or question.

You'd noticed from the start that the hair on her arms, shins, and thighs grew at a slightly faster rate than that of other women. Delicate long hairs spread everywhere. At first they emerged shyly from their point of growth, then reached half an inch and then a whole inch.

You'd surreptitiously watch her arms and say to yourself, "It's fine. They're coming up, but they're still short," reassuring yourself by thinking, "They're not revolting yet; they're just there. Short, delicate, smooth."

Once—it seems ages ago now—she was talking to you in that voice of hers whose musicality, sharpness, weakness, and intermediate position between delicacy and coarseness you'd almost forgotten. She was speaking of some new invention that had appeared in Japan, a cream for softening women's skin made from human fat, sperm, and crocodile blood.

You'd had your head bowed and had been staring at the places in the crook of her arm where the hairs were starting to sprout.

When she saw that you weren't going to raise your face to look at her, she stopped talking. After some moments, she went into your old bedroom, while you pondered the fact that as far as she was concerned, the progress and value of science should be measured by its ability to remove hair from her skin.

Afaf wasn't to be pitied at all, wasn't pitiful in any sense. She could discipline you as effectively as an experienced school principal, even though she'd been a bad student. She'd turn her back on you in bed, she'd show off to you her coarse skin and the luxuriant hair beneath her armpits without a thought, almost, indeed, with contempt for your lust and raging desire, with disgust for this person who wanted to have sex with her, then and there, immediately.

You resorted to her because you could do nothing outside the house and there was nothing else you could do with your ramping animal.

She's lying on her stomach, stretched out on the luxurious bed like a round-rumped mermaid, her long black hair thrown carelessly over her broad back, wearing her backless white nightdress, slit to reveal her full calves. The sight of her like that always excites you.

You leap off the bed onto the floor so that you can see her and look her over carefully.

You stand beside the bed, bent over, bewitched, swallowing your dry saliva, abandoning yourself to the pleasure of standing there and looking at her beautiful thighs and knees. Plenty of blood must run beneath that pink-tinged brown skin.

You convince yourself that the fragile hairs are no obstacle to passion; it's only the sharp dry hairs that you hate.

No sharp hairs are to be found on any part of her body when viewed from behind—her back and her wonderful backside, her thighs and calves and heels. You push your tongue out between your lips and suck on it lasciviously, trying at the same time to prevent your hands from reaching out for her buttocks when you aren't watching, of their own accord.

Afaf isn't asleep, she's only lying down, relaxed, her eyes closed, taking a short rest from her labors in the kitchen. She may be thinking she doesn't have a job that would shower her with money of her own, doesn't have a cell phone, doesn't have an expensive dress.

You know the sort of thing she thinks about when she lies down like that, but don't feel obliged to bring her such things. She, for her part, knows you don't have money but that never stops her from expecting you to get them.

Afaf punishes her stud because he isn't stud enough.

On her first birthday in your house, you went to five flower shops downtown. You were looking for a really nice bouquet of red and pink roses with white carnations. You checked four stores, but couldn't find carnations. After almost three hours of running around, you went back to Giza and made the rounds of the flower kiosks till in the end, in a small glass kiosk under the on-ramp to the flyover and almost invisible to passersby that called itself the Tamarind Kiosk, you found carnations set outside, next to the glass side of the kiosk—large white carnations whose little petals emerged from the body of the flower like a soft hymn.

The aged lady selling the flowers smiled at you like an old flower. People look like what they sell. You smiled at the woman and said, "You too are a flower."

She was wearing a wide green wash dress with lots of white, yellow, and red flowers on it. She was extremely generous and made you up a wonderful big bouquet of roses and carnations and put in lots of jasmine without being asked.

"It'll smell nice like this," she said.

You were wearing an expensive black jacket you kept for special occasions. The old woman said you were in love, and that your beloved must be very beautiful.

In your hands, the flowers felt like a huge chandelier and you paraded them for miles through the streets of Giza so that everyone you knew, and those you didn't, could see you carrying the flowers against your chest. You returned to the house in high spirits with your bunch of roses, a broad smile on your face. You couldn't wait to see to see her face at the moment you placed the flowers in her hands. You opened the door of the apartment carefully and went in. The house was dark, at ten in the evening. You didn't go over to the light switch in the living room but stole through the dark on tiptoe, reached the bedroom, and found her there, lying on the bed, in your favorite position.

Her head was buried in the mattress, her arms stretched to their fullest, as though she were hugging the cotton. Her back was a broad expanse, her backside a rounded dome, and her white nightdress was open at the calf. You were depending on the scent of the flowers to suddenly fill the room. You could smell it slowly permeating the particles of air.

The old woman was very clever. She'd known that roses are the herald of nights of passion, that jasmine is delicate and soft but that its smell is capable, unaided, of waking an elephant. You smiled to yourself. You left her alone, waiting until the smell of your flowers could suffuse the air of the whole bedroom. Would it disturb her? Flowers breathe, just like us. Roses breathe at night, and here were the two of you, in the night of your own room.

Don't you want to remember what happened when you touched her shoulder gently to wake her? Would you like to flee your pain? Did you find her dead in the room?

She was closer to dead than asleep. She was breathing, a captivating sleeping body exhaling poisonous carbon dioxide and a continuous snore, visited by dreams in which there was no place for you. Why then should you let her inhabit this life of yours? You were young, old man, and as sentimental as an adolescent.

You blew up and trashed your bedroom. You smashed the mirror on the dressing table and threw it to the ground, and you tore three doors off the clothes cupboard. Roaring like a wounded lion, you cursed her and used foul language and exited, leaving her alone in the house.

Are you afraid she may hate you? Are you afraid that one day she may slip poison into that delicious food of hers?

From your room of solitude you took to stealing in to see her sometimes, to silence the voice of your animal, while she performed her religiously mandated duty.

As the result of one such expedition you had Ahmad.

The one time you went to Alexandria for the summer, in the company of and paid for by your father and her mother, Ahmad drowned.

He wasn't yet three when it happened. He was a miniature of you, but much better looking and very good company and full of mischief. He drowned in the ocean, and his calls for help still ring in your ears.

———

Don't cry.

Afaf means nothing to you now. A woman who lives here, under the same roof, as do your mother, your uncle's wife and her daughter, and your grandfather's wife.

16 A GRANDFATHER

ON RARE OCCASIONS I think of my grandfather. He is resurrected from his darkness and nothingness and leaps into my head as I lie stretched out on my bed of loneliness, gazing at the ceiling, in my room on the ground floor. He's in his antique bed on the third and topmost story, so I'm separated from him by two high ceilings and there are approximately ten meters of high walls between us. Nevertheless, he is lying directly above me, his bed being in the same place in the room, in the corner next to the wall, right over mine. There he sleeps a deep, uninterrupted sleep, like that of the dead, while I experience constant panic, fear, and terror, here, day and night, in my self-imposed incarceration.

The "Hagg," who's never made the pilgrimage, is very old. He wears pajamas made of ancient flannel, pajamas that must be thirty, even forty years old. They're clean, of a washed-out color, and on his head sits his ancient dunce's cap. His huge frame fills the bed, his eyes still brightly glaring; they used to terrify me when I was a child. I can still visualize that glare, the glare of a cat's green eyes, eyes that glow in the dark, spreading terror all around. His eyes are large, wide, and green, now almost hidden beneath the many wrinkles of his face and the squares and triangles chiseled into his narrow brow.

The ancient blanket is draped over his long legs and huge waist with its globe-shaped paunch, which looks like a small child sitting in his lap.

My grandfather is absent from this world, the only movement he makes being from bed to bathroom, helped by his last wife.

A quarter of a century ago, a young girl came here to be cured of a fierce demon—an afreet who forced her to listen, day and night, to an infernal singing that made her dance, seemingly for no reason. He pursued her through the chambers of the mud houses of her village, chased after her in the dusty streets, the fields, the marketplace, and by the mechanized mill, made her listen to the strange music made by his instrument, which was of a kind unknown to humans, and by so doing made himself her master and owner. The music would start low and gentle, its rhythm intensifying little by little. The beautiful girl would smile and listen intently to the tunes, be transported, and start to sway as she walked, her nubile body moving of its own accord to the rhythm as though she could see her demon lover standing before her and smiling, moping and mowing, drunk on her dewy beauty, showing her, through his tunes, how enchanting he was, so that she became ecstatic, and melted, felt a warmth, an unbearable warmth, coursing in pace with the blood through her veins, and swayed and swayed from the depths of her being, sweating, feeling as though her hot head were about to burst, her nipples growing slowly erect till they were as hard as nails. Her lower parts would flow, froth, and foam with a warm liquid, she would moan with pain and pleasure though no man had entered her, no male member goaded her. Her bewitching body, her tender, innocent body, would clamor and she would shriek as the lust took possession of her every part. Seeking air and coolness, she would start to strip off her clothes in front of the crowd gathered around her, but she wouldn't see them as living bodies, she would see neither man nor demon; rather, she would feel his presence, she'd feel that he was there, and she'd hear the marvelous music growing louder and louder.

A sense of sublimity would take hold of her, a shining brilliance would radiate from her face, and her hands would gesticulate madly. Those long brown hands would pull off the wide black mantle that hid the patterned wash dress that concealed her many treasures. She'd throw the mantle to the ground as she swayed in ecstasy, her face empty in its delicious intoxication, as though the tunes had entered through her ears and taken up residence behind her eyes, behind her nose, between the bones and the skin, in the flesh, in the veins and arteries, as though the music had taken up residence in the black pupils of her eyes, the music that none but she could hear. After pulling off her mantle, she'd rip off her colored wash dress with its pattern of roses and little flowers, revealing her firm brown flesh, her shining shoulders, and her neck, tall and white as a palm heart, and the gleaming cleavage between her mighty breasts would reveal itself. Her breasts were full and strong, with erect brown nipples, her calves and thighs rounded and wide and shining, filling the place with a dazzling light. Naked but for a satin brassiere that failed to provide a decent covering for her breasts and white calico drawers that didn't cover her red and swollen pubes, she would dance, dance wherever she might find herself, at home, in the marketplace, in the streets and fields. The girl would scream and wail if any man approached her, pulling off his wide peasant gallabiya and throwing it over her exposed body to protect it from his eyes. She would wriggle like a mermaid trying to slip through the many hands outstretched to pin her to the ground, to stop her from her evil dance. Again and again the girl would scream, weep, howl, and wail, because the music had vanished, its player scared away by those surrounding her, panicked by the people holding her body down hard so that she couldn't escape them.

It may be that sometimes she asked to die, just so that that music wouldn't stop. It may be that she often prayed to God to kill her whole family, to clear the house of them, to fill the graves with them, so that they'd leave her alone forever in her paradise, with her afreet.

Her family lived in constant fear that her breasts would burst forth in the faces of the passersby, that she might on some occasion reach down to her drawers, rip them to pieces, and throw them in people's faces. The girl had been disgraced and she had been exposed to scandal throughout the village, her shame paraded from one end of the settlement to the other. But the demonic music never faded or vanished and would not leave her be.

The music of the wicked demon defeated all attempts by magicians, spirit guides, Righteous Friends of God, and masters of the dark arts to subdue and put an end to it. The demon's music drove away suitors, relatives, and everyone else, all coming to fear for her, lest she had fallen under the command of demons, and to fear her herself. She was possessed by an incubus, some mighty demon king.

Her condition kept her family in a constant state of depression, fear of scandal, and terror that some villain from the village might dishonor her and have his way with her.

In the end, counseled by certain men of good will, they took her to see that man of wide repute and high standing in that terrifying and mysterious world, my grandfather, Sheikh Issa, in his sacred aerie. They came to him as a last resort; it may be that they came to him only after having decided that, should the Hagg be unable to cast out the afreet, they would kill her and thus rid themselves of her and her demons forever.

The Hagg was their last refuge, and if he did not get rid of the demons, they would hide her in the good earth, which draws a veil over bodies, reputations, and honor.

The resourceful sheikh, of intimidating appearance, with his height and breadth, his white clothes and special black turban (which he had invented for himself), separated her from her family and spent some time alone with the girl in his chamber.

Outside, the family could hear the sound of incense being burned and of the Hagg mumbling and muttering, intoning in a low, gentle voice mysterious prayers and chants that went on and on. Then the voice of the Hagg rang out with a shattering high-pitched roar like that of a tornado and the girl let out a single long scream, after which everything went silent and those gathered around the door held their breath.

After a few minutes of awe-inspiring silence, they heard the girl laughing and giggling as though she'd never known laughter before.

A little later, the sheikh permitted them to go in. They could find nothing in the room that was strange or suspicious. In the middle was a large sofa on which was seated the Hagg, before him a beautiful stand made of turned wood and mother-of-pearl bearing a huge open copy of the Qur'an, and to his right an incense burner that emitted sweet-smelling scents of various kinds and numerous colors, like a rainbow. On the ground, at the sheikh's feet, the girl slumbered deeply.

When they saw he was not going to raise his face to look at them, they fell silent and stood before him submissively, filling their noses and breasts with the smell of musk and sandalwood, the colors that formed on the walls and ceiling forming a veil before their eyes.

My grandfather didn't speak for a long time, his eyes closed, and they continued to stand before him like statues of stone.

Finally, he raised toward them his white, aged face, brimming with godliness, and sketched a smile so slight that it might easily have gone unnoticed.

They continued to stand in front of him obediently, their hearts in their mouths.

Eventually, in a voice like that of a prophet, he pronounced, "Praise be to God. The girl is well."

Their faces beamed like dry earth that water has just reached following a long, soil-cracking drought. The girl's father and mother fell to the ground and started kissing the sheikh's hands. He abandoned his hands and feet to them until they had drowned them in the saliva of their long kisses and the family no longer had breath left to say "God keep you, sheikh! God honor you as you have protected our honor!" and so on till the last heartfelt prayer had left their guileless hearts.

"But," the grave, imposing sheikh then said, "the girl will never leave this place." He was silent for a moment, then continued, "I have cast out the accursed demon and he sits now in hellfire lamenting, but I cannot be sure that another will not possess her. If you want her to live and to avoid scandal, she must remain here and never leave my house."

"How can that be, Hagg?" they asked.

"I shall marry her according to the practice of God and His messenger," he replied.

My grandfather always speaks to people in classical Arabic, from which he refuses to deviate.

Sheikh Abdallah, Giza's marriage registrar, along with the friends closest to Hagg Issa's heart (and furthest from Sheikh Hubb el-Din's), came and the marriage contract between him and the virgin of sixteen years was formalized, with a bridal dower of just fifty piasters, twenty-five piasters to be paid in advance, payment of the remaining twenty-five to be deferred till the earlier of the two terminal dates (divorce or death).

The girl's family returned to their village of Sheikh Uthman, south of Giza, in good spirits, having preserved their honor and ensured forever that their daughter would be neither made naked nor the subject of scandal, thanks to her marriage to the celebrated, awe-inspiring Hagg. They had hidden her with something that was, to their minds, any way you looked at it, better than earth.

From that day on, she never left his room except to go to the market, speaking only rarely to his other wife. My aged grandmother died three years later without saying a word about her young co-wife, and the girl, whom my grandfather never addressed in any other way than "Hey, you girl!," remained.

She's about forty now. She's still a beautiful girl who hears the music of the demons and dances and strips off her clothes as she used to do when she first entered this house. Now she nurses her doctor, who is sunk in his own private world.

On occasion, each of us would ask when this man now so advanced in years would die and we'd be able to get our hands on his hidden treasure. My father and his brother were convinced that my miserly grandfather had hidden his life savings away somewhere, perhaps in the mattress of his bed or under the floor tiles of his room or in a belt around his waist. It might be so, but no one dared to ask him or to search his room. His sons had been waiting for his death for many long years, just as I had from the moment, many years ago, when they'd told me, "Your grandfather's not well." It was ages, decades, God knew how long, since he'd seen the street. He was simply there, a body all alone up at the top of the house, in his bed, sunk in his thoughts, illusions, and dreams, never giving the least sign to anyone, to anyone at all.

—

The Hagg circumambulates the world from his bed. He tells the girl of his great journeys that shuttle him from one continent to the next. He imagines seas and oceans he's crossed, ships and planes he's ridden in, terrors and misadventures that have crossed his path. He leaves his bed and returns to it with a new tale, which he tells the girl to keep her entertained, to stop her from ever leaving his room again.

The girl laughs and laughs, the same laugh that she gave first in that same room a quarter of a century before.

The voice of Sheikh Hubb el-Din rises, bringing the call to the prayer that will be held at the Mercy zawya. It reaches me in my room, my prison.

My grandfather hates that ascetic.

17 AN ASCETIC

I CAN SEE HIM STILL, in his jubbah, caftan, and turban, tall as a wooden electricity pole of the kind that's now disappeared, his chest and shoulders broad, his body firm, his face dark brown and pockmarked, the eyes unseeing, his moustache as luxuriant as an Upper Egyptian's, his long beard still black despite his fifty years. His walking stick of yellow cane, with its downward-curving crook, rises in the powerful grasp of his right hand, cleaving the air before him and descending to strike the ground in advance of his steps.

He walks in utter darkness, his heart full of light.

I was about ten and Sheikh Hubb el-Din was imam of the mosque in Bayumiya Square and master of the attached Qur'an school for children. His gentle, melodious voice was the thing I loved most as a child. At his hands I memorized about half the Noble Qur'an in two years.

Only Sheikh Hubb el-Din would be invited to recite in the large funeral marquees that in Giza were put up exclusively for the rich and important families.

The sheikh would set off to recite as though on his way to a wedding or a concert of classical music—in the fullness of his gravity and splendor, his striped satin waistcoat, caftan, and jubbah clean, and ironed to perfection.

Morsi the ironer gave the sheikh's clothes special care, that of a disciple and lover of God, not a paid professional. He would wash them, iron them, and perfume them with musk, then help the sheikh into them. Thus, in mosque or marquee, or on the street, the sheikh was always elegantly dressed, imposing, the smell of perfume wafting from him and from his clothes.

Sometimes the sheikh was led by a small boy, the grandson of his "mortal friend" Hagg Issa. I was that boy.

I'd pray the evening prayer behind him with everyone else at the Bayumiya Square mosque. After the prayer, I'd approach him as he uttered the concluding devotions and whisper politely "In Mecca some day, Master!" He'd smile, keep up his muttering, and then, leaning on his stick and my shoulder, use me to rise, like a camel, till he was upright.

As we passed through the large wooden door, I'd help him step over the raised lintel, then take his stick from him and tuck it under my arm while he placed his heavy left hand on my shoulder, and like that we'd set off together through the heart of Giza. I'd show off to my peers the fact that I was in the sheikh's company, making as though to stick my tongue out at any of them I might see. I'd make detours through the alleys, lanes, and streets with him, taking the longest way around so that everyone could see me leading "Our Master."

He didn't mind or get annoyed or fidgety. I'd look up at him and all I'd see would be a serene face seemingly smiling at my cheap tricks and my boasting. His lips never moved. In general, his words were few but precious.

When we got to a marquee where a wake was being held, I'd sit him down on the reciters' wooden bench with its decorative blue velvet covering and lift his feet up so that he could sit on it cross-legged, and he'd squat there like a statue of an Ancient Egyptian scribe. I'd straighten his white turban and his shawl, pour water into the glass in front of him, and keep hold of the bottle of cold water in case he should ask for more; then I'd position the microphone in front of his mouth, tapping on it to test it and breathing into it the words "Allah! Allah!" When I was satisfied that the microphone was properly positioned and the sound quality good, I'd seat myself at his feet, cross-legged like him, on the carpet, ears open to their fullest.

Sheikh Hubb el-Din recited the verses of the Qur'an with a veneration that shook men's hearts, a submissiveness that forced them to bow their heads. His voice was omnipresent, manifest yet hidden and internal, mysterious as the sound of the earth turning. It issued from the heart and soul, not from the mouth, gullet, vocal cords, or throat. My every limb strained to hear him, and my tongue would move, repeating the verses after him exactly the way that he recited them, at the same pitch and with the same rendering, tone, and commitment to God. I'd open my hands to their limits, place them over my ears, and, without moving from my seated position, sway to right and left, exactly like him. I would shudder and a melody of the utmost sweetness would course through me, my whole being filling with his celestial voice, and I'd enter a state of ecstasy, my eyes closed, my heart seeming to circle as though riding a shooting star, the saliva almost dripping from my lips.

He'd be reciting, his voice plangent as a curlew's, and then he'd go further and further, until he was no longer with us at all, leaving his listeners with nothing but the body and face of one who was no more among us, who had flown from our world to the highest heavens, entered Paradise, drunk of its rivers, its milk, honey, and wine, and beheld its dark-eyed maidens—a pious believer who had had commerce with them and known a pleasure and a heavenly ecstasy without equal here on earth.

The sheikh always began the first sequence of his recitation with the chapter called "The Believers"; for the second, he'd recite from "The Forgiver"; for the third, from his favorite, "Yusuf"; and he'd conclude with his gem, "The Compassionate." It was a rigorous order from which the sheikh never diverged and in which no substitutions were permitted, for he cared nothing for his listeners. He recited for himself, chanted for his own sake and no one else's, for his own pleasure and enjoyment only. And the strange thing was that people loved him for precisely that—for his obliviousness to their presence and indifference

128

to their existence. His blindness bestowed on him total freedom, making him dive deep into his own being, unconcerned by what was around him, unaware of anything but the image of his own soul suspended before him from the holy words. Whether the occasion was a rich man's wake, the fulfillment of a vow, or the celebration of a saint's day, our sheikh never compromised his probity or his conscience, or his four beloved chapters.

From just four chapters Sheikh Hubb el-Din created his far-flung fame, which was recognized not only in Giza but beyond its borders as far as the villages of Badrasheen and el-Ayat to the south and Bashteel and the Barrages to the north. Wherever he went, wherever the sheikh recited his four chapters, the exclamations of "Allah! Allah!" rose around him to the ceilings of the tents, the sighs and gasps of the connoisseurs, entranced by that beseeching, submissive voice, followed one upon another, and the tongues of the people rang out with "God grant you blessings, Sheikh!" after each pause, each silence, each terminal cadence.

Our Master held classes in the memorization of the Qur'an in the chamber belonging to the small school on the second floor of the mosque, from after the afternoon prayer until the sunset prayer. Following the latter, he would go home to rest until a little before the evening prayer. I'd walk him home, this time cutting straight through the market and taking the shortest route to his house, for the lanes and streets of the market area would still be thronged with people.

The market women sitting on the ground in front of their displays of cheese and molasses, limes and vegetables, the women standing in front of the handcarts, behind the crates of fruit, and at the doors of the stores large and small, the women sitting at the doors of their houses, would all stare at us, their looks trained upon us, winking at one another, ogling us shamelessly and displaying none of the manners appropriate to the passing of a sheikh. Sometimes even worse things would happen. One rosy-cheeked woman would lean over to another and whisper something in her ear, smiling. The other, after a small show of embarrassment, would allow her lips to soften into a broad grin as the first continued to whisper circumspectly, as though revealing terrible secrets, and then would laugh as she gave Our Master's towering body a stealthy once-over, her eyes coming to rest on his crotch and remaining glued there.

I would look at them with exasperation, resentment, and anger, as they kept up their staring and whispering, their nodding and winking. I'd try to rebuke them, silently, with an angry movement of my head and neck, my face red and ears burning, but they'd smile mockingly at me, striking palm on palm, their laughter rising. I'd get furious and brandish the sheikh's stick in their faces, making their laughter grow louder and lewder still. The sheikh heard their obscene laughter but nothing about him showed that he did so and he would utter not a word. Looking into his face, I'd see nothing there but serenity, contentment, and a radiant smile. Gently, he'd squeeze my shoulder to tell me to calm down and that we should keep going, and I'd bid them farewell with an angry look and curses that never left my mouth. All I'd hear, though, would be their lavish, raucous laughter behind our backs.

I knew that the sheikh's secret reputation as a lover and as the possessor of a huge member was almost as great as his public reputation for reverence and piety, the beauty of his voice, and the magnificence of his recitation. In fact, the sheikh, who had neither sons nor daughters, was known as "the three-legged man." Some said this was because he walked with two legs and a stick and some said other things. The malicious rabble put it about that he had gained the title after his last wife died of an excess of pleasure during a lovemaking that had lasted ten hours, when the sheikh had convulsed her with a shaft the length and thickness of the foot of a man of average height.

All I saw was a man sweet and refined, getting on in years, and alone.

The sheikh had married many women in the bloom of his youth, none of whom had borne him children or remained in his house for more than a year, after which it would be over for her—either because, divorced, she'd leave Giza entirely and disappear or because she'd be carried to her grave. So it was, until he married Sabiha, the last of his wives. Like the others, she bore him no children, but she was everything to him, devoting herself to him and taking care of him with inexhaustible love for a number of years until she died. After her passing, the sheikh had nothing more to do with women. His recitation became heartrending, low and sad, and he took to singing, when alone and sometimes at Buhluq's café on Priest's Alley, where they sold hashish.

At his private sessions at the café, the sheikh would dispel his sorrows among a small group of friends—my uncle Musa, Hasan Effendi the songwriter, Morsi the laundryman, and two or three other intimates.

He'd become merry, and sway and sing. He sang with intoxicating virtuosity the qasidas of Sheikh Ali Mahmud, his voice turned delicate and tender with the mawwals and duurs of Nazim el-Ghazali, and he chanted the taqtuqas, qasidas, and duurs of Sabah Fakhri. He never touched beer, the only drink served at the café, but would smoke a few bowls of hashish from a goza.

In the darkness of the night, toward three in the morning, the sheikh would return to his house, my uncle Musa and Hasan Effendi leading him by the arm. On the way, he'd always tell them the same story—tell them how, when on his own, he wept incessantly from grief, grief at the loss of Sabiha, who had died in his arms as she bent over his hand to kiss it, and of how he yearned to join her.

Hasan Effendi would leave them at the corner and set off in the direction of Station Road, where he lived, while my uncle would lead the sheikh to his green, single-story house that was next to ours, take him into his bedroom, and leave him. A minute later, I would hear my uncle's footfall as he climbed our stairs to his apartment.

I had been into Our Master's house so often that I knew the sheikh's house and bedroom were utterly dark, with no lamp to light them and no sun entering from the outside. A dreary house unshared with any, where no voice or other sound was to be heard.

Alone, the sheikh would stumble at length between the bed and the closet as he removed his caftan and turban. He'd nap for two hours at the most, then wake up of his own accord and go to the square to give the call to prayer.

Ten minutes after the death of Sabiha, the sheikh had forsworn women for the rest of his life, and not one, be she relative or maid, had entered his house. I knew that it was his habit to turn his tape recorder on and play over and over again his tapes of Sheikh Rifaat reciting, allowing his tears to flow onto the pillow while he moaned with a low-pitched rasp and allowed his strong body to collapse under that moaning of his soul.

He did this every night, before lying down on his stomach, pressing his body against his small, coarse mattress, and stretching out his arms as far as they would go, like a crucified messiah, a messiah who slept on a bed of thorns.

My uncle Musa says that at first the sheikh's sight had just been weak. It was an excess of weeping over the departure of women from his life that had sent him blind.

18 SAMIRA

I DIDN'T WEEP OVER HER DEPARTURE long enough to go blind, but I did come close to killing myself.

Perhaps if I'd been able to put an end to my life so innocently, if I'd possessed the strength to do that, I would never have reached the point I'm at now. My life would have been steadier, less punishing, more refined . . . a lot nicer.

I recall her, a grateful smile on my face, my eyes flashing and shining as they watch her phantom, my heart leaping in my chest like an innocent boy's.

Samira was the icon of my adolescent years, shining down on my head like a small sun. I feel a great longing for her, a longing to experience once more those same guileless emotions. Remembering her, I return to things I've almost succeeded in rooting out of myself—innocence, integrity, idealism, and the goodhearted naiveté I lost so long ago.

I summon her now and feel no pain, heartache, or bitterness; just a long ironic laugh at the expense of that schoolboy in the first year of secondary school, a laugh that rises from somewhere between my lips and my heart.

I think of her and am struck by a wave of nostalgia for those days that have gone forever, and of joy that I can still picture the delicate features of her face, her honey-colored eyes, her small fine nose, her short curly hair, the distinctively husky timbre of her voice.

The images I retain of her are many and dazzling. They follow one another slowly in my mind's eye like a reel of film that I've taken in my hands to scrutinize frame by frame.

She's sitting on the first stone step of the staircase of their house, her feet on the ground in front of it. Her trim body is settled on the stone, her legs are a little splayed, and her long toes peek out the end of plastic slippers decorated with a green rose, on the clean stoop. With water and soap, using a piece of sacking, Samira wipes down the steps every morning.

Her body relaxes as she sits, leaning at an angle. Her back rests against the yellow wall and her face is buried in a book of poems open in her hands. Her legs are long and slim and her sweet brown knees shine out under the hemline of her short white dress with large red dots scattered over it. From the transistor radio in her lap rises the voice of Nagat el-Saghira: "I'm waiting for you . . . I'm . . . ."

She's standing to the right of the wooden door to their house, which is open, chewing gum, hand on hip, her face tilted upward, eyes on the second-story balcony opposite, chatting with her girlfriend Asmaa, who is leaning over, resting her budding bosom on the balcony railings. Samira asks her, insistently and yearningly, what it's like at Cairo University.

"What do the lecture halls at the college look like? What do the girls wear, Suma? How do they walk and how do they talk? What do the professors say in the lectures? What are the boys like on campus? What are the latest love stories? Have you found a boy that likes you, skinny legs?"

"I'll tell you everything, you little minx."

Then Asmaa turns on the tap and nothing can turn it off again. While Asmaa gabs, Samira sighs, going "Yes, yes" over and over, and asking, "Okay, and then what? What happened?" She looks grave, and her eyes take on a faraway look, her hand straightening her hair, and she goes on chewing the bitter rush-gum, unaware of what she's doing, her small jaws moving mechanically. After a while she gets bored, fed up, and falls into a state of gloom. Sorrow, trying to hide behind a wan smile, sketches itself on her face.

At the end of the conversation, before turning her back on Asmaa, she lets out a great sigh, perhaps because she's never seen the university and has failed the secondary general certificate three times, perhaps because Boss Farag keeps her at home, waiting impatiently to be rid of her so that the honor of the twenty-year-old spinster can be preserved by marrying her off to the first man to knock on their door.

Some days, when I'd skipped school to saunter through the streets with Haris, we'd see her walking through the market in a tight-fitting green dress and high-heeled black pumps, strutting with the daring of a "girl from the neighborhood," her fat buttocks twitching as she swayed, a large, empty bag for vegetables swinging to the motion of her right hand. I'd just manage to drag Haris back and we'd follow her from a distance, making sure she didn't see us, as she made her way through the vegetable market without a glance at her father's store, buying meat from Gabr's butcher's shop, bending forward and to the side, picking out tomatoes, vegetables, and fruit, and returning to the house with a full, heavy bag, not having spoken to or haggled much with the sellers. Most of them knew her as the daughter of Boss Farag and Mrs. Teresa, and always addressed her as "Miss Samira." I called her by just her name, which I loved so much.

She's on the roof on a hot, moonlit night, seated on a large empty metal can, face in hands, pensive and grave, silently raising her eyes to the sky, and Shawqi and I go into his room, with a "Good evening, Samira" to her, though she doesn't reply. After a while we hear her sobs and quiet moans.

It's late afternoon. She and I are sitting on the stoop, in the light coming from the stairwell. She is reading quietly and I am sitting a few inches away from her. I rest my arm on the wooden banister and gaze at her, smiling. I've claimed that I have to wait for Shawqi to come back from the store so that he can explain the difficult algebra lesson to me and she's told me gently, "Okay. Sit down," so I've sat down next to her in silence, stealing glances at the page from which she's reading. I'm hesitating over whether to ask her why she likes poetry so much. I'm on the point of speaking but the words turn to stone on my trembling lips and I fidget where I sit. She is unaware of my presence and doesn't lift her eyes from the book. I indulge myself for long moments in looking her body over from top to toe, flustered and almost shaking. My eyes settle on her gleaming knees and stop there. I am at rest and unafraid, and I look like any good, well-behaved boy (ho-ho!), gazing shyly at the ground.

Shawqi's room, a month before the promotion exams. We're sitting opposite one another on the rush mat, our Arabic Language books and texts open on the low round wooden table between us. I'm looking in the direction of the open door and reading out loud to Shawqi, with extreme lack of enthusiasm, one of the poems we have to learn for Memorization:

Lodged am I upon unspeaking rocks,
And would that my heart like this unspeaking rock might be!

She enters carrying a tin tray with cheese and egg sandwiches and two glasses of tea. I'm suddenly overcome by ardor. My voice rises and rings out, and she smiles at me. I go on reading and try to jazz up my poetic performance with Qur'anic embellishments. My eyes meet hers, I get flustered, and the blood rises to my face. I make a mistake and start stammering: "and would that my . . . and would that my . . . and would that my head like this unspeaking rock might be!" She puts the tray on the table, leans toward me, and winks. Then she says, "You've got a nice voice but you're saying it wrong, love. It's 'would that my *heart*,' dumbo!"

She leaves, cutting an elegant figure, and I am covered in embarrassment and shame.

I'm standing at the threshold of the door into her house, sweat pouring off me from top to toe, heart pounding, mouth dry, face red, ears burning, and she's staring at me in astonishment. I stammer without producing a single word, making meaningless sounds, summoning up all my courage so that I can take from my pocket the thing I've spent all night working on. "What's wrong, Rabeea?" she says. "What's happened?" With trembling fingers, I place in her hand a poem I wrote about her, for her alone. I give her a pallid smile and turn and flee. I run till I get to my room.

Next day, as I was climbing the stairs to Shawqi's room, she came out from their apartment on the ground floor and stopped me. Her face was rosy and very beautiful. She looked into my eyes without saying anything for a while and examined my face closely, then stretched her hand out toward my hair and stroked it, saying with unforgettable sweetness, "I love you too. But . . . but you're still young."

Then she gave me a single light kiss on my cheek, which is all I ever got from her.

Her naked body shines and dazzles, her black hair is wet and loosened to fall over her face and onto her shoulders, her lips are as delicious as cherries, her small breasts are in my hands, and one of her nipples is in my mouth. Her hands are in my hair and on my back and a flood of water descends on my head and body from the showerhead. I gasp and shiver with pleasure and the soapsuds are thick and white and cover my left hand and the thing between my thighs.

Samira is in a white wedding dress, her right hand on Luqa's arm at the threshold of St. George's. Luqa, her cousin, has his big jaws parted as far as they can go, and his repulsive black face is joyful and glad. His gray hair is shiny, slicked with oil, and Samira is dwarfed by his hulking body.

Samira's face is brown and beautiful on the water under the Abbas Bridge, and a fifteen-year-old teenager looks at it and chokes as he weeps and tries to pluck up the courage to jump the iron railings.

I neither laugh nor weep at that scene now. I just long to see her, but she hasn't come back to Giza even once since she set off with Luqa for the ends of the earth, a.k.a. Canada.

Why didn't I kill myself then and have done with it? Why did I have to come this far?

19 A LOVER SURPRISED

THE SCANDAL WAS WAITING TO HAPPEN, foretold by the events of that day not too long ago. (Three months ago? Two? A month? Have you forgotten?)

Remember, ladies' man! Recall, my dear sir!

I went to her despite the peeling, despite the little bumps on my member from our last ravenous lovemaking, which hadn't yet healed and still hurt every time I moved or stood or sat, and even though I'd told her I was tired and afraid. I'd told her I couldn't take her any more and couldn't take myself any more and "I don't want you!" and "You'll never see my face again!"

It was Nashwa who'd put the rope around my neck, at our first encounter. She alone could bind and loose, she alone controlled the thick rope, which she could jerk on, pulling me to her whenever she chose. She might pull violently, dragging me in whenever she felt like it, whenever she wanted me, or let it out a little, according to her mood, depending on how bored or fed up with me she was, or how indifferent she felt toward me. Sometimes she'd cast me away from her onto the floor of the living room in her father's house or her bed or the kitchen tiles. She might discard me on Nile Street or Greater Ocean or in Giza Square and leave me free to roam, waiting for her next step, the thick rope firmly around my neck but without her delicate hand to pull me, drag me, and lead me, the free end hanging in a vacuum. I'd be free and independent, able to move as I wished and as my fancy dictated, but the rope would still be wound around my neck.

That day I went to her furious with myself, defeated by my inability to do without her, torn. I opened the door to her apartment with the key she'd had copied for me so that I could come to her any time I wanted and as an affirmation of something more than just passion: "Trust," she'd said. "A sense of security."

I entered her apartment with unwilling steps, but in the end I went on in and closed the door behind me as calmly as though it were my own place.

She must have heard the sound of the door closing from inside and known who the intruder was, but she made no move to welcome me, didn't utter a word or even say "Who is it?" until I reached her.

She was lying on the spacious bed in her bedroom. Her red nightdress was open at the front and had ridden up well above her knees. Her plump thighs shone with a pure brownness and in her hands was an English-language fashion magazine. She didn't lift her head from the page, just looked at me from the corners of her eyes. I said nothing. Fully dressed and still wearing my shoes, just as I had arrived, I lay down next to her on the bed and took a deep, audible breath.

The scene remained frozen like that for a long time.

When she'd more or less finished leafing through the magazine, she broke through her arrogant indifference to me and rasped out sarcastically, with that signature catch in her voice that she used to demonstrate her permanent mockery of me, "So you're back, champ! To what do we owe the honor?"

I participated along with her in gloating over me. I smiled to hide my embarrassment and self-disgust and bent over to kiss her, while she held herself as rigid as a rock.

After numerous long kisses on her head and cheeks, then her lips, and then between her swelling breasts, I repeated in her noble ear over and over that I was sorry for what I'd said last time, uttered many expressions of supplication and pleading, and sought her forgiveness and pardon. Turning away from me coquettishly, she whispered, in the petulant tones of a little girl, "Didn't you say you hated me and hated yourself?"

I was silent for a long time, fighting fiercely the need to burst into tears.

I moved close to her, took her whole body in my arms, and placed my head between her breasts. She closed her eyes and didn't push me away, didn't move, didn't say a thing. All I could hear was the sound of her heartbeats, which were regular and normal.

After long minutes—during which I almost fell into a quick sleep, like that of a suckling child, as I lay there embracing her—she let rip a gloating laugh that could have been heard at the end of the street.

"Didn't I tell you you wouldn't be able to do it, you weakling? You, do without me?"

I shook my head several times to deny that I could stand being separated from her and tried to find words to express what I felt and satisfy her conceit and monstrous femininity, but she didn't give me the chance.

She wasted no time on listening to me and changed the subject with astonishing speed. In a second, we were back as we had been, as though there had never been a wide rent in the fabric of our relationship, as though it had never happened. For her, I was a huge ear that had to be constantly fed with her words and endless stories.

She said her husband had returned the day before from his trip and the vague mission that had taken almost two weeks, that he'd gone over some bills and invoices and so on with her, given her extra cash for the coming month's expenses, kissed her tersely and quickly, apologized for not being able to spend the night with her, and departed on a new mission "without even taking a shower."

"Dear, dear!" I said, laughing.

"You're just a slob, so it makes no difference to you. You don't know the importance of a shower, or being clean, or stuff like that!"

She threw herself on me like a wild animal in heat. She covered my lips, neck, and chest in sucks and bites, her mighty thighs crushing the lower half of my body. She had no pity or mercy for my obviously inflamed animal. She made love to me at length, while I tried to bear the mounting pain, pressing my lips together so that my cries wouldn't emerge, and merely moaning. Eventually, I let myself give vent to my distress. As she let out her prolonged scream of lust, I too screamed with the terrible pain.

She left me and got up, after a long kiss of gratitude on my lips, and I turned over and pushed my face into the plushy mattress, quickly dropping off into a sudden deep sleep like a delicious, final death. There was a dazzling white light before my closed eyes and in my ears the sound of a copious and unceasing waterfall. I was happy in my coma and had no idea how long I slept, or was dead.

Her delicate fingertips were on my back as she gently woke me. I turned onto my side, raised my head toward her, and opened my eyes to find her completely naked, drops of water dripping from beneath her armpits, her elbows, and her hair, the smell of her body fresh and very subtle, her lower half fertile and fruitful as a bed of red flowers. She gave me a carefree smile, bent down to give me a long kiss, then twisted around, her naked body seen from behind extremely trim and beautiful. She opened her closet and put on in front of the mirror a white dress with little silver flowers, like an expensive wedding dress. She put it on with joy and a bright smile, and started to sing.

She pulled me by the hand and we went out to a restaurant in Zamalek, where we ate fish and shrimp and behaved like infatuated lovers. She gave me her hand and I took hold of it rapturously, stroking it as I gazed into her bold eyes, which she lowered in ecstasy as I told her, "You're very beautiful tonight."

She let out a long "aaah" as I told her, "My life had no meaning before I met you!" (as though it had any then). "You're beautiful," I went on. "The most gorgeous thing in Egypt today."

"Hah!" she said. Then, laughing sarcastically: "And what about Egypt yesterday and in the future?"

It was one of our favorite games: I'd speak words of love and passion and "stuff like that" to her, and she'd try to come up with the appropriate response. She'd made what she called this "romantic" suggestion to add an authentically lover-like nature to our nakedly physical relationship.

Once we got bored with the game, she started talking in an affectedly histrionic manner. She said she'd gone that morning to the offices of a large production company to demonstrate her acting talent to a well-known director.

The director, tall and thin as a reed, had been blown away by her from the moment he set eyes on her. Patting her captivating bosom, she said that he'd shown great enthusiasm and an immediate appreciation of her outer and inner acting potential and had gone on at length in praise of her matchless beauty and spellbinding voice, which he thought quite sufficient to justify giving her the lead role in an artistic work either on the stage or on the small or silver screens.

Nashwa, displaying her usual narcissism, insisted that the man hadn't been exaggerating or paying empty compliments and had done nothing more than state the plain truth. "Congratulations," I said. "Congratulations."

She sighed with genuine pain and mourning at loss of self.

"For what, damn it?"

"Heavens! Didn't you just tell me that the guy was bowled over by you and you were about to be launched on the path of glory and would be honoring stage and screen with your presence, bringing pleasure to audiences with your great art?"

"Forget it! You're totally in la-la land."

"Meaning what? There's no theater, movie contract, acting?"

"Of course not. I wish! I would have done you Taheya Carioca's belly dance tonight!"

"So what happened?"

"What you'd expect. What one always expects. The usual."

"How come?"

"He told me, like the charmer he was, 'Well, that's wonderful, Nashwa Hanim. It seems we're colleagues. I'm a Dramatic Arts Institute grad too. What do you say to going out with me tonight, colleague?'

"I told him, 'Sorry, I have a date.'

"He said, 'Work is more important.'

"I told him, 'Of course. But in fact my date's with my husband, because I only get to see him once in a blue moon.'

"'How can that be?' he said. 'Who'd leave a sweet little chickabiddy like you on her own?' A real charmer the rotten scrawny old goat turned out to be, right?"

"Absolutely. A rotten, puerile old goat who ought to act his age, and a bastard too."

"So . . . I told him, 'The thing is, my husband, Lord preserve us, is a police officer.' The moment he heard that his face turned red, then green, and then went through all the other colors.

"He asked me, 'A real live police officer?'

"I told him, 'Yes, and a high-ranking one too, for your information, not one from the marching band.'

"The man cleared his throat, put on a grave expression, like he was the minister of foreign affairs, and said to me, 'Nashwa Hanim, as you well know, art is a harsh taskmaster, but the life of an officer is harsher still. Nevertheless, we shall try to respect both callings. God willing, should I ever come across an appropriate role, I shall contact your good self.' I left him and went my way, after giving him a look a mangy cur wouldn't deserve from a poodle."

We laughed for a long time.

She cut our laughter off and suddenly went quiet and raised her face to look at something behind me. She bent forward, tapped the backs of my hands with her fingers, and whispered, "A friend of my husband's. Duha's brother. Behave yourself if he comes over here."

And he did come to our table. He was an elegant young man wearing an expensive suit and a necktie bearing the image of Leonardo's *Mona Lisa.*

Following a slight bow, a quick kiss on the hand of Nashwa Hanim, and a "How do you do, sir?" he studied my face, smiling with practiced confidence. Nashwa introduced me with all the seriousness of a lady running a cultural salon, saying as she gestured toward me, "Rabeea el-Hagg, broadcaster, a colleague of your sister Duha's at the radio."

His smile grew larger and broader.

He left us, creasing his brow with the frown of deep thought appropriate to an officer who was not to be made a fool of.

Did he see the terror on my face? Did he smell the fear that ran through my blood from my feet to my head?

Did he hear the sound of panic as my bones knocked against one another? Did he intuit what was going on between us? Did he hear the squealing of my flesh and skin?

I . . . I sank into the great ocean of horror, the well of fear that has no bottom.

20 FLIGHT

YOU KNOW . . .

that the best way to flee what you fear is to not flee at all, but to stand up straight where you are, like a man, breathe calmly, open your eyes wide, monitor your surroundings, be alert, and wait, steadfast and patient.

You wait for the switchblade to bury itself in your breast, for the length of its whetted blade to disappear into your heart, for the blood to spurt, to fall prostrate on the ground, your eyes wide open; or for a bullet to strike you on the forehead, between your eyes, so that the ground beneath your feet shakes and you fall on your back, a blackened corpse, in an instant; or you wait till they've got you cornered, are subjecting every part of your body to a vicious pummeling, thugs and bullies beating you to a pulp, and you look up at those surrounding you from where you lie at their feet in terror, look up at their faces as they pounce on you, their leader targeting his final assault at your poor thing, ripping it out by its roots, before they finish off what remains of you with a rusty knife.

Any method of killing, any of those described above, would be far better than to be killed without being granted even one second in which to view your killer's face, to know him, even to no possible end.

What I fear is that the blow will come from behind, that I'll have my head hacked off like a sheep's, in a killing whose perpetrator's face I never see: a blow to the skull with a hammer, hatchet, or mattock by an unknown assailant, or a slightly gentler death, by poison—just a small drop put into the food on my plate or into my glass of tea.

Or . . . or perhaps it would be better to be killed in a public space, in the middle of the highway, on one of the better-known streets of Giza, in Cinema Fantasio, in the marketplace, or on Bayumiya Square. What matters is to be killed openly, in plain sight, before everyone's eyes, and to see your killer's face.

EXIT

21 BLAST

HOW DID I GO TO SLEEP, and when? At what time did I lie down on my bed and sink into sleep, or death? How many hours did I sleep? What day is it? What happened after I entered the house just before the Friday prayer? What came over me after that long rant, that crazy debauch that went from sunset on Thursday till mid-morning on Friday? What happened after I swallowed that enormous dose of hashish and alcohol, after the copulation and the laughter, the eating and drinking, the chatter and the fear? How did I get back to the house? What had happened up to this point, the moment when I opened my eyes and became aware that I was alive, realized that I was on my bed and in my room? What were those ghosts, shadows, images that appeared before my eyes and in my head? What had opened the pit of the distant, and recent, past? Why had the lake of memories, sounds, and pictures overflowed its banks? What had made Samira, Sheikh Hubb, my father, my grandfather, Ahmad, and so many others take up residence in the pupils of my eyes, my brain, my room? Why had they come?

What had made them appear to me so clearly, to stand before me and stay for a while, moving around my bed, talking to me and gossiping about all those things while I listened to them in silence, opening my eyes as wide as I could to stare at them as their expressions changed, as their hands moved in signs and gestures, as they talked till their voices wore thin, grew gradually softer and lower, ended in gloomy silence, their words exhausted, their expressions stiffening as they fell silent, standing in place like statues in a museum or like old photographs, and then vanishing, slowly, slowly, before my eyes? What made them fall on me like that? Did any of them notice me as, staring and appalled, I hung on their words? Did I talk to them? Did I say anything to them? If any sounds or words did exit my lips, if I did in fact speak, or rave, did anyone but me hear my voice? Did I babble on for long? Did I make a spectacle of myself? Did I give away all my secrets, all the infamies I'd committed over the course of my life? Did I say anything about Nashwa, about my affair with her, about Anwar Gabr, about my fear, my horror, my shameful cowardice? Did I?

Many were my questions concerning that madness.

The last things I could remember—vaguely, and in shaky, blurry images like shadows or reflections on water—were coming back to the house and finding the sun's rays streaming in through the wide-open windows and filling the place, the Friday Qur'an reading on the radio's General Program coming loudly from the kitchen and filling the house, and the many noises made by Afaf as she moved over the kitchen floor making lunch. I said something I don't remember to my mother, kissed her hand, crossed the living room to my room, and stretched out on my bed. I felt a disturbance and pain in my belly and a strong urge to vomit. With difficulty, I got up off the bed, placing one hand over my mouth and the other on my belly, went out of my room, and, moving with difficulty, crossed the living room, entered the bathroom, and bent over the basin. I emptied my guts once, twice, three times, four times. I voided my innards again and again, seconds, even long minutes, between each bout. My body shook and convulsed each time the contents of my guts were expelled. I vomited so long that my stomach and intestines seemed almost to be coming out through my mouth and nostrils. I remember that my body went into spasms and flailed and twisted, and that I was bent over, supporting myself with both hands on the white basin. The large basin filled with the revolting filth that had come out of me, its rusty metal filter clogged with lots of hard little bits—meat and lumps, dark fluids, black and glutinous—the level in the basin rising and rising so that the filth of my guts spilled over onto the crotch of my pants, onto the front of my shirt, onto the legs of my pants and my feet and the tiles beneath them. The smell was acidic, stifling, rank as the dung of some beast. I felt as though my limbs would detach themselves from my body. I felt that my guts were about to burst like a balloon and my head explode and everything in it fly off in little shards and stick to the ceramic wall tiles; that my entire being was about to collapse and fall to the bathroom floor like a deflated water skin. My whole body felt as though it were about to go off like an explosive charge, inert but ready to burst asunder at any moment. And I remember that I left the bathroom staggering, incapable of seeing what was in front of me, and walked the few steps from there to the living room and then to my room, supporting myself with my right hand on someone who was shorter than I. And I remember that I lay on my back on the mattress like a dead, stinking animal, a worn-out rag, my eyes bulging and fixed on the ceiling, my mouth open and dribbling saliva onto my chin like an imbecile, a retard from whose lips flows a copious supply of drool. At the beginning, my head was an empty white space containing absolutely nothing. I remember that I was thinking about nothing, nothing whatsoever. I'd become just hollow and empty and calm and silent, like someone long dead, all of whose flesh, fats, and limbs had dissolved, leaving only a few carious and fragile bones. All the same, I wanted to speak, to say many things, to myself and to an unknown other, though, while my mouth yawned open like the mouth of a well, my lips wouldn't perform the movements necessary to form sounds. My mouth was open and I didn't know how to close it and I can't now remember the stories I wanted to tell or the images I watched erupting without warning inside my head—throngs of people who had leapt into my brain and in front of my eyes, as though returning to life from the nothingness of the past, travelers long departed who returned and entered my room and took it over. I remember that I was full of fear and horror and wanted to say that to someone, wanted to hear myself, hear my own voice, hear myself speak. And that I lost consciousness, was away for a long time. I didn't sleep, I was just away, and I and the wood of the bed became one—wood, or brick, or cement, or sand, like the walls of my room, and . . . .

Wow! How did I make it back?

Here I am, still alive!

I lift the blanket and stand, feeling debilitated. The sun's rays fill my room and make shapes on the ceiling and the walls, fall on my face and my clean white sweatsuit. I wake like a dead man returned from the grave. My mouth is dry and my bladder hurts, as does my back, from having lain on it so long. I stretch and feel my back, suspecting I may have ulcers and skin inflammations. I go to the bathroom, empty my bladder, and relax. I take off my underwear, noting that it is dazzlingly white, stand in the bathtub and take a long shower, closing my eyes and letting the water pour in a torrent over my head for long minutes. I feel that my body is clean and light and I am refreshed and alert. My body is as fresh as that of a newborn child, my head emptied of everything, my stomach a void, as empty inside as a new water skin.

I was thirsty and hungry, very hungry, and felt I could eat anything. I left the bathroom, water dripping from my hair, the towel around my neck, went into the kitchen and sat on a wooden chair, resting my elbows on Afaf's worktable, a square wooden table with a white marble top. Afaf was washing the dishes and pots and pans with rolled sleeves and a frown. I sat there for a few moments, remembered I was thirsty, stood and opened the refrigerator, drank a bottle of water at one go, took out a plate of white cheese and two cold loaves of bread, and sat down to eat.

Afaf, who was totally absorbed in washing the dishes, finally noticed my presence and abandoned her typically deep concentration on the washing and rinsing. She turned and looked at me from the corners of her eyes with annoyance and reproach, her hand pausing. She advanced the two steps between us, removed the plate with the cheese, took away the loaf that was in my hand and the other that was next to the plate, and put everything back in the refrigerator. Then she opened the wooden doors of the kitchen cupboard and placed numerous hot dishes in front of me, one after another.

"Thank you," I said, seeming to hear my voice for the first time. It was low and weak.

"Welcome back, sir!" she replied.

I looked at her, trying to work out what she meant. She sat down opposite me and gave me a small smile while placing her hand under her chin.

As I consumed, ravenously and greedily, the meat casserole, okra, and rice, Afaf broke the long estrangement between us and decided to talk to me like a good wife. She spoke a lot, with much verbosity and many digressions, and told me everything that had happened after I returned to the house last Friday in the late morning.

Afaf said I'd come back a few minutes before the call to the Friday prayer and had gone to my room to sleep, as usual without speaking to her. I hadn't been in there long, though, before I came out again and staggered into the bathroom. I'd almost fallen down in the living room next to my mother's wheelchair. I'd left the bathroom door open behind me and from the kitchen she'd heard the sound of me retching and vomiting. She'd come to see what was the matter and had found me suffering torments enough to make a disbeliever take pity. My eyes were tomatoes, my face yellow as turmeric, my mouth open as wide as it would go, my jaws jerking open and shut. I was vomiting yellow, brown, and red fluids, bits of rancid, black meat, and threads of dark red blood with a foul smell, like feces. She stood next to me for a few moments, patting my back and shoulder, taken aback by my appearance, then ran quickly to the kitchen, mixed salt and water in a bowl, picked up a glass, and went back to me. She made me drink three glasses of salt water, at which point I was ready to puke up the wall of my stomach and my guts. When I'd gotten out everything that was in my stomach, she placed my arm on her shoulder, put her arm around my waist, and physically dragged me from the bathroom to my room. She took all my dirty and befouled clothes off me, dressed me in a clean set of underwear, made me comfortable in my clean white sweatsuit that I wore around the house, and stretched me out on the bed. She left me for a minute and went to the kitchen and came back with a glass of warm milk. She took my head on her bosom, opened my mouth, and made me drink the milk, to cleanse my stomach of any poison left in my insides.

She said that, my head on her bosom, I'd closed my eyes and fallen quickly asleep, while she opened my lips and put the edge of the glass of milk to my mouth and made me slowly drink; that I looked like someone who'd taken rat poison, my face bloodless, my complexion wan, my whole body exuding from its pores the smell of alcohol and hashish, along with other strange and unpleasant odors.

She said that after she'd lined my stomach with milk to cleanse it of the poisonous microbes, she'd covered me with a blanket, closed the windows, pulled down the blinds, and left me to rest and sleep. She said I'd slept for about two nights and three days, during which time she fed me nothing but milk and a few spoonfuls of honey, and that I'd been semiconscious most of the time and had sometimes opened my eyes and mouth and talked nonsense, uttering disjointed words. She hadn't understood a thing but I'd said a lot of enigmatic stuff about herself, my father, Ahmad, my grandfather, and a lot of women. She also gave me a heartfelt sermon, in which she said that I ought to thank Our Lord and pray to Him often because it was He, the Glorious, the Almighty, who had been behind what had happened and had made her become aware of my presence and go to me and save my life, and that I should thank God and make penitence to Him, for the Omnipotent One, glory be to Him, had rescued me from certain death.

She told me I'd been sleeping as soundly as a baby that morning too and had felt nothing of the thing had happened, and that what had shaken everyone, the whole of Giza, had had no impact on me in my bed.

My mouth dropped open in surprise and I asked her, in a voice that had recovered some of its strength, "What happened in Giza?"

She said the whole of Old Giza—the square, the houses, the streets, and the people—had been shaken early in the morning, that at about six in the morning everything had swayed for a short while, that she'd been awake, as usual, and was in the kitchen boiling milk for me and making my mother's breakfast, the bells for the mass and the hymns audible from the church of St. George, as they were every Sunday. She'd heard a resounding crack and a simultaneous large explosion and the bathroom tiles had moved beneath her feet for a few moments. Terrified, she'd let out a scream and beaten her chest and thought that a violent earthquake, like that of '92, had struck Giza and Cairo. She lay down on the kitchen floor for what seemed like ages, silent and quaking with fear, but hadn't felt another shock or heard another crack or explosion, so she'd gotten up, scared out of her wits, and, muttering, "Protect us, O Lord, protect us, O protector!," had entered her bedroom and snatched up her headscarf, all the while reciting under her breath, "When earth is shaken with a mighty shaking . . . ." Then she left the house to see what had happened and found people running in the direction of the project housing behind the church. She said the people had come out in their nightclothes, with sleeping dust still in their eyes, running and trotting through the streets as though it were doomsday, as though they were the dead who'd been awaiting the moment of release from their graves, and they'd formed a crowd on Durri Street and in the cramped square in the middle of the project blocks where the dumpsters stood on the corner of the street and next to the walls and in the corners of the square. When she got there, she'd been caught up in the crowd and found herself close to the huge iron dumpster on the corner of Sabri Basha Street and seen that it was glowing red, burning hot enough almost to melt its metal, a smell of burning and gunpowder coming off it, and around it piles of black garbage bags, filth, and plastic that popped as it burned, sending out a choking, nauseating smoke. Close to the heap of garbage, the remains of two children, their bellies split open, lay in a pool of blood that had mixed with the dust, their guts coming out, their necks severed, the blood pouring from them as if from a faucet opened to its fullest, their faces bloody and disfigured, their eyes glazed and open in terror and surprise.

She said she'd screamed and cried out loud in terror at the horrible sight and burst into tears and wails as people gathered the remains of the two children and covered them with whatever old newspapers they could find, and that my uncle Musa had taken her under his wing and saved her from fainting and falling on the ground in front of everyone and brought her back to the house hugging her to his chest as though she were a terrified little bird and that she'd been sobbing and sniveling, her whole face bathed in tears.

Afaf wept as she told her tale and put her head between her hands. I'd stopped eating long before and was listening to her despondently.

I went over to her, took her in my arms, held her to my chest, and patted her on her shoulders and breast.

Amid her sobs, she whispered that, for all my faults and sins and everything that had happened between us, I was a good man and generous and that I mustn't put all the blame for our son Ahmad's drowning on her because it was God's decree and his fate and He, Great and Glorious, was merciful and forgiving and capable of compensating us and giving us sons and daughters, and that we had to have hope and trust in Him, the Almighty. And why couldn't we go back to our life together, like a good husband and wife, and that He, the Almighty, would be generous to us, God willing, if we only had faith.

I kissed her head and was about to exit the kitchen and leave her alone to continue her housework, when she stifled her tears and said that something else had happened, about two hours ago. I looked at her expectantly.

She said a young police officer in plain clothes had come to the neighborhood and asked a lot of people about what had happened that morning and that he'd entered our building, stayed a long time in my uncle's apartment, and talked to him about the suspicious explosion. The policeman had asked him if he'd seen anyone messing around with the big dumpster, and whether he thought there might be political motives behind the blast. She said he'd rung the bell to our apartment on his way down from my uncle's and talked to her and asked her about the incident, so she'd told him everything she'd heard and seen. Then he told her, "Good. Very good. Thank you very much," and asked her about me, mentioning my name and job, so she'd told him I'd been sick for three days and was in bed asleep. "Dear, dear. I really hope he gets better quickly," he said. He told her that he knew me personally and would have liked to see me but that as I was, unfortunately, sick and had been sleeping at the time of the incident, there was no need to wake me or disturb me. He asked her to give me his greetings so she'd asked him to be so kind as to tell her his name, and he told her he was Captain Asaad, brother of my colleague Duha at the radio. As he was leaving, he told her that his friend Lieutenant-Colonel Anwar Gabr remembered me and had mentioned that we'd been at the same school together, and that he sent me his greetings—lots of greetings and salutations.

22 AN OLDER MAN

I WANT TO WALK THROUGH THE STREETS. I have to get out of here, and damn the consequences. Three days and two nights I've been stuck here in the house like an old man too sick to move, like "bones in a basket," as the saying goes.

The house is stifling me. Even the air I'm breathing chokes me.

Full of forebodings and lassitude, like a rat coming out of its hole, I quietly open one half of the building's sliding gate. The gate has two leaves of wrought iron painted with black shellac. It still looks nice, with all its squares and triangles and circles, and it's solid even though the paint is flaking and there's some crumbly rust at the bottom. I cross the old marble floor tiles and the threshold, two hesitant steps putting me outside. In the street, the light of the late afternoon sun dazzles my eyes and I put my right hand in front of my face, lower my head, and bend forward, like a man no longer young.

Bank of Athens Street, where we live, runs for only about three hundred meters. Most of the houses are in the European style with three or four stories and built with load-bearing walls of masonry and red brick. The walls are high, the ceilings tall, and the balconies small, with iron railings that curve outward, and on the façades are reliefs and ornaments inspired by Greek and Roman legend, now mostly worn away and indecipherable. The windows are wide and tall, the leaves of the shutters thick and green, and behind them are panes that were originally of Belgian glass of the highest quality, bits of which are still painted with colored decorations of flowers, trees, and birds. In the old days, women were experts at making designs on window, door, and balcony glass.

In the 1930s, the two best-known landmarks on the street were Christo's print shop and the Bank of Athens. The print-shop building still stands—large and roomy and consisting of a single story, above which hangs an old green signboard from which the name Christo has disappeared, though the words "Print Shop" remain, faded but legible. Rising damp has taken hold in the print shop's thick stone walls and the large corrugated-iron door bulges, spotted all over with ancient rust. It has been closed from the time I first set eyes on it, from the time I first went out onto the street as a kid. The Greek bank building, though, had been demolished long before I was born, leaving the name of the Greek capital on a street sign hung on the wall of the first house. Its place had been taken by a yellow, six-story apartment block.

Before the July revolution, the street's residents had been a mix of Greeks, Egyptians, Italians, and Armenians—merchants and employees of the government or of companies, skilled workers, effendis and beys. Following the Tripartite Aggression in '56, most of the foreign residents sold their houses for peanuts and left Egypt, either to return to Europe or to emigrate to the Americas, and all that remained of them in Giza were a few old people; most had died and gone to their graves, their remaining living representatives a few women of great age living isolated lives in the same old houses as before. My mighty, crafty grandfather bought our house in '57 from an Italian tobacco expert called Marco who worked at the Eastern Tobacco Company. He got the whole house with its three stories and small garden, now gone, for just thirty pounds.

The street is some five meters wide, with some twenty houses between the two sides. Because it's a side street between Durri and Nasser, it's somewhat off the beaten track. Durri is an important street, very special and well provided with security personnel and soldiers distributed here and there, sitting on wooden benches in front of its two long-established churches—the Church of St. George and the Church of the Brothers, which belongs to the Coptic Protestant community. It is a quiet, well-to-do street that for six days of the week sees few pedestrians. On Sundays, it's very crowded, with people coming from all over to pray and visit the two churches. Nasser Street is known for having the Ahram Publishing Company's advertising office, as well as the offices of the *Gumhuriya* newspaper, the Abu el-Dahab confectionary company's kitchens, and three Internet cafés, and it leads to Ahmad Mahir, the largest and best known of the market streets.

Our old-fashioned street is a little island of calm in the midst of the waves of noise that extend the length, breadth, and height of the nearby market. In our street, elderly vendors silently, calmly, and at known times place their aged customers' milk, bread, newspapers, vegetables, and fruit in baskets lowered by ancient ropes from small balconies and via stairwells. The veteran vendors know precisely the requirements and needs of each customer. They put their goods into the baskets and leave, presenting them with the account at the end of the month, or as occasion arises. The itinerant peddlers who fill the other streets for all of the day and a part of the night do not make their rounds here.

From time to time, a cart strange to the neighborhood passes by loaded with seasonal fruit, its aged donkey or horse led by a vendor in a gallabiya and shawl, usually an Upper Egyptian, who calls out his wares using an abbreviated code that everyone understands, eking out a living, or Old Man Salama the junkman, pulling along behind him with his left hand his ulcerated donkey, which in turn pulls a cart with a small closed wooden compartment, and holding up in his right a portable loudspeaker into which he joyfully bellows "Bekyaaa! Bekyaaa!"

And most Friday afternoons, a praise singer, no longer young, who plays a large tambourine without jingles, stops for about an hour and praises the Chosen Prophet in short poems in popular language, his voice shaky and weak. He wanders down the street with slow steps, raising his tambourine in the air and striking it with a veined hand and long brown fingers. He stops before the doors of the houses and under the balconies and sings of his love for God's messenger and the people of his House. Once done with his praises and chants, he lowers the tambourine, letting it dangle from his right hand, and walks over to Aziza, where he gathers the skirts of his wide gallabiya and seats himself in a dignified manner, stretching his long legs out before him and leaning his back against the wall, using for this purpose a small cement bench built into it just before her corner. He takes a tin box from the pocket of his silvery waistcoat, opens it, and busies himself rolling a cigarette. Aziza puts a glass of black tea with lots of sugar into his hand, saying happily, "May God make you rich, Sheikh Marawan. You honor all Giza with your presence!" Aziza is very fond of him, responds with delight to his singing, and always greets him with a free glass of tea. The tambourine lies on the bench next to his right hand, and certain persons, always the same, go and place in it what they can afford, the praise singer smiling at them, his eyes narrowing, the wrinkles and folds of his face multiplying as he does so, his dark-brown face relaxing into a joyful expression. In gratitude and thanks he raises his hands over the white shawl tied around his head after the manner of a snake-charming dervish. He drinks his tea slowly and noisily and smokes his cigarette with patent enjoyment. After the tea and the cigarette, he stands up and resumes his wandering and singing, walking off with slow steps, striking the tambourine and chanting, in the direction of the "Two-thirds Off" market.

And there was another stranger to our neighborhood, a very strange person indeed.

I see him now, as I do whenever I go out, sitting in his usual spot opposite our house, three meters from our door.

There he is—exactly opposite the door that I have opened and closed. An older man, who sits there from early in the morning until the dark has thickened in the streets, at the time that Aziza leaves and Farghali closes his grocery.

I smile, out of pity for him and myself.

I look at him, stare hard at him, search his face, clothes, body, outward appearance, and general demeanor for some clue—a clue obviously well concealed, camouflaged beneath his strange appearance, that he has been hiding since he first arrived and took up position here. I've tried many times to examine him closely, to show him friendship, to get close to and talk to him, to find out what makes him tick, but he refuses to look at me, won't say a word to me, and all my efforts to find out about him behind his back yield nothing. I can get nowhere.

His presence fails to send me any message, either by conjecture or by intuition. He's there, that's all. His presence is pure and gratuitous, devoid of any purpose, meaning, or significance. He takes no notice of anyone, pays no attention to anything around him, just stays the way he is, with himself, always the same, a small riddle, enduring and firmly ensconced.

I look at him, somewhat in awe, but he barely seems to see me. He's far away, absorbed in his long contemplation of stone and iron and of the hyacinth vine, dry of leaf and stem, on our ground-floor balcony. He doesn't lift his face to look at me, pays no attention, as usual, to my hand raised in the air by way of greeting.

He is a man in late middle age who resembles me somewhat in a few of the things that characterized me when I was twenty.

This older man sits five meters from Aziza's tea stall, which occupies a gap between two walls at the intersection of Bank of Athens and Nasser, before him a number of fizzy drinks boxes set one on top of the other, the topmost spread with newspaper on which are packets of paper tissues of different sizes and brands. He sits behind these on a wooden deck chair, silent as a statue, with lovelorn face. His gaze is fixed on our house, and behind his head is a rusty corrugated-iron door, the door of the electrical appliances store that is always closed.

The whole scene repeats itself as predictably as the successive risings and settings of the sun. For ages, the man has been a fixture as unlikely to move as the stones of which the houses are made.

Silently and indifferently, the strange man follows with his eyes the falling of the sun's rays on the wrought iron of the balcony and tracks the opening and closing of the doors, windows, and balconies of our house and the appearances and disappearances of its inhabitants. His eyes focus most on the hyacinth vine on my balcony. My mother planted it years ago, when she was young, when she heard and spoke, in the hope that it would grow and grow and cover the whole façade of the three-story house with its broad green leaves.

Throughout, the face of the older man remains unchanged—pleasant, kindly, fixed on our balcony with its iron, its vine, and its closed door. From time to time, he adjusts the strap of the expensive watch on his left hand and stares into space, his handsome brown face relaxed and content, enjoying the unchanging vista that he has created by himself for himself. The man is silent most of the time and speaks to no one but himself. He never fidgets as he sits there; he just sometimes hums, growls, wets his lips, dreamily and gravely smokes a cigarette, or, in a hoarse voice, utters a few disjointed words and obscure phrases: "I didn't want it to be like that."

Sometimes he lets himself go, gives full rein to his restless spirit as it wanders its private world: "Really, it's a crying shame."

His reproachful voice is gentle and low.

Frequently, groups of people, mostly children and adolescents, disturb the serenity of his silence and abstraction and, for a laugh, try to get a rise out of him by snatching the packets of tissues and running off, but he says nothing and doesn't leave his place. They mock him and insult him, cursing him for a sphinx, but he isn't shaken. They kick the dust of the street in his direction till his face, hair, and clothes are covered with it, and run off laughing while he sits there stolidly, neither moving nor uttering a word. Aziza comes and curses and screams at the miserable bastards and wipes his face and hair and tries to make him feel better with a few words.

Aziza puts a glass of tea for him on the edge of the box with his goods, next to the packets of tissues.

"Come on now, old buddy. What's up with you?"

The man remains silent and gives no sign that he hears her.

"You're an odd fish. Why don't you tell me, so I can help you?"

He raises to her a face like stone.

When she leaves, clucking and tut-tutting, he talks to himself.

"The fact is it's strange, very strange. But what I am supposed to do about it?"

When things get too much for him, he raises his voice a little and complains to an illusory person: "She handed me a bitter cup, cousin!"

The older man dresses as elegantly as a new suitor. His black pants are clean and pressed and his olive-green shirt is of classic cut, its cuffs buttoned. His white mustache is thick and he has a large nose over thin lips. What hair remains on his head is carefully combed and unassumingly parted to one side.

His long neck moves slowly to right and left: "I didn't want it to be like that."

He takes a last sip of tea and Aziza comes to take away the empty glass. Later, she'll bring him a cup of sugarless coffee, which he drinks slowly but never looks at. His wide eyes are connected by invisible threads to the immutable image inside his head and before his eyes — our house.

On his way into and out of the house, my uncle smiles to him, raises a hand in greeting, and says "Good morning" or "Good evening." The man doesn't raise his hand in response, but a slight smile appears on his face. Sometimes my uncle stops in front of him for a while and looks at him, striking one palm against the other out of pity for the man's condition. "There is no power but with God! Hang in there, friend!" When he sees him sitting there in his usual place at the end of the evening, in the dark, as he returns from his evening out, he stops in front of him, lets out a sudden laugh, and says mockingly, "There, there. Get a grip, buddy. Good night!"

My father ignores him completely, as though he can't see him. He gives him none of the greetings he hands out to all and sundry on every street, not one of the "peace be upon you"s that are forever on the tip of his tongue.

Each day, for long hours, this strange older man sits in his place, through all four seasons of the year, in cold and in heat, pretending to sell paper tissues but not selling any, paying not the slightest attention to his pathetic trade.

In the last part of the evening, his brown, sharply sculpted face and prominent nose, shaped like an old-fashioned crutch, disappear from the street. Sometimes the face of this strange man jumps out at me. I see it when my eyes are closed. I see its tightly drawn skin, strewn with small dark spots—the rigid face of a dead man in whose eager eyes alone does life stir—those wide black eyes through which he communicates the essence of his existence.

My misgivings about him have never disappeared. I fear him!

On occasion, Farghali the grocer will address him from his store on the opposite corner, smiling and waving: "Hello, hello! Anything for the gentleman?"

The older man, whose name nobody knows, does not reply.

Farghali keeps an ear out for anything the man may say. He picks up the few widely spaced words the man produces—a single word or two; one phrase every hour or two—and refuses to leave him alone, sending him glasses of tea with Aziza, self-importantly shouting, "A tea for the gentleman, Aziza!"

The glass arrives in a trice, but the man refuses to take it. He shakes his head. Aziza proudly puts her hands on her hips, pleased at our friend's haughtiness.

"Don't you mind, Farghal. He doesn't accept drinks from anyone."

Farghali answers her with an idiotic laugh and keeps on sending over his tea, which the man never accepts.

When did the man first appear on our street? Where did he come from and where does he go to spend the night? How does he live and in what house does he sleep?

No one knows and no one cares, except Farghali.

Farghali, who always struts around in colored shirts and delights in the thought that he's Giza's very own fashion encyclopedia, will explain to you the secret of his creepy commiseration with the man's plight by telling you, "Listen. He's a real gentleman. There isn't a more distinguished or better dressed person in the whole neighborhood."

The older man is indeed distinguished and above reproach. Who'd have thought that such a person would turn up here, all of a sudden one morning, to sell paper tissues to the passersby? It's a trade that can't make more than three, four pounds a day and each day the vendor spends around twenty pounds on his tea, coffee, and cigarettes!

Farghali has spent months trying to uncover the man's secret. Recently he confided to Aziza the information he'd gathered, which he swore was true. The man's name was Nabil. He was originally from Alexandria and he'd taken early retirement from a large company. That was it.

The older man whom Farghali the grocer called Nabil confirmed nothing and denied nothing. He spoke to no one except his phantoms and had no interest in anything except our house, on which his eyes were glued.

Sometimes I'd notice the ghost of a smile on his face if the curtains in our house shook, or if a new light appeared.

What's he to me? Let him sit there. Let him rock himself and chew over his sorrows and wretched, unobtainable desires.

As I passed him, casting a glance at his pathetic little setup, I thought of myself on that distant night when I returned to Afaf bearing my wretched bunch of flowers, the night when Afaf slept with her back to me and I smashed up the bedroom and its contents.

Perhaps this Mr. Nabil is the wretched suitor of some woman living in our house. Who knows? Perhaps one day, ages ago, a woman bestowed a glance on him, smiled at him from one of the three ancient balconies, and left him living the dream of an impossible passion. Beautiful, delectable women dwell in this house—my uncle's wife, her daughter Muna, Afaf, my grandfather's wife, and my mother. Or maybe this suitor has come to butcher me, is the hired killer who will one day spill my blood on my doorsill. Who can tell? Life is a black casket—black and closed like a tomb locked with a large iron padlock, which should never be opened because if it is the evil genies will come out of their lamps.

His eyes are still glued to our house and he is unaware of my presence. He doesn't see me as I stare at him.

"I didn't want it to be like that."

I left him talking to himself and went my way.

23 BUTCHERS

I TRAVERSE THE HEART OF GIZA unconscious of my surroundings. I walk through the crowds like one wading through a wilderness of reeds, scrub, weeds, and thorns. My feet mechanically traverse the alleys, lanes, and streets. My legs know the way on their own by virtue of familiarity and the habit of long years.

I reach the market. Battles and fights here are daily, have no end, and are never settled. As soon as one is broken up, another erupts, usually only a short time after the first has been set to rest and in more or less the same place and for the same familiar causes, or causes that are continually renewed.

At the entrance to the vegetable market is a small butcher's shop three square meters in area. It has no sign bearing its name. Along its high ceiling, dozens of iron hooks, empty now, are hung at differing heights. A few minutes earlier, the remains of entire carcasses hung from the hooks, a vast crowd before them.

From the time of the dawn prayer till the arrival of the first customers in the market, the hands of the ten butchers working in the shop are busy flensing and boning, chopping and dressing and otherwise preparing the meats for sale. A butcher takes a carcass weighing three hundred kilos on his back, disappearing beneath it, and, without looking, maneuvers the base of its neck so as to impale it on the hook, sets it straight with a movement of his shoulders and back, then pulls himself out from beneath it, steadying it with his hands until it stops swinging. He sighs comfortably, without panting, his features showing no sign of fatigue.

"It comes down to sinew, not muscle," says the big boss, Hasan el-Shafei, founder and owner of the small shop, which is why the butchers who work there are sinewy and don't have huge bodies or rippling muscles.

In el-Shafei's shop, they display the beast's flesh as is, naked, not covered with white muslin, so that the customers and passersby can all see the pure fresh redness of the meat and the large blue official stamps that confirm that the slaughter was performed legally and in keeping with the government's technical standards, as well as in the prescribed religious manner and according to the rules of Islamic law, and that it took place at the Saqyit Mekki abattoir under the supervision of a specialized veterinarian.

Pride in the quality and freshness of their meats, and honest practice, were traditions in the Shafei family. Every day they'd bring to their shop no fewer than ten carcasses, slaughtered at the abattoir before dawn, and hang them up with much rejoicing, commotion, and fuss, and they'd hang there from the hooks, taking up the whole shop, too many to count and making the visitors to the old market drool, especially those who only went there once a week to buy a couple of marrow bones for two pounds or a quarter of a kilo of stewing beef for five—things that were available only at el-Shafei's and absolutely out of the question at the large butchers' stores in Giza, of which there were about thirty, or at the Gabr Butchers chain stores.

El-Shafei's meats were classified and carefully sorted, each part of the animal's flesh being expertly, slowly, and precisely separated and each having its own price and value for connoisseurs and lovers of meat with means, as well as for the less affluent masses. Nothing, not one part of its flesh, went to waste, not even the offal, bones, or gristle.

In front of the store, a long line would grow spontaneously out of nothing, extending till it almost reached the cold-locker of the large butcher's opposite el-Shafei's, a branch of the Gabr chain. All day long, men, women, and children would form a crowd that kicked and shoved with its elbows and shoulders, screaming, shouting, and quarreling as though in front of a bakery selling five-piaster loaves of bread, the victorious taking their order wrapped in brown paper like that used to make cement sacks and setting off in high spirits, dreaming of how good the broth, crumbled bread with meat, stew, and boiled meats would taste. The unlucky ones who reached the butcher's chopping block too late would return to their homes as mournfully as if they'd lost a loved one. By the time of the afternoon prayer, the store would be scrubbed down and completely empty and the last bit of gristle, the last bone, would have been sold, would have entered mouths, and would be making their way toward the amazing stomachs of the mighty people of Giza.

The store had two main characteristics that accounted for its resounding reputation and the scramble for its products—the freshness of the meat and its relative cheapness. The store was small and had no cold-locker, despite the tons of meat on offer every day: all of it was sold, and once that was done, the store shut up shop and closed its doors. The sale of all the meat and the absence of a cold-locker meant that nothing stayed in the store overnight, this being the best means of assuring the freshness of the meat, which the empty stomach would absorb gratefully even if the eater did not care to savor what he was eating for long, connoisseurship being a luxury in which most of the people of Old Giza did not indulge. El-Shafei's prices were relatively good too, especially for stewing beef, which was unrivaled at any other butcher's. A kilo of veal or lamb cost five pounds less than the price shown in the list in the front window of Gabr's store. And this was the main cause of the continual battles in which the butchers of the Shafei family, blessed with the love of the masses for their meats and the store's low prices, became embroiled with the Gabr family, owners of the larger store with its giant glass cold-locker that occupied a larger area than the store itself, so that part of it was on the street.

Toward the end of the afternoon, or, more precisely, just before four, when the Shafei family would be on the verge of closing their doors, their last bone having gone, it was quite normal to see the workers of the Gabr family store, on the other side of the street, who rarely sold to any but the elite, and the elite of the elite at that, trying to get a rise out of them with phrases such as "Donkey meat all gone, then?" or "All sold out and ready to go home early!" or "Donkeys slaughtering donkeys to sell to donkeys!"

The Gabr family boys would use such expressions as a secret code to alert any of them that might not be aware that they were about to launch an attack on the Shafei bunch.

Boss Hasan el-Shafei rarely came to the store because he was busy making deals to buy cattle from the provinces. The store and all the buying and selling were delegated to his eldest son Fu'ad, who, though not yet thirty, was as grave and dignified as a man of seventy.

Tell those who come and those who pass
El-Shafei's meat's straight off the ass!

The chants of the Gabr family's workers increased in volume at a gesture from Gamal Bey Gabr, who was standing in front of his store in his elegant Parisian suit and whose heavy scent obscured that of the meat, fat, and grease, while Mr. Fu'ad el-Shafei would hold the hand of Scarface, the oldest and huskiest of his workers, trying to calm his anger and whispering in his ear, "The daily performance. Don't let it get to you," and then turning to the rest of his workers and saying, "Lock her up, boys! We're sold out, praise God."

The meaning of the latter, coded, phrase was "No one leaves the store without a knife or a pistol!"

On the other side of the street, Gamal Bey would have lit his pipe and started puffing clouds of smoke from his elegant nostrils. Knuckle-bone, the puniest of the Gabr family workers in both body and standing, would now come out, a knife almost as long as his arm in his hand, and shout into the space between the two stores: "The donkey butchers don't have a man among them. Filthy, slovenly apprentices!"

At this, on cue, out would come the brave, hot-tempered lad Tripes (whose mother had wanted him to grow up to be a devotee of Sidi Ramadan but who'd dashed her hopes and made his way in life with his knife) to defend the Shafei honor—and it had to be him because, like Knucklebone, he was short, with a puny body, and more or less the same size as his opponent (approximately, that is, of the same weight class). It wouldn't do at all for the veteran Scarface, for example, who was much taller than him, to challenge Knucklebone.

The duel would now begin, each of the two bosses, who were of similar ages, following it from the safety of his position in front of his shop, watching with as much pleasure and enthusiasm as they would a wrestling match on Egypt TV's Channel Two. The basic principle of the fight taking place before them was to hurt without wounding or drawing blood—this was the basic rule of engagement that both Knucklebone and Tripes sought to apply as strictly as they could.

Tripes would move into the middle of the space separating the two stores, while Knucklebone would keep up his foul-mouthed insults, each staring into the other's eyes, each wary, each brandishing his long knife in the air, their waists braced with thick leather belts tied over their blood-smeared gallabiyas, and each wearing tall rubber boots down which were stuck a number of cleavers and boning knives. Tripes (he whose mother had hoped he'd dedicate his life to Sidi Ramadan) had never been wounded in his battles with Knucklebone, aside from a few superficial scratches on his neck and face (whose premature wrinkles made it look like tripe); the cleft that divided his thick lips in two wasn't Knucklebone's doing—it was how the Good Lord had made him.

The opponents face each another, a distance of two meters between them, and start bellowing and exchanging threats:

"I'll cut you to pieces!"

"The dogs will have bones for supper tonight, you c**t!"

"You son of a b***h, I'll slice up your mother's . . . !"

". . . !"

". . . !"

This verbal head-butting continues for about half an hour, during which they compete at showing off their knowledge of the dirtiest and most obscene insults current in Giza. The crowd that has formed a circle around them now includes plainclothes police informants, so they up the ante a bit, each pushing the other back with a shove to the chest, like judo practitioners. Their shoulders make contact and the knives are raised into the air. Knucklebone bluffs a blow to the head, to which Tripes responds by feinting a kick below the belt. The two part and close in, grapple and separate, the crowd lapping up the scene. Knucklebone and Tripes each have their admirers, so of course the voices of the masses rise with cries of "Let him have it, Tripes!" and "Teach him some manners, Knucklebone!" and "Tripes! Tripes!" and "Make mincemeat of him, Knucklebone!"

Mr. Fu'ad's mood quickly sours. He finds the spectacle boring and leaves his closed store, his workers, armed with knives and cleavers, surrounding him with all the pomp and circumstance of a governor of Giza or a famous businessman on Station Road. Gamal Bey continues to watch the fight, having achieved his objective of spoiling his opponent's mood and bringing his work day to a close with insults to and ridicule of his meat. The combatants are still circling and turning like Greco-Roman wrestlers, each feinting at the other and dancing around with his knife. Tripes is an expert whistler; he whistles like a carter giving directions to his donkey and this makes Knucklebone's anger exceed all bounds, especially as he realizes that Tripes is sending him a message whose gist is "That's it, that's enough. The bosses have gotten tired of it, mama's boy."

A greenhorn, if his glance happened to fall on these two puny men in their blood-smeared gallabiyas and with their white boots stuffed with knives, would think he was about to witness with his own eyes the demise—swear to God and hope to die!—of one or both of them, and that the affair was going to get bigger, with the Shafei and Gabr family workers joining in, and that there'd be a battle, with much carnage. But if he were to look to his right and his left he'd see that most of the other butchers in the market were standing here and there finishing off their customary tasks with their usual calmness, chatting with the venerable police informants of the market and smoking and swapping jokes.

In the end, the combatants raise their weapons, throw themselves into one another's arms — "I'll kill you! I'll finish you! I'll slice you up!" — and fall to the ground, their knives held high. Neither has put a scratch on the other. At this moment, the police informer Masaoud approaches them, slaps first Knucklebone on the face ("because he's a bastard and makes problems for his boss and gives him a bad reputation") and then Tripes, the pothead ("because he smokes weed and can't hold down an honest job").

Each of the combatants gets to his feet, pretending to be furious and sticking his knife in his belt, and leaves the middle of the road, the battleground, with the composure of a military commander who has torn his enemies to shreds. Tripes makes for Loza the fishmonger to smoke a cigarette in proximity to her mighty buttocks, and Knucklebone heads for the interior of the Gabr family shop, to go on boning the top-quality, unsold meat. Masaoud will go to Gamal Bey to collect his "tea money" and a reward for having intervened at the right moment, thus preventing a massacre in the market that would have led to only God and the government knows what, or so Masaoud the informer insists as he enters the Gabr family shop. Gamal Bey, with the tips of his fingers, places ten pounds in the informer's hand and nods to Knucklebone, who has prepared a package of bones and gristle. Masaoud, proud as a rooster in a flock of hens, takes the package, holding it against his chest like a bunch of flowers, and struts off in his black gallabiya and brown skullcap, the bamboo cane required by tradition upright in his hand.

As a long-time observer of this daily scene, it should have been nothing to me but a source of entertainment and amusement. Now, however, it had become a source of terror, a rehearsal for a killing, for Gamal was Anwar Gabr's eldest brother.

I look into the faces of each of the butchers, trying to find in them a sign, a symbol, a meaning or mark. I search for *my* butcher, the one who will kill me one day. He doesn't have the shape of Knucklebone or Tripes or even the largest and fiercest of them. They are ordinary butchers, whose job is to slaughter animals and chop up meat that will go into bellies; which of them, though, will turn into a butcher of men and chop up a body that will go into the belly of the earth?

My own, criminal, butcher is a veteran when it comes to his crimes, a criminal in his invisibility, in his self-concealment, in his vanishing. If he were to appear to me once, just once, if he were to open his mouth and bare his fangs, I'd struggle against him till the snuffing out of the last spark of life.

24 FANTASIO

MAHMUD HIMEIDA AND LAYLA ELWI are two huge, panic-stricken, horrified faces covered with dust and dirt looming above Cinema Fantasio. The main billboard is mangy, large, and square, its chalky colors dominating the upper façade of the entrance to the cinema on Sanadeeli Street. The upper parts of the yellowing walls are covered with more advertisements for *I Love the Movies*, the same panicked faces repeating themselves in an infinite number of smaller posters, some pasted on top of each other, that are distributed all over the walls of the featureless ancient building. The walls are dirt, damp, and ooze water, and there's a dark discoloration at the base.

On either side of the cinema's entrance are a cigarette kiosk, an offal cart, and a stall selling headscarves. The scarves are colored and diverse, conforming to the type of religiously approved contemporary headwear commonly seen on the streets and lanes of Giza. The owner of the stall is an older Upper Egyptian from whose scandalous attentions and endearments not one pretty girl or woman is allowed to escape; a nice old man with a face spotted and burned from the sun that falls on his head all day and a long black silk scarf wound around a tightly fitting white skullcap. Each time a full bottom goes by, he sucks on his tongue and repeats rapturously, his spittle shooting from his broad mouth, "What a body! What a body! God grant you more!" He says this over and over, following the bottom with a long stare until its owner disappears from sight into the crowd. He doesn't address his endearments to thin women, old women, or ugly women.

I Love the Movies was taken off at most movie houses after a celebrated battle among the makers of the film, the Church, and the censor but has never left the third-rate theaters, where it will go on playing for all eternity. Nashwa had seen the movie at the Cinema Fatin Hamama in Manial. I hadn't entered the Fantasio since I was in middle school. The last time I'd gone in, with Haris, we'd watched three movies: *I've Got the Wallet*, *The Big Boss*, and I can't remember the name of the third.

I bought a ticket for five pounds that gave me the right to watch three movies in a row and stay in the cinema from six o'clock until twelve. The aged ticket seller gave me a special, ambiguous, look, as though reviving some old understanding between us. He pressed the fingers of my right hand as he handed me the ticket with an unctuous smile and gestured toward a dirty black drape behind which lay the theater. No sooner had I passed the drape, holding it away from my head with distaste, than I was assailed by a pungent reek of urine. I went into the darkened auditorium as though entering a huge public urinal.

On the screen the credits were coming up. From the first glance I could see that the picture was out of focus and very bad, while behind me the projector in its cubbyhole droned away, buzzing on and on like an endless frog concerto. I tried to see what was at my feet so that I could sit, lifted what I took to be the seat of the nearest chair to me, and sat down. I fell through the middle of the bottomless frame onto my backside, landing heavily on the hard cement floor. It hurt, and I tried to get up as quickly as possible, more concerned about what I looked like and my lost dignity than the pain. Bursts of laughter at my discomfiture and delight at the comic scene rose behind me. I took a number of steps and sat down gingerly on the first chair on the other side and began to watch the movie, into which I wished to sink, losing myself totally.

I heard a loud, petulant voice at the back and looked around.

A youth was standing in the middle of the back row and calling to "Umar," who was sitting in the front row.

"Umar! Umar! Let's go!"

Umar didn't answer.

"Yoo-hoo! Yoo-hoo! Let's go, kiddo!" he protested coquettishly, with a shake of his slim body.

Umar turned around and contented himself by making over his shoulder a gesture of palm and fingers meaning "Wait! Wait! A little longer!"

I started to become aware that small creatures had entered my pants and were crawling up my legs. With loathing I struck at my pants and legs, using both hands and making sounds of disgust.

The audience was preoccupied with things other than the movie. I couldn't hear the dialogue or follow the plot. Scenes and images followed one another in succession like ghosts swimming in gray space, but I determined to stick it out and enjoy the semi-banned film.

"Excuse me. Excuse me, young man." The voice was extremely soft and sweet.

I turned to look at him. He was standing to my right, leaning with both hands on the back of my seat and moving his right leg winsomely back and forth. He lowered his eyes, looking closely at my face.

"Yes?"

"I'd like to get past."

"There's lots of ways you can go. Why don't you go around that way, Hamada?"

He simply moved aside the leg of mine that was blocking his way and said, "My name's not Hamada, Amr. It's Mimi."

"Okay, so go around some other way, Mimi."

"La-di-da! I want to go this way, mister. What's it to you?"

He passed his huge bottom slowly over my lap, rudely making his way past me and uttering a little sigh.

The sound of the waiter tapping on his tray as he circulated through the theater selling snacks created a background music as loud as that of the movie and I glared at him angrily—a thin, even emaciated, individual with a ballpoint behind his ear, who tapped on the tray with his bottle opener and with his other hand dragged behind him a crate of cold drinks. He'd make directly for the couples, totally ignoring the occasional singles such as myself, and force a bottle of Pepsi into the customer's hand, stretching his mouth wide open in a broad smile.

At the ends of most of the rows, couples were sitting, hugging and sticking their bodies up against each other, the smoke from their cigarettes forming a cloud above them and their sweet smiles making the scene extremely romantic. The movie kept on rolling, emitting sounds and pictures, but I couldn't see, hear, or understand a thing.

Mimi, who was sitting five seats away from me, started to try to attract my attention, moving his lips as though sucking in air and looking at my crotch. I smiled to myself, embarrassed, and devoted my efforts to following the movie, ignoring Mimi's moves and games.

When the film was about halfway through, as far as I remember, the youths standing at the doorway to the toilets began to increase in number and form themselves into a line that was a little longer than it had been at the beginning of the movie. Elegant white gallabiyas stood next to shiny shirts and tight jeans, brown peasants' caps next to Upper Egyptian scarves and gimme caps. Most of the clientele fell into the uncertain age bracket between twenty and forty. They were very dressed up and extremely clean, as though come to attend a wedding or a ballet at the Egyptian Opera. Cell phones never stopped ringing and conversations took place among them in soft whispers, though their bodies, hands, and eyes played the most conspicuous role in communication, agreement as to the next step, and the final coming together of two persons in holy matrimony.

Mimi had placed his hand on his crotch and teased out of it a low swelling that raised the light fabric of his pants slightly, and his short, soft fingers now started to play there. He looked at me with beautiful green eyes like a lovesick swain while Layla Elwi wept for the death of Mahmud Himeida. I couldn't understand why he'd died so early on, when the movie still had a ways to go.

A couple passed in front of me in a state of felicity, on their way to the middle of the large silver screen. For a moment, they took up the space occupied by Layla Elwi and Mahmud Himeida, who had his head on her lap. In place of her copious tears falling on the dead man's face, we saw the two lovers holding hands and facing the audience. In a sudden attack of passion that seemed to take them unawares, they turned to face each other and embraced. The two youths were approximately the same height. One was wearing a white gallabiya, the other a green shirt, very tight pants, and a gold chain that gleamed on his naked chest. The one wearing the gallabiya bent over his friend, took him in his arms, and, placing his hand on the back of his neck and starting to caress it, brought his lips close to the other's and gave him a deep, long-lasting French kiss. A long silence reigned in the theater, which had followed the scene with concentration and affection. The kiss was perfect, sweet and slow, and accompanied by the fondling of backs, buttocks, and thighs. When the lips parted, enthusiastic, extended applause resounded through the auditorium in a display of admiration and encouragement. The two lovers smiled shyly, drew apart, and, still hand in hand, made their way toward the toilet with the flirtatious manner of a pair of film stars, having performed their roles much better than Layla Elwi and Mahmud Himeida. Mimi had been fiddling with his pants. Now he took out something small and, in an agony of impatience, signaled at me with his head in the direction of the toilets. I scowled at him as angrily as a lion affronted by a vile insult.

The foul smell had turned my stomach and for a few moments I felt nauseous. Fighting the urge to vomit that seemed about to overwhelm me at any minute, I stood up and ran, bent over, toward the toilets, one hand on my belly, the other over my mouth. Mimi watched me, giving a shrill laugh of malicious pleasure, striking his forehead with his palm, raising his feet in the air, and shaking his slim body in his seat, pleased as punch. At the entrance to the toilets, the couples waiting to enter were whiling away the time with light kisses and soft touches. There were about five of them, full of pride in their bodies and their love. When they saw me put my hand over my mouth, they made way for me. I passed them and found myself in front of a single, closed latrine. I could hear moans and sighs and cries of pleasure coming from inside. I turned my face to the other side of the intervening space. Someone

179

was lying on the ground and another was moving on top of him, slowly and with deliberation. For a second, my eyes met with those of the youth on the ground. He was suffering an unbearable pleasure.

I left by the back exit without emptying my guts, feeling as though my clothes had become saturated by a penetrating odor of urine and feces that would cling to my skin forever.

25 CD

WALKING ON SAAD ZAGHLOUL, I called Simone's cell phone. I told her I needed her and wanted to see her. She sounded pleased to hear from me and cheerful. She told me it was only three days since we'd been together and asked if I'd missed her so soon, saying with laughing coyness, "Have you fallen for me, baby?" "You can think whatever you want," I told her, but said that I truly needed to see her, within half an hour if possible, and asked her to come to Haris's room. She said she was at home in Maadi lying in bed being deliciously lazy and cracking her knuckles but, for me, she'd get up, take a quick shower, get dressed. Then, "Abracadabra, I'll be with you, baby." She said she'd give me a call in half an hour at most, that I should wait if she was a little late, and that she hadn't forgotten and knew exactly how to get to that elegant room, that hermitage full of naked women, "you lady-killer you!"

I was amazed she didn't object or hesitate, and had agreed after just a couple of words.

Sunday night. Haris has been at work at the Thutmose Bar for hours and he'll go on working till the last customer leaves and the bar closes its doors, to the sound of the dawn call to prayer.

I stopped somewhere near the middle of the street and patted my pants a few times to be sure I had the key to Haris's room. I climbed the ruinous stone stairs, opened the door, and went in. The white lamp was on—Haris must have forgotten to turn it off—and both windows were open to their fullest. Unusually, the room wasn't clean and well-arranged. There was a lot of dust on the rugs, floor, pillows, couches, computer table, and over the picture of Lauren under the glass. The cushions were thrown around chaotically on the couches and by the walls. On the table were the remains of stale food on paper plates. Newspapers and magazines had been dropped here and there, and Haris's couch, which he used for sleeping, had been moved from its usual place. Piled on top of it were dirty clothes, sheets, and blankets. The glass ashtrays were full to overflowing with ash and cigarette ends and some were thrown down on the couches and rugs and in corners. Haris must be in a really bad mood.

I couldn't find it in me to clean the room, wipe off the dust, and set some limits to the mess. I put the sofa bed back in its place, beat the dust off it with a magazine, and made it up. Closing the windows, I sat down for a smoke, contemplating Haris's naked girls pinned up on the walls. I was thinking that women were my basic problem, the root cause of the disastrous situation I was in, that I should have nothing more to do with them, and that I shouldn't want Nashwa and should forget her forever.

Daydreaming, I didn't hear the sound of her footsteps as she climbed the stairs. The repeated ringing of the tweetie-bird doorbell roused me and cut short my ruminations. I got up, wishing myself a happy fuck, opened the door to her, and smiled into her face. I kissed her on both cheeks and told her jovially, as I looked her over from the front of her hair, which was covered by the usual deluxe colored headscarf, to her high-heeled shoes, "What's all this? You're looking beautiful today!" She kissed me on the cheeks and said, "*Merci*." Then she examined my face for some moments, smiling.

"You look like you're under a bit of strain."

"Me? No way! I'm feeling great."

"Always, O Lord!" she said, and sat on the couch, crossing her right leg over her left so that her black skirt was hiked up and rose to the midpoint of her white calf. Happily, I sat down next to her.

"So what's up, pretty lady?"

"Not much, baby."

She looked around her at the dust and mess and smiled. "Poor bachelors!" she said sympathetically. She made a "what can one do?" gesture with her hand in front of my face.

"I'm married," I said.

"Really?" she responded in her sexy voice. "Seriously?"

"Yes, married, and have been for a long time. What's so weird about that?"

"Nothing. There's no such thing as weird, baby. Nothing seems weird to me any more, hasn't for ages."

"I still find it weird. It amazes me."

"Well, of course. I mean, you're still a kid, and a sweet, innocent one too, baby."

The words were uttered sarcastically and flippantly and I stood up without thinking.

"Innocent? Innocent? What do you know about me so you . . . ?"

She interrupted me, jabbing the fingers of her right hand at my chest: "Shush! It's clear as daylight. I don't need to know more than I already do. Why did you get up? Sit down."

I pulled myself together and sat down next to her with a huff of disgust. Slowly, with gentle movements, she took off her shoes and socks, giving me a cunning and naughty smile. She took a cigarette from my pack, put it between her red lips and wagged it up and down, so I lit it, gazing at her. Her face looked a bit strained and tired. It was beautiful without makeup, and as innocent as an adolescent's. When our eyes met, she flinched a little and turned and faced the back of the couch to escape my look.

"Don't play with me like that," she said.

"Why not? Don't you like to play?"

"I love it. I like all sorts of play, but . . . ."

"But what?"

"But nothing. Just stop glaring at me like that, that's all."

Afraid she'd get mad, I changed the subject.

"By the way, I'm sorry. There's nothing to eat or drink."

She blew out a cloud of smoke.

"It doesn't matter. I ate at home and I don't drink this early."

The mention of food and drink excited me.

"So . . . ?"

She shook her head, playing dumb. "What? What?"

Hesitating and a little embarrassed, I said, "Why . . . don't you get on with it?"

She was silent for a while, her eyes shining. It looked to me as though some wicked idea was going through her mind. Suddenly, she let out a long, resounding laugh and stood up, parading her body in front of me. At the speed of light, she removed her red blouse, her skirt, a short white nightshirt, and her red panties, and stood there hand on hip, stark naked. "Let's go, baby, let's go," she said in a neutral tone and with humiliating nonchalance.

A bucket of cold water. Lots of little ice cubes falling over my head all at once. My body went rigid and a shiver ran through my limbs. I turned to the cushion behind me, closed my eyes and, putting my hand over my face, held my breath and went as silent as a statue.

The silence between us lasted many long minutes. I heard her laugh. Then she gave another obscene whoop, even louder than the first. When eventually she finished laughing, she sat down next to me, wiggled her body over until she was up against my thigh, and put her hand on my hair. I opened my eyes and found her looking at me strangely. "Didn't I tell you?" she said. "You're an innocent."

Another bucketful of water, colder than the first, over my head.

She put her hand on the back of my neck, pulled my head toward her breast, and said, "You need to suckle, not do it."

I pulled my head away quickly and erupted in a loud laugh that shook my whole body. Tears of laughter in my eyes, I asked her, "How . . . hee-hee . . . do you know?"

"You're all babies, baby, and you, especially, are the babiest baby I've ever seen."

A sudden gloom descended on me and I sat there in silence, jiggling my feet and blowing out smoke. I almost forgot her existence and lost myself in my thoughts. She too said nothing for a time. Then she stood up, gathered her clothes, got dressed, sat down again beside me, and asked, "Are you mad at me?"

"Not at all. It's just . . . I guess I'm a bit tired."

She leaned over me and started undressing me slowly and extremely gently. I don't know why Simone tried, and tried with great patience and determination several times, though without success. In the end, I became exhausted and fed up with the attempt, as the dead man never awoke and was never going to that dark night. I was totally impotent and didn't much care. What had happened to me didn't make me sad at all: I'd be dead in a few days at most.

Simone didn't worry either and reverted to her wanton sarcasm. Laughing, she said, "So what? You just relax. Being friends is nice too," and she set about trying to build up as much of a bond of friendship between us as she could.

"Sex isn't everything," she said, and then roared with laughter to indicate that she meant precisely the opposite, so I got angry.

I was overtaken by feelings of hostility toward her. Her flippancy was brazen and total.

"Right, sex isn't everything," I said, "but you, poor thing, don't have a choice. It's your destiny and fate. Poor thing, if only God would give you a second chance!" She smacked her lips with a musical popping sound and said, "Tsk tsk! I like sex a lot, and as far as I can see a prostitute's life is super attractive. It's so great I even stoop to hanging out with innocents like you."

This time, I was the one to burst out laughing.

"Innocent? Again?"

"Naturally. Compared to me you're a total innocent. I, kiddo, am a star, a major star . . . but modest with it."

"What?"

"You don't believe me? Don't you watch porn CDs?"

"Frankly, not often. Very rarely."

"So you wouldn't know, baby."

"I can't say I've heard of you."

"You didn't happen to see the CD with Amr?"

A memory flashed through my head, illuminating the darkness of my brain. I gazed at her face for a long time without saying anything. Impossible! Incredible!

Very calmly, she ordered, "Don't glare at me like that."

It was a CD showing an eminent person, a very eminent person, that had been leaked to the porn market to discredit him, and which had almost put paid to his career and broken him. In a matter of days, it had become the best-known local porn movie.

I hesitated a little and then said, "Yes, but that's old stuff. People have almost forgotten it. I remember. What about it?"

"I'm the heroine, my dear sir!"

"*What?*"

"Yes, me."

What had happened to make this courtesan of the great fall from her perch and descend to the street, dragging herself in person through the dirt of the squares, streets, apartments, burrows, and caves, and giving herself up to copulation with "every prince and pauper"? She could, at the very least, have found regular employ within that respected institution designed for local porn stars such as herself— that traditional, highly organized institution that starts with the aged madam or refined pimp who hunts for clients in bars and nightclubs, discotheques, hotels, and the like and goes on down to the thug, who terrifies everyone and imposes his rule, protecting the working woman and lending her a certain prestige. This vital institution creates a female who is supported, respected, and naked, stretched out on the bed in her well-guarded nest. The only ones who walk the streets are the aged, the ugly, those recently thrown out of brothels, those new to the trade, and amateurs. The good-looking professional, the grande dame, stays at home, safe among her bodyguards and entourage, her beauty products and the tools of her trade, and even if she's an amateur who works purely for her own personal pleasure, the preceding is the setup best fitted to her project, the most appropriate and convenient.

Simone told me, for my information, that she'd become fed up and had grown to hate the pampered life she'd been living. She'd come to despise the pashas and beys all slicked down with oils and expensive perfumes and had reached a point at which she could no longer put up with the very rich, the ones rich beyond the capacity of the imagination to comprehend. She'd come to hate the affected youths and older men and their insane sadism. She could no longer stand such insatiable people and their satanic contrivances for obtaining preternatural pleasures and sensations from a woman's body—a human body that they treated like a cut of meat set out on their ever-groaning table and that, after they'd sucked on the bones till they gleamed in their whiteness, they'd throw out the window into the middle of the street without an ounce of regret for her fate, before opening their jaws once more to devour the next hot meal. Much loathing and hostility showed on her face as she said that even to look at one of them struck her with terror, with panic and fear, and she became distracted, saying nothing, training her eyes on the wall and withdrawing into herself. I too said nothing and watched her, thinking about her.

After many long minutes, she smiled, her gloomy ruminations dispelled, and whispered dreamily that she wanted to live as a regular prostitute of the middle class. Life on the streets was more sensual, more of an adventure, more conducive to pleasure!

If Simone's tale is turned back to front, the truth behind the carefully designed cosmetic lies she told becomes apparent. From a class perspective, Simone belongs to the lowest rung of the upper class. She has an implacable lust that is fed by her blooming youth and magnificent body, which she grants gladly to her many lovers. Technically, she hadn't really been a professional: all she would accept were expensive presents wrapped in love, infatuation, and passion. She might really have loved that man, the "porn star" now vanished behind prison bars. She'd given herself to him utterly, his sadism and endless new inventions had fascinated her, and the pleasure she'd gotten from him had been enormous. But after the scandal of the CD, which had been snatched up by teenagers who had poured out so much semen, uttered so many moans, and performed so many jerk-offs before its images and over her body, her whole class had ostracized her. Her lovers had fled and left her on her own, not returning her repeated calls, paying no attention to her excuses. As far as they were concerned, she'd caught the mange and it might spread from her to their poodles and expensive cats, so they banished her forever, and she found herself alone, as utterly alone as a corpse in the grave. The nicely brought-up girl who'd become the star of every computer in the country thought she should do something different. She couldn't withstand the longing for sex, to which she'd been addicted since she was fourteen, and her natural and irresistible lust, so she decided, after long and deep thought, to spit out those who had spat her out, to devote herself to taking vengeance on them all by making her body the plaything of a lower class, a class in eclipse and an enemy. And because Simone had no experience with prostitution as a profession, or with its ways and institutions, she'd thought she could remain a free individual, the way they'd taught her in the British schools whose hard exams she'd passed. She'd thought her will, her body, and her life could be hers and hers alone. This is why she'd turned to roaming the traditional hunting grounds—Pyramids Road, Arab League Avenue, Cairo's luminous downtown, and all the other paradises of predators and prey. With a bit of acting, some basic modifications to her appearance—that of an affluent woman of the upper classes—she was able to make herself look like a prostitute of a special, refined type, the sort you might run into on the streets behind a hotel or discotheque; and by virtue of her awareness of the nature of the Egyptian street, she was able to produce a shorthand of symbols in her outer appearance, by acquiring the headscarf of the day and the cheap perfume, and by an exaggerated use of the English-peppered language of the street. Indeed, she'd gone over the top in acting the role, though not totally abandoning a certain aristocracy of manner . . . baby!

This is the story I imagine Simone is hiding so skillfully, never even admitting it to herself and concealing it under a mask of "I choose to live according to my own whims, as a simple act of personal freedom."

I told her all this. I explained my theory to her, which I'd come up with on the spur of the moment, with a great deal of crudeness and boorishness, but she showed no sign of annoyance or anger. She admitted nothing and denied nothing and was silent for a long time, looking into my face and thinking.

After a while she smiled an extremely kind smile and said she needed a friend like me and that we could become real friends, talking on the phone and checking up on each other. We could go out together and have tea at a café and chat and smoke the water pipe that she adored. "We could be friends for real, baby."

My cell phone rang. It was Haris and he sounded very down.

26 UMM EL-MASRIYEEN

I BOUND DOWN THE STAIRS, almost fall as I stumble on impact with the edge of the last step, and exit, rushing from the darkness of the entrance to the Gabr family's ancient house into the lights of Saad Zaghloul. I run toward the square, slowing down a little when I get to the corner with the La Manche restaurant. I turn left on the crowded sidewalk and follow its many twists and turns, pushing my way through the throngs of passersby and the vendors' stalls by keeping my right hand extended in front of me to move the people aside and moving my shoulders and waist. I swerve right and left and my foot catches on the wooden support of a stall selling variety goods. My leg hurts, but I keep running; I'm panting, holding my hand to my chest. I gasp for breath, opening my mouth, and wipe off the sweat with the end of my shirt. I don't stop till I get to the corner of Station Road. I pause for a moment to catch my breath and look for him. I see him in the middle of the crowd, in front of Zeezu's kushari restaurant, looking restless. He looks at his watch, then in the direction I'm coming from. His shirt's white, his bowtie red, his pants black. I move toward him. Panting, I ask him, "What? What's up with Shawqi, Haris?"

He shakes his head gloomily. "I don't know exactly. Shawqi's at Umm el-Masriyeen."

We walk fast, going south. We're almost running. We don't exchange a word the whole way from Station Road to Umm el-Masriyeen. We enter via the hospital's main gate in a state of terror, desperate to find out what's happened to Shawqi but also a little hesitant. All the same, we push on, thinking about what to do when we meet his father.

We find him standing alone, leaning against a wall at the entrance to the surgery building, blowing clouds of smoke from his wide nostrils. His turban is dark, his gallabiya large on his huge body. In one hand is a cigarette, in the other a walking stick pressed into the dust. Furious, he fixes his eyes on us as we approach. The second we reach him, before we have time to say a word, he blows up in our faces, as though we'd stepped on a hidden mine. He shakes his stick in our faces, yells, curses, and hurls abuse and insults. He accuses us of being a gang of wise guys, spoiled brats despite the gray hairs that have started to appear, before their time, on our heads. He claims we're the ones who long ago messed up his son, ruined his life, made him a hardened drunkard and drug-taker, and made his large intestine burst. He swears by the Living Christ he'll break our skulls if we go anywhere near Shawqi again or if he sees us anywhere near his house. He waves his stick and orders us to get out of his sight and go to hell. Like naughty schoolboys, we're overcome with embarrassment, stammering and confused, and bow our heads, at a loss for words. People gather around from all directions, attracted by Boss Farag's deep, loud voice. We've become something for everyone to gawp at and still he keeps up his tirade. Haris tries to calm his anger, says quietly and in a conciliatory tone that we are exactly the way he's described us, that we're spoiled brats who deserve the worst, but "that's not what matters, Uncle. What matters now is Shawqi, that we set our minds at rest regarding our brother Shawqi. What happened, and how?" He screams in our faces, "Shawqi's in the operating room. His intestine burst. Happy now? May the Lord save him and take you all, you bastards!"

Someone brings him a chair and sits him down, patting his shoulder and saying, "Take it easy, Hagg, take it easy. Sit down. Sit now." He sits, catching his breath. The mouths of men and women sprinkle over his head phrases intended to make him feel better: "May he get well soon, a thousand times over!" "God willing, everything'll turn out fine!" "May he leave here cured and in the best of health, amen, O Lord!" "Just think of his poor mother, friend!" "It's just a moment of trial and will pass." "It's a very simple operation. My brother had it only yesterday and today he's fit as a fiddle." "His poor mother, you poor thing!" "What operation exactly is your son having, Hagg?"

At great length and in great detail, Boss Farag explains to everyone what had happened to Shawqi from the moment he entered the house on his return from work at around eight p.m. until the moment he entered the operating room, plus our criminal role in driving him to the point where his intestine burst and the details of last Thursday night's party. I said nothing. I looked at the ground and tried to stay and put up with it all so that I could go up to the operating room and pick up any news about the operation, but I felt oppressed, very oppressed, and knew I had to get out of there immediately. I turned my back on them, went out onto the street, and walked northward trying not to cry. The words his father had poured over everyone's heads as he gestured, raising his stick in the air and striking the ground with it, rang in my ears.

"Shawqi—my only son, my only man, a youth who's hardly begun to live his life—lies now in the operating room between life and death. No one knows whether he'll come out of it dead or alive. Two hours ago he was happily sitting with me at the dining table. He came home from work at the pharmaceuticals company in Sixth of October City at the usual time like any other day. He ate dinner with me just fine and for the first time he talked about getting married. He broached the subject with me and was as shy as a little boy. He told me that he was sick and tired of being a bachelor and wanted to marry a pharmacologist called Dr. Janette who works at the Greater Giza Pharmacy. I told him, 'That's wonderful, Shawqi. She's a lovely lady and her family are good people,' and I was very pleased. I want to see his children before I take off, see children growing up before my eyes. I told him, 'I'll do everything I can to help you, dear boy. The money's there, don't worry about that side of things.' He's all I have after Samira left and has been away in Canada so long. He ate till he was full, kissed my head, and told me, 'You've always been good to me, Boss Farag, you dear, kind man!' He went up to his room on the roof to sleep, hardly able to contain his joy. After a while I heard shouting and wailing. I went up the stairs, terrified at what might have happened to my darling boy, and found him writhing on the floor squeezing his belly with his hands and screaming in fear. I was afraid too. I called the ambulance right away and brought him to the hospital. Lord save him! Lord save him and take those jinxing bastards!"

Shawqi's intestine just blew up and almost killed him, without warning, without reason. Death has no reason. Death is just death.

I reached Fishawi's café in Giza. I raised my hand in greeting and said, "Good evening!" to my uncle, who was sitting in the midst of his gang of friends.

As usual, my uncle was totally engrossed in a round of chess. When he plays chess, he forgets the world around him and moves his lips as though chewing some delicious candy. As I was looking for an empty place, he raised his head from the board and shouted, "Come here, Rabeea, sir! Come sit here!" He didn't wait to hear what I'd say and went back to his white and black board, his pawns and his queen, his knights and rooks, and the battles in which, absorbed, he'd whiled away some half his life.

I sat at an empty table outside the café and ordered tea and a water pipe.

27 TRAVEL

HARIS ARRIVED before I'd finished my tea. He sat in the empty chair on the other side of the table and looked at me with his sad face, biting his nails as he talked.

He said I'd done well to leave and that Boss Farag had kept up his curses and insults and humiliated him before the whole hospital. He'd come close to rising from his seat, taking him by the throat, and breaking his head open with his stick. He also said that it would be two hours before Shawqi left the operating room.

"Our Lord be with him!" I said.

Haris said he was totally stressed out and was going to his room to sleep for a couple of hours; then he'd go back to the hospital to find out the result of the operation and try and see Shawqi. I looked him straight in the eye and said in the neutral tones of a newscaster, "By the way, I was at your house, in your room."

In a normal voice, almost indifferently, he said, "Fine. Who with, kiddo?"

"With Simone. Isn't that what she's called?"

He cursed me from the depths of his heart: "You son of a bitch!"

He said no more. I raised the mouthpiece of the water pipe to my lips and started taking long drags, one after another, expelling clouds of smoke from my nostrils and mouth that the air carried toward him. Waving his hand in front of his face, he said, "Keep that stuff away from me, please."

"Sorry," I said and stopped puffing, nervously wagging the mouth-piece in my hand.

He took a sip from his glass of tea and said, raising his face to look at me, "Rabeea, I . . . I got the visa and I'm leaving."

Total gloom settled over me.

"Lauren says hi. I was talking to her on Messenger yesterday. She asked after you and Shawqi. She really is a nice woman."

I looked at him questioningly.

"She's got a good heart . . . and . . . she loves me."

I didn't say anything.

"She's started looking for work for me. She says I just need to take a few English courses and do some training and be a bit serious and organized and I can be a proper barman. The nightclubs will be falling over themselves for me and—"

In spite of myself, I interrupted him, looking him straight in the eye, and said, "You don't say!"

He looked away and smiled to hide his embarrassment and went back to biting his fingernails.

A few minutes later his expression had changed and he was staring into the distance like a dreamy adolescent. "New York, capital of the world. . . . A city for all people. People of every kind, color, religion, language, and race. No one cares what color your skin is or what your face looks like or asks, 'Where are you from?' or 'Where are you going, black boy?' and you get back what you put in, in full, with respect, and . . . ."

"Do you really believe that stuff?"

"It doesn't make the slightest difference whether I do or don't. I'm going. I want to sleep."

I stood up, took him in my arms, and hugged him, patting his back.

In a low voice, our bodies just a hand's width apart, Haris told me I'd better watch my back and be very careful, that I was exposed and compromised and the stink of the business was everywhere, and he was afraid Anwar Gabr was going to take revenge. I asked for details: how did he find out what was going on between me and Nashwa, how had Anwar found out and what did he mean to do, and . . . ?

He interrupted, saying, "Nothing can ever be hidden. I've done my duty and warned you. Watch your back well."

With that, Haris set off with his long stride in the direction of the square and I sat down and stared at his back.

Should I be afraid of Haris too? Fear him? Would it be his hand that reached out for me, a couple of hours before he left the country? He was on the officer's payroll as a guard; why shouldn't he be on his payroll as a killer too? Nothing's black or white. It's all one color, the color of the blood that would, for sure, be spilled—nothing less would do. I hadn't told Haris I was innocent. I hadn't denied the charge. I hadn't disavowed her and I never would, but I still didn't deserve to be punished! I hadn't announced to him that I surrendered to Anwar, to do with me as he liked, and I hadn't told him I was desperate and I hadn't promised anything. I'd never keep away from her and I'd never forget her, so they might as well forget about me. It was nothing new for someone like me to live in constant fear and terror, fear of being killed and of dying, every instant, every minute. The whole thing was very simple. I might die suddenly in the most ordinary of circumstances at any moment in my daily life, be hit unintentionally by a car, go to sleep and die of a stroke without ever waking, or my large intestine might burst like Shawqi's, I might die in a crash in the broadcasting-company bus on my way to or from work, drop dead for no reason, be hit by a bullet by mistake, drown in the bathtub when I was stoned, be killed any other way, die any other death that had nothing to do with the officer. Why was I such a coward? I still wanted her and so was afraid of losing her. Death in and of itself isn't frightening. I was afraid of dying because I still wanted to live, still wanted her, wanted Nashwa. I smile at the thought of her and I'm happy when I imagine her with me and belonging to me, me alone, and that's quite enough to make me not want to die.

Uncle Musa put his hand on my shoulder and sat down opposite me, saying with a smile, "Hey! What are you brooding about?"

"I'm not. I'm fine."

"Come on, out with it. What's wrong, son?"

I said nothing but gazed at his face, on which prison life and harsh experience had engraved the wrinkles and folds of suffering. My uncle had eased up long ago and ceased to be involved in life in any way. Would he go back to it now for my sake and because of my predicament?

"Tell me. I'm the one who raised you, Rabeea, or have you forgotten that? Wasn't I the one who said that kid will be something big, a broadcaster to be precise, a famous broadcaster and . . . ?"

I smiled at my uncle, who'd become jolly and good-natured once he'd given up political work and had achieved the calm of an addict who's stopped snorting heroin.

"It's Muna's birthday tomorrow. You have to come."

"Muna? How old would that make her, Uncle?"

"You've forgotten how old she is too? Don't tell anyone. She'll be twenty-one, if you can imagine. Do you know how I begot her?" My uncle laughed.

"I don't. I don't know about such things!"

We laughed together, slapping palms.

"I begot her, can you imagine, during a short vacation between arrests."

My uncle stood up and straightened his old-fashioned suit. "Let's go. Aren't you coming home?"

"Just a little longer."

As he got up to leave, he asked me, "Will you be reading the seven o'clock news tomorrow?"

"God willing."

"Right. So come along now, boy, and get some rest."

"Give me just five minutes, Uncle, and I'll see you there."

"Whatever you say. Good night."

A good night? Where was I going to get that?

"You too," I whispered in a subdued voice as he turned his back on me and left.

Kagha was on the wall of the café opposite me, smiling and very happy, looking out from the poster for his first album, *Don't Ask, Hanafi!*

28 DROWNING

It's much better if a person ends up alone. I want to be totally alone. Sit on my own and smoke and think calmly and without pressure. But where?

About two in the morning I found myself on the Abbas Bridge. It was still bustling. The weather was pleasant and refreshing and there were lots of people: singles, couples, families, sitting on the low plastic chairs drinking tea and hot chickpea broth from small carts parked the length of the bridge. Amateur fishermen were casting their hooks with their long lines into the water and the lights were low and danced on the surface of the Nile.

I keep my distance, in a semi-dark spot next to the old wall that runs parallel to the shore; I jump up on top of the wall and sit on the broad stone. Before me is the Nile and a few meters behind my head her white building. What's Nashwa doing now? Is she there in her room? Alone in her parents' apartment? Who's with her, who is she with? Or maybe she's in the marital apartment in the Gabr family's tower block on Greater Ocean, to the south. What's she thinking about? Is she thinking about me? Is she yearning for me?

I want to push myself to the point of collapse; total, utter collapse. To be reduced to nothing, like a stray dog. To destroy my whole life, all its details large and small, with one shove, at one go, forever. Once you've been killed, there's nothing. After death, there's rest, in the form of a sleep that is very, very long and comfortable. Bodies, bones, and spinal columns cause no discomfort there: the back will by degrees have dissolved, so there'll be no need to fear the pains that come with long sleep. I shall lay myself down in the dirt and a black sky will shelter me. I shall have no senses. I shall slowly dissolve and blend into the surface of the earth, perhaps appearing thereafter in the shape of a cactus or a flower on a stem or wild grasses sprouting among the graves. Why, when we feel love exploding inside us, do we immediately, then and there, want to die? I want to run from everything, including myself. He's an idiot, an utter idiot, the pupil who disgustingly and naively repeats his mistakes, and I've repeated a vast number of mistakes and sins. I fall into the same error over and over again. But it's not a crime for a person to shiver and hurt from a bitter coldness in the bones even when the sun is scorching; it isn't stupid for the heat to rise to one's head and floods of sweat to drip from the body in mid-January because of a glance that has fallen out of the blue on one other particular face. Maybe because I came across her unexpectedly, I discovered in her that desire embodied, that perfect animal body, that I had wanted from the moment I first smelled the smell of the female—her pungent, acidulous smell, the smell of sour milk; the skin, the breasts, the sweat under the armpits. Nashwa wanted me too, as a barren woman wants a child, a barren woman who wants nothing but a child, for which she's prepared to burn everything in her path and tear the world to pieces with her claws, slaying everything that stands in her way—an insane desire, natural and furious. She wants me, and I want her, for no reason, with no hope. I want to flee from her, to destroy my life with my own hands. I will do anything that brings me closer to her because I am sinful and sick. I fell in love with her despite myself, despite everything, because I want her and I desire her and I want to have sex with her now, here, in front of everyone, forever.

If I jump into the river now, my body will pop up in a few hours. In the early morning I'll be floating on the water, my body puffed up, my pants a huge balloon, my shirt a dirigible, my face the color of the weeds at the bottom of the Nile and its black silt. The current will push me slowly northward until I snag, tilted and stretched, on the stanchions of the Abbas Bridge, green face to the sky, foul-smelling, bobbing like a glabrous sheet of cork. People will gather on top of the bridge and look at my corpse; a few students on their way to their institutes and faculties, some laborers and office workers, will pause in dismay and gaze at the new victim. The faces of some will turn pale and they'll compose them into expressions of pity, twisting their lips. Some will bewilder themselves trying to guess the history that the anonymous floating corpse carries within it. Softhearted girls will avert their faces, letting out small cries of distress that will escape through the fingers they have placed over their mouths. Their distress will be plain to see but they will not leave or stop looking. A long silence will reign over the crowd standing on the bridge watching the movements of the body. They won't go until they are sure that the routine procedures for dealing with a bloated corpse in the Nile are underway. They won't do anything. They will simply watch in silence the inflatable dinghies of the river police, who will take their time in getting there: they don't want any problems either. One of them, in a rubber dinghy close to the Giza Sporting Club, observes from a distance, hoping that the current will carry me on, will push me past the Abbas Bridge so that I keep moving in the direction of University Bridge, where I'll be outside his area of responsibility.

After a long while I, in turn, take pity on all of them, feeling their gorges about to rise and seeing on their faces the signs of nausea and imminent vomiting. I leave my corpse where it is, on the surface, and go toward them from the direction of the Ophthalmia Hospital, calmly and with dignity, hands in pockets. I cast a glance at the floating body and at their necks dangling over the water. Approaching them I say, in a neutral, mechanical voice like that of a robot, "Don't be afraid. Don't worry. The body's mine."

TOMORROW

29 WASHING THE BODY

T<small>IRRRRRRRRRRRR</small>!

The old black alarm clock on my bedside table rang. The sound was loud, long, and continuous, and filled the entire room.

Five a.m. Monday, the day of my return to work after the short vacation I'd taken to be free for love, for Nashwa, for . . . .

The six days, with their seven nights, were over—the worst and blackest days and nights of my life, though blacker and darker lay ahead. I would continue to flee so long as I breathed.

I was no longer alive.

Looking at my face in the oval mirror over the washbasin, I took off my pajamas, undershirt, and white underpants and stood there naked as the day I emerged from the darkness of my mother's womb. I was aware of a pleasurable feeling of oneness with my body, the delight of stripping off the cover and exposing oneself. I felt the light-heartedness that goes with being free, like a child, of the heaviness of clothes. I felt the luxury of total nakedness.

I shaved my upper lip and my chin of the hair, which had grown very long, then did so again.

I turned and opened both shower faucets, hot and cold, as far as they would go. I removed the long, kinky hair under my armpits and gave my pubic hair a close shave, using new shaving cream and a new razor. When I was done, I threw the razor into the wastebasket in the corner.

With the tip of the middle finger of my left hand I distributed small round dots of mint-scented cleansing cream over my chest and belly and shoulders and stood in the bathtub under the water that gushed from the showerhead. I rubbed down every part of my body with a new loofah, white and rough. I explored and washed, with excessive care, every fold, nook, and cranny between my fingers and between my thighs, in front and in back, and from my ears to my soles.

Under the constant fall of water, I washed once, twice, and a third time with thick soapsuds, shampoo, and cream till my skin shone and was soft and red. I became clean as a polished mirror, pure as a returning pilgrim, as a believer on his way to the next world.

I lifted my head up and back, slowly moved my neck on its axis from right to left and back again, closed my eyes, and lost myself in the sensation of the darkness of my naked body. For a deliciously long time, I let the jets of hot water fall onto my hair, face, and body, onto my chest and back. I took deep breaths and held the air in my chest, then opened my lips and exhaled slowly, my exhalations and inhalations following one another like the sighs of a gentle wind, the echo of the sound of my breathing returned by the white ceramic walls and low yellow ceiling. The current of water flowed scalding hot over my chest and back, gushing over every part of my skin, and I lost myself in a delicious numbness, my head empty of everything.

I look at my belly and concentrate on the atoms of water. I become aware of a weak steaminess infiltrating the air of the bathroom, of a softness and lightness moving through its spaces and slowly spreading. Gradually, it collects above the glass of the mirror, whose shiny surface disappears beneath the wisps of steam. The steam takes the form of warm soft tongues that enclose me, mount around me, coming from right and left, from the floor tiles to the ceiling. The four walls of the bathroom vanish, along with the door, the mirror, and the ceiling, little by little disappearing from sight behind the white cloud of steam. All the pores of my body are open and stimulated. My eyes are closed in the merciful darkness. My body is light, extremely light, fed and watered, completed.

Slowly, very slowly, my body dissolves. Time vanishes. The place vanishes around me, above me, below me, to the right and left of me. Everything is become a white emptiness, a forest of white clouds flying and racing, its sky white steam, its air a thick, extended fog, a nebula, a never-expiring nebula, a neb . . . uuu . . . laaaa!

30 CROSSING

I PUT ON MY BEST BLACK SUIT and sprinkled it, and my cheeks and neck, with drops of Gucci perfume. Happy with life and the morning, I left for work.

At a quarter to six in the morning the square is virtually empty and relatively quiet, the sounds few and far between. The normal noise and clamor of the day have yet to begin. The streetlamps on the flyover and the illuminated signs on the façades of the buildings still provide the square with pale yellow light and the sky is still gathering up the threads of darkness. The sun hasn't risen over it yet.

At such times, the square seems like a vast, encompassing limitlessness. Its department stores, shops, and smaller outlets are closed and just a few people walk the streets, scattered here and there. Office workers and laborers walk with long strides toward the bus, minibus, and microbus stops, and a few schoolchildren and students, especially girls wearing dark-blue school uniforms, move in the direction of the schools and the university.

The few cars cross the square quickly, going in all directions—to the university, to Murad Street, the Abbas Bridge, Pyramids Road, southern Giza.

In front of the Cinema Fantasio entrance, on the white and black curbstones, sleeps Burhan, an old army blanket pulled up over his huge body, a bundle of newspapers under his big head. In front of him, extending for three meters, is a display of newspapers—mounds of Egyptian, Arab, and foreign dailies and magazines in Arabic, English, and French, set out on upturned fruit crates.

I took copies of the three newspapers off the palm-frond crates and put them under my arm. Pulling his hand from under his head, I opened it and placed the money in it. He felt it with fat fingers and closed his grip on it. He never opened his eyes and went on with his sleep, snoring quietly.

I turned my back on him and went to the corner of Sanadeeli, where I waited for the shift bus, as usual.

Cold, refreshing breezes pass over my face and ears and hair.

Smiling, I walk in the direction of Abdu's.

The small iron bilila stand is parked in front of the Bank of Egypt. Its rich smells and the thick steam rising from the large metal pot draw me, as does Abdu, with his white face, red hair, and long bushy beard. Very naive, he works with enthusiasm and a permanent smile of welcome for his late-night and early-morning customers.

The taste of the wheat and milk remind me of my childhood in the streets of Giza, when, before going to school, we'd eat bilila on the other side of the square, in front of the underpass, by the Sphinx School's high yellow wall. Old Khadra would put a huge pot on a low, round wooden table. Wrapped in a black shawl, she poured the wheat and milk into small, deep plastic bowls.

"One with kunafa, Abdu."

"Coming up, Mr. Rabeea!"

I look at my watch. I still have a quarter of an hour before the bus arrives.

Daylight has started spreading slowly from the east, the direction of the Muqattam and the Nile, and I eat slowly and with pleasure, the taste of the milk and wheat as good in my mouth as when I was a child. My heart feels light and I'm in a good mood.

"Will you be reading the seven o'clock news, Mr. Rabeea?"

Abdu's voice is low and gentle.

"God willing," I reply.

"So how about putting something into the bulletin about Abdu's bilila?" he says, and we laugh.

The broadcasting service bus arrived, driven by Shaaban.

With a "Good morning, Shaaban," I leapt in beside him and we set off toward the Abbas Bridge to cross over onto Manial.

"It's the morning and the power is God's," puffed Shaaban. "What kind of shit is that to start the morning on?"

He pointed to the side mirror beside me.

"Take a look, sir."

I looked in the mirror to my right and saw a gray Volkswagen microbus trying to overtake on the right.

"Sorry, Mr. Rabeea, but duty calls."

Shaaban, determined to annoy the microbus driver, started swerving the car right and left to prevent him from passing.

I too was thrown from side to side. With my right hand I held onto the door and with my left onto the back of Shaaban's seat.

A coarse voice I knew rose from the microbus behind us. "Moof ofer, moof ofer, broadcafting boy!"

I made a sign to Shaaban not to lose his temper or answer back.

The head of Sayyid Uqr emerges from the window. "Go on, moof ofer for the king! I want to get by, mama's boy."

Shaaban looked at me in exasperation, a puzzled question in his eyes.

I yelled, "That's enough, that's enough! The news! The news! Think of the broadcast, Shaaban!"

The old man's voice got louder: "Get on with it! Pull over, affhole!"

"I swear on my father's grave," hissed Shaaban, "I'm going to get out and cut him into little pieces, the son of a . . . !"

Panicked, I screamed, "Forget it, Shaaban! He can go to hell. The broadcast!"

Agitated and furious, Shaaban pulled over to the left and made way for Uqr.

Uqr passed on my right, snorting and guffawing and wagging the middle finger of his left hand.

"Ha-ha! I'm the king, affholes!"

His microbus was rocking from side to side as though made of disconnected bits of metal and glass held together by cheap glue. Swaying and jangling, it almost came apart on the flyover, squealing under its elderly driver's crazy, reckless driving.

I imagined the microbus exploding from the inside like a huge time bomb, its doors, windows, and seats flying into the air, along with the bloodied bodies of its passengers, before it could get to the other underpass, the one at el-Malik el-Salih.

Shaaban glared at me with a furious, resentful expression. "What's up with that guy? What's going on?"

I said nothing and turned my face toward the Nile, so he shut up.

After a couple of minutes of saying nothing, he said, "You know what?"

"What?"

"No one knows what it's all about."

I nodded in silence.

"No one knows what any of it's about," Shaaban kept repeating to himself in a low, shaky voice the rest of the way from Qasr el-Aini to the Radio and Television Building on the Nile. "No one knows anything."

31 HIGHLY CONFIDENTIAL

WHEN THE UNIVERSITY CLOCK RANG the strokes of seven a.m., I was in Studio 12, the live-broadcast studio. I was sitting on my seat behind the microphone, the pages of the news broadcast in my hands, complete, after I'd checked them once, twice, three times.

I was poised to begin the newscast with the first item of the summary when Mahdi, the director, behind the glass wall of the control room, suddenly stopped. He stood up straight in a panic and waved both his shaking hands to tell me not to say anything or start reading the newscast.

As the sound of the clock striking faded, and without allowing even an instant of silence, Mahdi, with amazing speed, put on a musical interlude timed to last precisely twenty seconds, ejected himself from his place, and leapt toward me. From his pocket, he extracted a piece of paper that had reached him seconds earlier and was stamped "Highly Confidential" in red. Opening it quickly, putting it in my outstretched hand, and placing his index finger in front of his mouth, he whispered, his whole body shaking, "A Very Urgent news item."

I ran my eyes over the two lines in surprise and shock. A sudden chill ran through my body and a feeling of utter depression afflicted me for a few instants. The music was about to end. Clearing my throat quietly and making my voice as professionally neutral as I could, I started to read the astounding, Very Urgent, news:

"Ladies and gentlemen, this is the seven a.m. news bulletin, read to you by Rabeea el-Hagg . . . ."

GLOSSARY

101 dominoes: a form of dominoes in which 101 points are needed to win.

Abd el-Wahhab: Mohammed Abd el-Wahhab (1900–91), musician and composer, known as "the singer for important people, kings, and princes."

Abla: term of address and reference for an older woman such as a relative or teacher.

Ahmad Munib: Nubian musician (1926–91) who adapted the pentatonic music of his homeland to a classical Arabic modal regime.

al-Ahram, al-Akhbar, and ***al-Gumhuriya:*** three major daily newspapers, all government-owned; sometimes referred to simply as "the three papers."

ashura: a sweet pudding of whole wheat traditionally eaten on the tenth day of Muharram, the first month of the Islamic year.

audible prayer (Ar. *salah jahira*): those of the five daily prayers (sunset, evening, dawn) during which the imam and the worshiper recite certain passages from the Qur'an in an audible voice.

baba ghanoug: eggplant-and-tahina dip.

Bekyaaa: an attenuation of the call of the junkman who goes through the streets with his barrow or cart crying "rubabekya," from Italian *roba vecchia*, "old things."

Bey: a title for a man, formerly official but now purely social and used to indicate respect or to flatter.

beys: men of upper-middle-class standing or appearance.

bilila: boiled wheat with hot milk, usually eaten for breakfast in the winter.

Copt: a member of Egypt's native Christian minority.

"dirty kerosene . . . broken-down trains . . . sharks in the Red Sea" (p. 44): the references are to two historical incidents: the burning to death of more than 350 passengers bound for Upper Egypt in a second-class train with barred windows in 2002 and the drowning of over a thousand passengers on a ferry that sank while crossing the Red Sea from Upper Egypt to Saudi Arabia in 2006.

duur: a responsorial musical form.

effendi: an Egyptian man who wears European clothes; a title of respect afforded such a man.

Farghal: nickname for Farghali.

Feast of the Breaking of the Fast: the Islamic feast celebrating the end of the fasting month of Ramadan.

fiseekh: a kind of cured fish consumed mainly at the feast of Shamm el-Naseem, on the Monday following Easter Sunday.

Friday prayer: the noon prayer on Friday, which Islam recommends be prayed collectively.

fuul (rhymes with pool): fava beans, a staple of the Egyptian diet, usually eaten stewed.

gallabiya: a full-length gown, closed in front, the daily dress of many Egyptians.

Giza: a city on the west bank of the Nile, forming part of the Greater Cairo metropolis and home as of 2006 to some two and a half million inhabitants.

The Gondola: a song by Mohammed Abd el-Wahhab.

goza: a handheld water pipe for smoking tobacco or hashish with a water container made originally from a coconut (goza), but more often today from a jam jar.

the Greater Ocean: the reach of the Nile between Giza and Roda Island; Greater Ocean Street in Giza is named after it.

Hagg: title of respect for a man who has performed the pilgrimage to Mecca.

Hanim: title of respect for a married woman of high social standing.

I Love the Movies (Bahibb el-sima): a movie (Usama Fawzi, 2004) whose social, religious, and political audacity made it controversial.

July revolution: the revolution of 26 July 1952 that overthrew the Egyptian monarchy.

Kamananna: title of a song sung by the comedian Mohammed el-Heneidy in the film *Isma'iliyya Rayih Gayy (Ismailia There and Back)*.

key money: an under-the-table payment to a landlord in return for a lease at an artificially low, or controlled, rent.

khamasin: a wind that blows from the south in spring and is often hot and dust-laden.

Khawaga: a title today used most commonly of non-Muslim foreigners but formerly also used of Coptic merchants.

kunafa: baked, threadlike noodles; often used, crumbled, as a topping for bilila

kushari: a dish of rice and lentils topped with fried onions.

Maadi: an affluent suburb to the south of Cairo.

Mahmud Himeida, Layla Elwi: lead actors in *I Love the Movies* (see above).

el-Malik el-Salih: a district of south-central Cairo.

La Manche: a fuul restaurant supposedly started by an Egyptian long-distance swimmer who swam the English Channel in record time in the 1950s.

Manial: a district of Cairo at the southern end of Rodet el-Manial island.

Maryutiya: a large irrigation canal that runs south from a point close to the Pyramids, southwest of Giza.

mashrabiya work: traditional ornate turned-wood lattice work.

mawwal: a type of popular song.

Mercedes Phantom: nickname of the Mercedes S320 (1991–98).

miluha: salted, pickled fish.

mish: a seasoned milk-based liquid culture in which cheese is fermented, the final product consisting of lumps of fermented cheese in a thick liquid.

mulukhiya: a leafy green vegetable (Jew's mallow or *Corchorus olitorius*), prepared as a slightly viscous soup.

the Muqattam: a range of limestone cliffs to the east of Cairo.

Nagat el-Saghira: singer and film actress (b. 1938)

Nazim el-Ghazali: an Iraqi singer (1921–63).

Omar Sharif: an Egyptian actor (born 1932).

the Protected City: i.e., Cairo.

qasida: a long poem in classical Arabic, often set to music.

qulqas: taro (*Colocasia antiquorum*), an edible tuber.

Sabah Fakhri: a celebrated interpreter of traditional Arabic singing styles, from Aleppo (born 1933).

Samalut: a town and administrative center in the Upper Egyptian governorate of el-Minya.

Saqar: in the Qur'an, one of the names of Hell.

Saqqara: site of the step pyramid of Djoser in the desert south of Giza, and a nearby town.

shaabi: a genre of song popular since the 1970s and much condemned by the cultural establishment (literally, "popular, of the masses, low-class").

Shaabolla: pet name of Shaaban Abd el-Rahim (born 1957), a leading exponent of shaabi song.

Shamm el-Naseem: a popular Egyptian festival falling on Easter Monday.

Sheikh Ali Mahmud: a celebrated Qur'an reciter (1878–1946).

Sheikh Rifaat: Sheikh Muhammad Rifaat (1882–1950), a celebrated Qur'an reciter.

Sidi Ramadan: a Muslim saint, with a much-visited tomb in Giza.

siwak: a small, sweet-smelling stick with a softened tip used to clean the teeth.

Sixth of October City: a satellite new city to the northwest of Giza.

Snake Canyon (Shaqq el-Ti'ban): an area of quarries in the rocky hills east of Cairo.

Struggle in the Valley (Sira' fi-l-Wadi): first movie (1954, Youssef Chahine) in which Omar Sharif took a starring role.

taamiya: fava-bean patties, falafel.

Taheya Carioca: a celebrated belly dancer (1919–99).

taqtuqa: a form of song popular in the first half of the twentieth century, consisting of couplets sung by a soloist that alternate with a choral refrain.

"The place is his, the singer's his, and he who names his own singer doeth no wrong, ha-ha!": a parody of the proverb "He who disposes of his own wealth does no injustice."

"The trembling hands of the fearful and hesitant will never find the strength to build": quotation from a speech by President Gamal Abdel Nasser.

the three newspapers: the three government-owned newspapers (*al-Ahram*, *al-Akhbar*, and *al-Gumhuriya*) that jointly dominate the printed media.

Tradition: a saying or act of the Prophet Muhammad, to be taken as a guide to understanding or an example to be followed.

Tripartite Aggression: invasion of Egypt in late 1956 by British, French, and Israeli forces following Egyptian president Gamal Abdel Nasser's announcement in July of the nationalization of the Suez Canal.

Wafd Party: the dominant political party in Egypt during the 1920s and 1930s, dissolved along with all other parties by President Gamal Abdel Nasser in 1953.

Yusuf: twelfth sura (chapter) of the Qur'an, which tells the story of Yusuf (Joseph) and his sojourn in Egypt.

Zamalek: a wealthy neighborhood on the northern half of the island of el-Gizira in the Nile at Cairo.

zawya: a small mosque inside an apartment or other building.

Modern Arabic Literature

The American University in Cairo Press is the world's leading publisher of Arabic literature in translation.

For a full list of available titles, please go to:

mal.aucpress.com